The Assassin Chicago

JIM WEST

Acknowledgments

Thanks to all the people who helped make this book a realistic depiction of what life in the gang/drug world is really like. That includes how they interact with one another, the suppliers, and those agencies that are sworn to prevent them from harming the public.

Unfortunately, preventing the gangs and their drugs from harming the public is proving to be an almost insurmountable problem. Countless resources have been spent and numerous lives lost trying to control the drug problem, and we're no closer than we when started the War on Drugs.

The first attempt to regulate drugs was in the 1800s, with the levying of taxes on opium and morphine in 1890. In 1971, President Nixon declared the War on Drugs. In spite of him declaring drugs Public Enemy Number One, the problem never seemed to get resolved. The estimates of drug expenditures by the Rand Corporation in 2010 were $40.6 billion for marijuana, $28.3 billion for cocaine, $27 billion for heroin, and $13 billion for meth. That's almost $109 billion.

To effectively stop illegal drug use in the United States, unacceptable steps would have to be taken. We would need to use the same methods as the cartels that supply the drugs, and the public would never accept the total elimination of entire families, including every man, woman, and child who has any relation to the primary targets. This would be necessary for each of the major gangs that control the drug activity in each of the major cities. The carnage would be horrifying, especially in light of today's unparalleled access to everything with the ever-present smartphone.

If we're to ever slow down the proliferation of drugs and gang activity, it will take extraordinary methods. This book is just a suggestion of one method. All it takes is for those in a position to make the hard decisions to use assets that are always available.

As always, thanks to John Fleenor for his tireless attempts at making this book readable. My special thanks go to the outstanding men and women of the Chicago Police Department and the task forces that try to control the gangs and drug activity within their cities, a never-ending, thankless, and extremely dangerous endeavor. Thank you.

Other books by Jim West

DNAlien

DNAlien II

DNAlien III

Genocide by GMO

Living Within a Strange Mind: Volume I

Living Within a Strange Mind: Volume II

The Making of an Assassin: Atlanta

The Assassin: Baltimore

Prologue

Tuesday, the Eleventh

"American 2263, climb and maintain 10 thousand, turn left to 040, and contact departure 126.5," came the instructions as they were approaching five thousand feet after taking off from the Dallas/Fort Worth Airport (DFW).

"Climbing to 10, left 040, and 26.5," Jim Lashley said as he looked at Captain Rob Sproc. Seeing Rob select 10 thousand in the altitude window for the autopilot and 040 in the heading window, Jim dialed 126.5 into the second radio. Switching the radio, Jim pressed the talk switch on his control yoke and said, "Departure, American 2263, with you passing 7 for 10, heading 040."

"American 2263, roger. Continue climb to 280 and proceed direct Little Rock," came the new clearance.

"American 2263 up to 280 and direct Little Rock," Jim acknowledged, watching Rob make the appropriate changes to the altitude and GPS. "Any ride reports?"

"Nothing but smooth," came the answer.

Rechecking that everything matched what Jim knew to be the headings and altitude settings, he slid his seat back a few inches and waited for them to pass ten thousand feet.

Rob double-checked that the autopilot was performing correctly and slid his seat back and picked up the phone from between the seats. "You got it," he said, looking at Jim.

Jim merely nodded and waited for Rob to press the call button, which caused a chime in the cabin of the airplane as they passed ten thousand, which ended the sterile period. Rob then began his normal spiel about seatbelts, flight attendants, ride reports, estimated landing time, and thanks for flying the friendly skies.

As soon as Rob had replaced the phone, Jim turned on his overhead speaker and removed his earpiece and microphone. A quick click of the radio toggle switch on the control yoke confirmed the volume on the speaker. Rob did the same and leaned his seat back to a more comfortable position. Taking the Styrofoam cup from the holder beside his seat, he made a face as he took a sip of the now cool coffee that he had gotten before they had been pushed back from the gate for the flight to Chicago O'Hare or ORD.

"You got the jet," Jim said as he picked up the open can of Mr. & Mrs. T Bloody Mary mix. Pouring the last of it into the plastic glass, he added a dash of jalapeno powder and stirred it with the short plastic straw.

"Roger," Rob said as he hit the chime button twice and picked the phone back up. "Hi, Millicent," he said when the flight attendant in first class answered. "Could you please get me another cup of black coffee?"

Hearing her response, he eased the half-full cup into the trash bag that rested on the back of the center pedestal. As soon as she knocked on the cockpit door, he pressed the button that unlocked it and turned to greet her.

"Thanks," he said, taking the steaming cup from her.

"No problem," she answered as she turned to Jim. "Anything for you, Jim?"

"I'd like chicken-fried steak, mashed potatoes, and gravy, please," he said, smiling.

"Tabasco?" she asked, smiling back.

"Got my own," Jim answered. "But thanks."

"Then I guess you better take it with you when you go to Denny's after we land," she retorted. "I may have a snack bar or two, maybe some fruit, if you guys are hungry."

"I'll wait until we get to the hotel," Rob told her. "They have a pretty good afternoon lunch buffet."

"I'm good also," Jim told her. "I had a blueberry muffin at the airport before we left Phoenix."

"And you didn't think to bring me one?" Millicent joked.

"I bought enough for Rob and the ladies who came with us to DFW," Jim answered. "Didn't your first Captain or First Officer (FO) bring you anything?"

"Not everyone is as considerate as you guys," she said, turning to leave. "Just call if you need anything."

"Cute," Rob said as the door clicked shut.

"As a bug," Jim agreed, sipping his drink.

"Do you know her?" Rob asked, smiling at Jim.

"I've flown with her before," Jim admitted, nodding. "But you know how it is. Nowadays, we change crews every leg, and even though she's based in Dallas, odds are slim that I'll fly with her again this year. Maybe not even the next."

"Yeah," Rob agreed. "Used to be we'd all stay together for the entire month. Now the flight attendants are changed out almost every leg."

"I know," Jim said, nodding. "Different rules for how many hours a day they can work, and the company tries to extract every minute of work possible."

"I know," Rob said, shaking his head. "Not as much chance of romance when you don't even get to know their names."

Jim laughed as he heard instructions for a radio change. "Probably for the best," he said as he reached for the radio talk switch.

After waiting for Jim to make the frequency change, Rob asked, "Doing anything interesting this evening?"

"Not really," Jim answered, even though he was going to coordinate the execution of the top two leaders and kidnapping of the third highest of the five largest gangs in Chicago later that night. "How about you?"

"Meeting a friend for dinner," Rob responded. "You're welcome to join us."

"Thanks, but I'm going to have a beer and maybe catch a movie on TV," Jim answered. "I was pretty busy the few days I had off, and I just want a quiet night at the hotel."

"Okay," Rob said as he scanned the instruments for any indications of problems. "Just call later if you change your mind."

Chapter 1

On Saturday afternoon, Jim Lashley was washing his vintage 1962 Corvette in the driveway just outside of his garage when a black Suburban pulled to the curb at his house in Mesquite, Texas.

Noticing the extremely dark tint on the windows, he knew immediately that his old friend and mentor, Retired General Gene Barker, was inside. Gene was now a top-level executive for a well-known international security firm named Black Water and traveled all around the globe ensuring that whatever contract Black Water was fulfilling, enforcement was swift and effective.

Putting the sponge into the bucket of soapy water, Jim hosed his hands off and dried them on his Wranglers as Gene was getting out of the car. Walking across the grass to meet him, Jim said, "Sort of taking a chance that I'll be home when you arrive unannounced, aren't you?"

"I was pretty sure you'd be here," Gene answered, shaking Jim's outstretched hand. "You just got home yesterday from a trip, and your beautiful wife, Jennifer, is at work. Where else would you be?"

"I've got a life outside the airlines and a secret life that my wife knows nothing about," Jim retorted, smiling. "Care for a glass of tea or something stronger?"

"I was thinking that we'd take a quick drive down to that little pizza place you like," Gene answered. "I haven't eaten, and I seem to remember that they have excellent lasagna. Maybe we can have lunch while we discuss a couple of things."

"Sounds good to me," Jim said as he turned toward the house. "Just let me lock up, and we can take the 'Vette."

"Let's just take my car," Gene told him as he walked over to admire the sparkling paint on the old Corvette. "Still looks good though."

"Thanks," Jim said as he locked the front door. "This is the only car that I've ever owned that actually makes me money the longer I drive it."

"I understand," Gene responded as he led the way to his car. "But it's a little impractical for me."

"Probably draws too much attention for you anyway," Jim said as he opened the passenger door. "People would see you coming for miles away."

"And then you'd do what? Run around behind the house and try to avoid me?" Gene joked as he started the car. "I really doubt that. I'm sure you enjoy the little adventures that I involve you in. Just think of how dull your life would be without your association with me."

"I'll have to admit that ever since you got me into the Marine Aviation program, it's been pretty interesting," Jim told him as they pulled from the curb.

"Just think of all the exotic places you've seen. Those once-in-a-lifetime experiences," Gene reminded him as they sped down the street.

"Exotic?" Jim said, laughing. "Let's see. Ever since you got me involved with Black Water and their enforcement arm Dark Water, it's been almost anything except exotic. There was that little country halfway around the world where people were trying to kill me. Then there were all those trips to that godforsaken, snake-filled, scorpion-infested mountainous desert land of thousands of terrorists who were trying to kill me. Yeah, pretty exotic."

"That's all in the past," Gene told him as they pulled into the parking lot of Venice Pizza and Pasta. "You've had it really easy these last few years, working for Black Water's domestic organization, Muddy Water. Plush hotels, fine restaurants, charming people to converse with. All in all, I think you should be showing a little more gratitude."

"I'll admit it beats the hell out of most of the overseas stuff," Jim said as he got out of the car. "And yes, I do get a little bored with everyday life when I'm home."

"Better not let Jennifer hear you say that," Gene said as they entered the restaurant. "I'm pretty sure she'd take it personally."

"She knows me well enough to understand," Jim replied as he waved at the owner and headed for the back room, where he knew they wouldn't be disturbed. "And she also knows that I'll never get bored with her."

Almost immediately after they had picked a table as close to the back as possible, their waitress came with glasses of water, silverware, and two menus.

"Do you know what you'd like, or do you need to see the menu?" she asked as she put everything on the table.

"Not for me," Jim told her as he reached for the water. "I'd like the lasagna and a Dr. Pepper."

"I'll have the lasagna and a glass of unsweet tea," Gene said, smiling at her.

"I'll be right back with your drinks," the waitress said as she picked up the menus.

Once she was gone, Jim asked, "What brings you down here besides the chance to take me out to lunch?"

"I suppose you expect me to pick up the tab for lunch," Gene asked, taking a sip of water.

"Well, you're the one who asked me out, so yeah, I expect you to pick up the tab," Jim retorted. "I don't imagine it will strain your budget too much."

"I suppose you're right," Gene said, nodding. "But I expect something for my generosity."

"And that would be----?" Jim asked, leaning back in his chair.

"What do you know about Chicago?" Gene asked, looking at Jim.

"I know it's cold in the winter, crowded, that they have some great art and history museums, cold in the winter, crowded, have great pizza, very cold in the winter, and very crowded," Jim proclaimed, smiling.

"True," Gene responded. "But what do you know about the political and criminal activities?"

"Let's see," Jim began. "Pretty much liberal as far as I can determine based on how long it's been since they elected a Republican mayor. As to the criminal activity, I'd say that I'd rather spend another one-year tour in the mud in Vietnam than a night on the streets of Chicago."

"Pretty much on target," Gene said, nodding as the waitress rounded the corner with their drinks. "And I think you're going to become much more informed as to the situation in the Windy City in a few days."

Chapter 2

As soon as the waitress had set the drinks down and left, Jim said, "I'm assuming that this is going to be more than a geography lesson or civics class."

"Indeed," Gene answered. "We've been tasked with a very delicate operation to assist the Mayor of Chicago, the Governor of Illinois, the DEA, and the Department of Homeland Security."

"Some pretty heavy hitters," Jim remarked. "Just why does such an auspicious group of people need our services? They undoubtedly have the funding and other resources to do just about anything that I would think we could do for them."

"They do," Gene admitted. "But as with our operations for Black Water and both Dark Water operations overseas and our work with Muddy Water here at home, we have the unique ability to remain out of the public eye, while they, the government entities, have complete deniability."

"So what's so important that you're down here expounding on their problems?" Jim remarked. "And by 'they,' I'm assuming it's primarily Chicago's problem."

"Yes," Gene answered as the waitress rounded the corner with their orders and a basket of bread. "And by the other entities, I'm sure you can tell that the problem has been elevated to a very high level yet remains unresolved."

As soon as the waitress was gone, Jim asked, "Just what is this problem that can't be resolved within the framework of the agencies involved?"

"Simply put, drugs and gangs," Gene answered as he took a piece of the warm bread and spread butter across it.

"There are drugs and gangs in every town across the country," Jim countered, taking a forkful of the steaming lasagna and waiting for it to cool.

"Nothing like Chicago," Gene lectured him. "I'm guessing that you've noticed the number of shootings and homicides every year in Chicago. It's way above just about anywhere else, and there are over five hundred murders every year. And over two thousand shooting incidents."

"That's a lot," Jim agreed as he finally tasted the lasagna. "But the kill rate per attempt is pretty pathetic. Still, why can't the Chicago Police Department handle it? I'd bet they have a pretty good force and probably some very experienced officers. I mean, look at the St. Valentine's Day massacre and Al Capone. Hell, they've had more experience in gang or mass homicides than any other place that I can think of."

"That's all true," Gene admitted. "But the environment is different today. Politics has a lot to do with what the Chicago Police can or can't do. But regardless of the why, we've been tasked to lend an assisting hand."

"Do we have people within the organization who have better insight or experience dealing with their situation than they do?" Jim asked.

"Not necessarily," Gene admitted, shaking his head. "But we bring anonymity to the table. We don't exist. As you well know, the only public face of our operation is Black Water, and they're just another security firm that's available to anyone who can afford their unique skills and expertise."

"If we don't have the expertise, how does the company expect us to plan and mount an operation that seems to have stymied one of the premier police forces in this sort of politically charged atmosphere?" Jim asked.

"First off, it's not just an operation. It's more akin to running fifteen separate operations and some collateral operations that involve hundreds of potential additions to the main objective," Gene answered.

"Just what have we been tasked with?" Jim asked as he thought about the enormity of coordinating such a massive operation.

"Eliminating the drug problem in Chicago and a major hit to the gangs that effectively run the crime," Gene announced with a slight smile on his face.

Jim sat back and stared at Gene for a moment and finally said, "So we're expected to do something that the CPD, the DEA, and Homeland Security can't handle. And just how much time do we have to execute this minor little task that the War on Drugs has unsuccessfully attempted for years now?"

"A couple of months," Gene told him, taking another bite of the lasagna. "Maybe six or seven weeks."

"Let me ask," Jim said, shaking his head. "You've waited this long to come to me for what reason? Because you're positive that I can accomplish in a couple of months what the rest of the most experienced police and other law enforcement professionals haven't accomplished in years?"

"You'll have help," Gene said, grinning. "We've already done most of the heavy lifting. You're just now coming into the picture because I've selected you to do two simple little things."

"And those would be?" Jim asked, shaking his head.

"First, I've convinced the big boys in all the aforementioned organizations that you are the perfect person to be in charge of our operations," Gene said seriously. "And what I mean by that is you will be the final authority to execute the missions."

"You said two simple little things," Jim told him. "Not that coordinating fifteen separate operations and potentially hundreds of other additions isn't simple, I'm hoping that the second little thing is truly simple."

"Compared to the first little thing, it is," Gene told him. "All it involves is you and your team taking out a single individual."

"My team," Jim remarked, shaking his head. "And is this going to be like the other assignments? My 'team' consists of me and an occasional female operative who's mainly there to distract the actual target?"

"Sort of," Gene admitted. "Do you think you need more than that?"

"I'm not sure," Jim said, returning to his meal. "You really haven't told me much. Let's see if I have this right. Chicago has a problem that the CPD, the DEA, Homeland Security, and the offices of the mayor, the governor, and whoever else is involved need me and some random female to resolve. Do I have that right?"

"Close," Gene admitted, smiling again. "But the female isn't random. As I'm sure you know, nothing is random regarding our operations."

"Okay, who's this nonrandom female?" Jim asked.

"You're going to have to wait for that," Gene answered. "We're working on it, and if everything comes together today, you'll find out next Friday when you attend the briefing at the headquarters."

"And you know I'm available to run halfway across the country on short notice because . . ." Jim remarked.

"Because I know your schedule," Gene answered. "And I know that there will be a company jet sitting at Love Field on Friday morning waiting to take you to Quantico."

"How many days do I need to plan for?" Jim asked, shaking his head.

"I'd plan on three," Gene told him. "But if everything goes as planned, we'll have you home Saturday evening in time for you to take Jennifer out for a nice steak dinner. On the company this time."

"When will I ever learn?" Jim said, looking at Gene. "I could have ignored you when you drove up. Just kept washing my car. Pretending I have a normal, boring life as an airline pilot and loving wife."

"You'd be bored, all right," Gene said, signaling for the check. "You're an adrenaline junkie just like me."

Chapter 3

After Gene dropped him off back at his house, Jim returned to washing his car. He was just finishing waxing it when his wife, Jennifer, pulled into the driveway.

"Got time to wash mine?" she asked as she got out.

"Sure," Jim said, smiling. "I'll take it down to Royal Car Wash, and it will look like a new car when I get back."

"You mean that you'll spend hours washing that old thing of yours and mine gets a drive-through?" Jennifer asked, watching Jim wipe the last hint of wax residue from the hood.

"Afraid so, my lady," Jim said as he admired the glossy shine. "This is more than a car. It's more like a family heirloom."

"I know how you feel about it," Jennifer remarked. "You've been driving it since I first met you in Florida. As a matter of fact, we've driven that thing across half of the United States together."

"And you enjoyed it immensely," Jim retorted.

"No, I enjoyed being with you immensely," she said, shaking her head. "But I never enjoyed riding in that thing. No air conditioning. A heater that barely works. Rides rougher than a wagon with no springs. And there isn't enough room in it for more than a small purse."

"That's not true," Jim responded, opening the door. "The heater works excellent in the summer. The air conditioning is unbelievable in the winter, and you've never been in a wagon with no springs, so you can't compare the two."

"I still think I like my car better," she said as Jim started the car and pulled into the garage.

"Honestly, I would rather drive yours if we had to go more than a couple of miles," Jim admitted as he walked back to where she was standing. "Now do you really want me to wash it?"

"No," she said, putting her arms around his neck. "I think it's supposed to rain tomorrow, so it would be a waste of time. I think it's good enough for us to take out to dinner tonight. I think I'd like to go to Outback Steakhouse."

"Sounds good to me," Jim said, nodding. "I haven't had a good prime rib in a long time."

"Good," Jennifer said, heading for the house. "How about we get cleaned up and have a drink before we head out?"

"Sounds good to me," Jim answered, following her up the steps. "I'm sure I have an unpleasant aroma that wouldn't be appreciated among the dining public."

"It's not appreciated among anybody," Jennifer said, smiling. "Even when you were hanging around down in Florida when we first met, it was tolerated. Never appreciated."

"Yeah, flight suits and warm humid days did sort of bring out a certain air," Jim remarked.

"Don't forget the smell of jet fuel that seemed to soak into your flight suit every time you flew," she remarked as they went into the house.

"I hardly noticed it," Jim told her as he headed for their bedroom. "But at least now, I don't reek of sweat and gas every time I come home from a trip."

"No, you've turned into a real gentleman," Jennifer said as she walked into the master bath. "I'll be out in a few minutes, and you can do your five-minute routine where you get most of the grime off. Oh, I almost forgot," she said as she slipped her blouse and jeans off. "There are a few things in the back seat that I picked up at the grocery store. Can you please bring them in while I shower?"

"Not a problem," Jim answered as he headed back through the house. "Anything else I can do to make your evening more enjoyable?"

"We'll see," she said, smiling. "If you hurry, you just might be able to get back here before I finish my shower."

Chapter 4

Leaving the house, they headed west on Kearney Street until it became Gross Road before passing beneath Loop 63. A few miles later, they passed below U.S. 80, and Gross Road became Gus Thomasson Road.

As they approached the area where Outback was located, Jim said, "There's a Hooters! Are you sure you wouldn't rather eat there?"

"Are you sure you wouldn't rather sleep on the couch tonight?" Jennifer asked sarcastically. "You can go to all the Hooters you want to when you're palling around with your buddy Gene. If you ever want to see 'Hooters' around me again, you'll keep driving to Outback."

A few minutes later, as they were awaiting their orders at Outback, Jennifer asked, "So anything interesting happen today while I was working?"

Taking a sip of his beer, Jim answered, "Not much. Gene did drop by, and we went to Venice Pizza for lunch."

"What did the General want this time?" she asked.

"Something about wanting me to go up to Quantico next week after I get back from my trip," Jim answered.

"I assume that you told him you'd go," Jennifer said, shaking her head. "I don't know what you guys do when you go off on your *little adventures*, but I do wish you'd spend more time at home when you're not out flying because of your job. I mean, I had to put up with your overseas stuff when you were still in the Marines. And now that you're gone three or four days a week with American, I'd like to have you home the rest of the time. Not running off when you're supposed to be home with me."

Jim set his beer back on the table and leaned closer, saying, "You know that General Barker is the man who made everything we have today possible. And once or twice a year, he asks me to come help with some problem where he thinks I can give him a little advice. Yes, he could probably resolve whatever the issue is without me. But I think he looks at me as a sort of surrogate son and wants to keep in touch. For all he has done for me and you as well, I don't think that a few days a year is too much to ask for." Leaning back in his chair, he continued, "And you know that he looks at you as a family member as much as he does me. Without his help, I wouldn't be flying for American Airlines, and we wouldn't be living the lifestyle we have. He's the reason we met, and I still believe that I owe him a debt that can never be repaid."

Jennifer waited a few seconds to respond and finally said, "I know how you feel about him. And I know how he feels about you. About us. And I know that he's more than just a former Marine commander to you. He's as much of a father figure to you as you are a son to him. I know this." Waiting to judge his reaction, she finally continued, "I'm just asking that you consider my feelings before you commit to one of your excursions. I don't ask what you do when you go off with him because I know you'll never tell me. I have my suspicions, and I think that some of it still has to do with some of the things you did before you retired from the Marines."

Jim reached across the table and took her hands, saying, "No, I can't always tell you what I'm involved in with General Barker and his organization. And I know that not knowing what we do is one of the things that bothers you." As the waitress was placing their orders on the table, Jim asked, "What would you like for me to do? Stop helping him? Refuse the one man left in my life whom I have total respect for?"

"No, I'd never ask for that," Jennifer answered as the waitress left. "Your unwavering loyalty is one of the things that I respect about you. I just want to have you for the few days you aren't gone flying. I married you to be with you."

Jim tilted his head slightly and asked, "What if you could go with me some of the time? Would that make you happy?"

"What do you mean go with you?" she asked, surprised that going with Jim was ever an option when he went to meet Gene.

"I mean what if you could go to Virginia with me when I'm working with General Barker?" Jim answered. "I'll be busy most of the days, but we'd still have some time in the evenings to go out. Sort of like a mini vacation."

"What would I do during the day?" Jennifer asked, getting a little excited about the chance to go with him.

"I don't know," Jim told her, knowing that the battle was half won. "Go shopping, go to museums, just be a tourist."

"Do you really think the General would let me go?" Jennifer asked, still having not touched her food.

Jim smiled and pulled out his cell phone, saying, "Let's find out." Dialing the number for Black Water from memory, he asked for Gene when it was quickly answered. Once connected, he said, "Good evening, General." After pausing to hear Gene's reply, he continued, "Do you think it would be all right if Jennifer accompanied me Friday when I come up to see you?" Listening to his response, Jim nodded and said, "Yes, it would be a tremendous help. I was sure that you'd understand. And I assume that there's no problem with her being on the plane."

Hearing that there would be no problem and that a hotel room in Alexandria would be booked for them, Jim said, "Thanks, sir. I'll see you before noon on Friday." Hanging up, Jim smiled slightly and asked, "Do you need to do any shopping for new clothes before we vacation in Virginia?"

Chapter 5

The following Friday morning, Jim was not surprised to hear the shower running when he awoke at five o'clock. Smiling, he slipped out of bed and headed for the kitchen to start a pot of coffee. Once there, he saw that it was done and that a pan of cinnamon rolls was in the oven.

Walking back into the bedroom, he noticed that the shower had stopped running, and he called out, "I had thought that maybe you might need a hand with something in the shower!"

Jennifer opened the door, smiling, and said, "Maybe tonight if you're a good boy. Now I'll be done here in about fifteen minutes, so you start packing and make sure to get the rolls out of the oven when the timer goes off."

"You do know that we have plenty of time," Jim told her as he headed for the guest bathroom. "We don't need to be at Love Field until nine o'clock."

"I know that," she answered as she turned from the door. "But I want to make sure that I have everything I need, and if I don't, then we'll have to stop somewhere before we get to the airport."

"You are aware that Alexandria has stores," Jim remarked, knowing that it was a futile argument.

"And I may need to go shopping when we get there," Jennifer said as she started wiping the moisture from the mirror. "That's why one of my suitcases is only half full."

"Not to state the obvious, but we're probably coming back tomorrow evening," Jim said, realizing that it was time to just shut up and let her do whatever she had in mind.

"Maybe," Jennifer said. "But what if you don't finish your little discussion or the weather is bad? Or maybe I just want to spend another day there."

"I'll make sure the rolls are taken out on time," Jim said, resigned to losing another battle. "I'll pack my suitcase when I get back and take a quick shower."

A couple of hours later, as they were heading to the airport, Jennifer asked, "Who else is going to be with you and the General?"

"I'm not sure," Jim said truthfully. "It depends on what they've called me up to discuss. Sometimes it's several people. Sometimes it's just two or three of us."

"What are you discussing this time?" she asked, looking at Jim.

"I'm not really sure," he said, wondering where this conversation was going.

"Really?" Jennifer asked. "Even after spending time talking to Gene the other day? Not a clue?"

Jim took a quick glance at her and answered, "I have a clue. But I can't talk about it. You know that, so why do you ask?"

"What's so secret now that you're not in the Marines anymore?" she asked. "I've never really understood why you can't talk about what you guys do."

"It's because the organization that Gene works for has several contracts with different companies and even some other countries as well as the United States," Jim started to explain. "Even I'm not always sure who they're working for when we're discussing issues. I just know that he expects me not to discuss it outside of the group."

"One of these days, I hope you'll really let me know what you're up to," Jennifer told him as they were pulling into the airport.

Parking in the Business Jet Center just off Lemmon Avenue, Jim shut off the car and turned to her, saying, "Look, there may never be a day when I can tell you what Gene and his company are doing. Just as there were things that I did in the Marines that I can never talk about. I just want you to know that it isn't because I don't trust you. It's just that they trust me, and if I ever break that trust, then I'll feel as if I let them down. Just as if I were to ever do something wrong to you, I'd never forgive myself." Jim waited a few seconds for her to realize that she wasn't ever going to get an answer that would satisfy her and said, "Now would you like to take a private jet to Virginia and have a nice but short vacation, or would you rather stay home, wondering what a couple of old Marines are talking about?"

Jennifer shook her head and finally smiled, saying, "I guess I'll just have to learn to live with not knowing what you boys are up to. Probably just a chance to drink beer and talk about the good old days anyway."

"Mostly," Jim agreed as he got out of the car and opened the trunk. "But now let's go see if our plane is here and if we're sharing it with anybody else."

"You mean that there may be other people on *our* plane?" Jennifer asked as Jim took out the suitcases. "I was sort of hoping that I might finally get a chance to join that exclusive club you guys always talk about."

"What club are you talking about?" Jim asked as he piled the suitcases on a nearby luggage dolly.

"I believe you call it the Mile High Club," she said, smiling and heading for the terminal.

Chapter 6

After landing at MCAF (Marine Corp Air Field) Quantico, Jim and Jennifer were met at the terminal by General Barker and an unknown man standing behind him.

"Welcome to Quantico," Gene said, taking Jennifer's hand as she stepped from the small jet. "How was your flight?"

"Very interesting," she said, smiling and thinking about the uninterrupted two hours during the flight. "I've never been in a private jet before. I could get spoiled."

"Not a chance," Jim said, joining them and shaking Gene's hand. "The General doesn't share his private airplane very often."

"Sometimes it's necessary if we need to get people here expeditiously," Gene told them as he signaled for the man behind him to go get the bags that the pilots were removing from the plane. "Granted, it's only an hour or so from the civilian fields, but since I know you guys want to get back home as soon as possible, that hour can be used more productively here instead of in a car driving. Now since time is an issue, let's get your bags to the car, and Jennifer will be taken to Alexandria while we get to work."

"Good morning," the other man said as he grabbed Jennifer's suitcases. "I'm Billy, and I'll be taking you to the Alexandrian Hotel."

"Good to meet you," Jennifer replied as Jim followed them, carrying his own suitcase. "How far is it to the hotel?"

"Only about thirty or thirty-five miles," Billy answered as they approached the dark Suburban. "I'll have you at the hotel in about forty-five minutes or so."

"When will Jim be coming?" Jennifer asked, turning to Gene.

"I'm planning on being at your hotel with your husband at about seven o'clock this evening," Gene answered as Billy loaded the suitcases in the Suburban. "And I've made reservations for us at the Chart House restaurant for eight o'clock."

"You'll be joining us?" Jim asked as he loaded his suitcase.

"Of course," Gene said, holding the rear door open for Jennifer. "You think I'm paying for your little vacation and fine dining without joining you?"

Smiling, Jennifer remarked, "I'd love to have my favorite two men in the world taking me out for a luxurious meal. How fancy should I dress? I may need to go shopping before you come get me."

"It's pretty casual," Gene said as Billy slid into the driver's seat. "Not quite jeans and T-shirts like some of your restaurants down in Mesquite. I'd say slacks and a nice blouse would be appropriate."

"I'm not sure I brought any nice blouses," Jennifer said, smiling at Jim. "Are there any good clothing stores near the hotel?"

"There are several upscale women's stores in Old Town," Gene answered. "Most of them are within walking distance of your hotel. And it will give you a chance to see some of the historic district while Jim and I are busy here."

"Speaking of being busy, we should get started," Jim said, kissing Jennifer as the car started. "I'm sure you'll have fun shopping while we slave away here."

"And I'm sure you two will have just as much fun talking about the good old days," Jennifer remarked. "Just please get Jim to the hotel in time to clean up. And please don't you guys drink too much before we go to dinner. After a couple of beers, you guys start reverting to your Marine Corps attitudes."

"You'll be impressed with our refined air of culture," Gene told her. "We've become gentlemen and no longer the mud-crawling heathens you keep referring to."

"And you already know how pretty I can be when I clean up," Jim added. "Ever since I retired and joined the airlines, I've learned to extend my pinkie when I'm sipping my tea."

"Yeah, yeah, yeah," Jennifer told them as she reached for the door to shut it. "Don't forget that I've known both of you for too many years to acknowledge. And beneath those refined manners you're alluding to is the same knuckle-dragging, beer-guzzling Gyrene I fell in love with. Just try not to embarrass me here. I'd like to have at least one city where I don't have to apologize for my dinner companion's behavior."

Chapter 7

As soon as Jennifer had left, Gene signaled for another Suburban to pick up him and Jim.

As they sped toward the Black Water headquarters, Jim said, "I suppose I'm going to learn more about Chicago and meet some people who are going to tell me how we're going to accomplish the impossible."

"Close," Gene said as they approached the first set of gates leading into the windowless facility. "Today you'll be briefed on the overall plan. There's too much to really get a firm handle on all aspects, so let's just say that this session will be to show you the enormity of the problem."

The first set of gates closed behind them, and a Marine Sergeant approached the car. Gene handed him his ID and waited as he checked it against the names on the clipboard he was holding. After getting clearance, the second gate opened, and they drove to Gene's reserved parking slot.

Entering a code in the pad beside the door, Gene looked up into the lens of the camera mounted above it and waited for the buzzing that let them know the door was unlocked. They entered a small room with a window where another Marine sat, and once again, Gene showed his ID. Once cleared into the facility, they crossed the large lobby and headed down a hall to one of the briefing rooms.

As they entered, Jim noticed most of the tables were already occupied and the people seated there were busy reading folders in front of them as they ate from plates with sandwiches and chips. Gene led him to a table with three chairs and a stack of folders on the table in front of each. Seeing his name, Jim quickly looked at the other names to see who was joining him. He saw Gene's name, but the other seat remained blank.

"You've got about five minutes to grab something from the buffet if you're hungry," Gene told him as he headed toward a group of people at one end of the room. "We'll get the briefing going as soon as I confirm that everyone is here."

Jim walked over to the long table covered with platters of fruit, sandwiches, salads, and various meats. After selecting a roast beef on rye with Dijon mustard, a small bag of chips, and a glass of unsweet tea with lemon, he headed back toward his table.

Not recognizing any of the faces around the other tables, he set his food down and picked up the top folder. The first page appeared to be an organizational chart like you would see on any company. The only thing that made it obvious that it was not a Fortune 500 company was the title on the page. It simply read *Gangster Disciples*. A quick glance at the remaining folders revealed the same format for *Vice Lords*, *Latin Kings*, *Black P Stones*, and *Black Disciples*.

Even though not recognizing any of the names, he knew that what he was looking at were obviously the names of gangs from the Chicago area. Mentally tying the conversation at Venice Pizza back in Mesquite to the folders, he suddenly understood the enormity of why Gene had come to get him involved. Replacing the folders, he had barely taken a bite of his sandwich when Gene came back to the table.

"Had a look at the folders?" Gene asked, setting a plate of salad and fruit on the table.

"Just a glance," Jim said, picking up his glass of tea. "Enough to show me that somehow you've managed to become entangled in something that I severely doubt can ever be resolved."

"How do you know?" Gene asked, smiling at Jim's perception of what they had been tasked to do.

Jim took a chip from his plate and studied Gene for a second before answering, "I believe it was Richard Nixon who had started trying to get a handle on drugs back in 1969. He started it by declaring that drugs were Public Enemy Number One. I remember this because I was up to my ass in mud and Viet Cong. I had an entirely different view of who my number-one enemy was."

"Trust me, I know the history," Gene told him. "I was also over there. Not in the field like you were, but I knew the drug problems and what we were doing to try and combat it. It was the following year that the DEA was founded. Then it became the War on Drugs."

"I know you were over there," Jim said, nodding. "If you hadn't been there at the right time, we wouldn't be sitting here today. But my point is that after thirty years or so of the weight of the U.S. government trying to get a grip on the drug problem, which I'm sure this is ultimately leading to, you're trying to convince me that along with these few people in this room, we are going to solve the age-old problem."

"By 'age old,'" Gene countered as he took a slice of apple from his plate, "I'm guessing that you are referring to something besides drugs."

"Of course," Jim said, nodding. "Drugs are just the current manifestation of what I'm talking about. My biggest point is that whether it's prostitution or any other so-called vice, it comes down to trying to regulate man's desires. Hell, you might as well declare war on sugar. Look at how obesity is killing almost as many people as drugs."

"I agree in part," Gene admitted. "But you don't see gang members killing one another over a Snickers or a Butterfinger. We all know that we can't stop the drug activity in Chicago or any other city or country. This goes back too far in history to even contemplate it. Just look at the opium dens hundreds of years ago. Man will always seek ways to step back from his mundane reality through something. Doesn't matter if it's drugs, alcohol, or some sexual pleasure. And that includes compulsive overeating. There will always be something that gives man pleasure that's detrimental to his health."

"Then why are we here?" Jim asked as a man wearing a white knit shirt stepped up to the podium at the end of the room.

Chapter 8

"Good morning, everybody," the man at the podium announced. "Please take your seats so that we can get this started." Waiting a few minutes for the last of the stragglers to get their plates from the buffet and take their seats, he continued, "As I said, good morning. I'm Mr. O, and I'll be briefing you today on this operation. Please feel free to just call me O. I'm sure most of you have had a chance to review the folders at your tables, but I'll be covering most of the basics quickly just to make sure all of you have an appreciation for the enormity and complexity of what we're proposing."

The large screen behind him lit up with the names of the same gangs that Jim had noted in his folders.

"Here, you'll see the same names as in the folders. These five gangs represent about 90 percent of the drug trafficking in the city of Chicago. There are close to one hundred various gangs within the Chicago area, but they are a minor part of the problem the city is experiencing." Pausing as everybody was looking at the screen, he continued, "The drugs are a real issue, but most people don't understand the scope of the problem. They see the escalating number of murders and shootings and don't really connect that to the root of the problem.

"Now before I get much further into the issues, a part of the problem is our city leadership. They—meaning the Mayor, his staff, and most of the city council—have, for too long, been more of a hindrance to the police than a supportive partner. The laws and most of the court system seem to be trying to resolve the violence problems with social measures. This has frustrated both the leadership of the Chicago Police Department (CPD) as well as, and more importantly, the cop on the street. The lack of support from the top down to the CPD has resulted in many of the street officers being less than enthusiastic regarding getting involved when they are literally risking their lives just to watch the system release some of the worst offenders. Morale is at an all-time low, and this exacerbates the problems. Okay, back to the problem and how Black Water and you here at Muddy Water propose to resolve it."

The screen changed to a list of well-known organizations. "Here, you'll see some but not all of the governmental departments that have been involved with this project for well over a year," O told them as they saw the number of organizations. "The FBI, the DEA, the Department of Homeland Security, the CIA, the Defense Intelligence Agency, Border Patrol, Immigration and Customs Enforcement, the Federal Communications Commission, the National Security Agency, and too many others to mention in the short time we have."

The alphabet list filled the screen as O gave everyone time to see how extensive the network of intelligence gathering had been.

"Now most if not all these agencies are unaware of where and for what purpose the information they provided to this group is being used," he continued. "They merely received tasking to provide whatever information they had or could obtain regarding certain individuals or companies. That list was compiled in cooperation with the staff here at Black Water, and the information was used by the senior staff of Muddy Water to develop the operation that we're about to get into," O said as the screen shifted to the gang Jim had seen in his first folder.

"The Gangster Disciples, an all-black and mostly South Side gang, has ties to legitimate businesses and even some well-known athletes and is the first one we'll discuss," O said as everyone opened their folders.

Pausing while everybody pulled out the pages, he continued, "The leadership is shown in your folder, and I'll skip reading all the names. However, each team here has been assigned a different gang, and the information for the specific gang will vary within your folders. The total list of gangs is provided only to inform you of how well Chicago has been divided and controlled by these people."

"I'll use the Gangster Disciples as a representative of each gang, and you can see how the organization fits your specific assignment," O said as he referenced the names on the screen. "As you'll see, they are as well organized as any Fortune 500 company. And they would probably be listed on the stock market if it weren't for the business they're in. It's estimated that there are over thirty thousand current members, although we'll never know how many there really are.

"First, the head of the Gangster Disciples is like the Chief Executive Officer, or CEO." O said turning toward the screen. "He lives outside of the city but controls his gang with an iron fist. This is common throughout the other gangs and the upper echelon of their organizations. Even they don't want to live where life is as cheap as it is on the streets of Chicago.

"The number-two guy is like the Chief Operations Officer, or COO. He controls the day-to-day operation and can step in whenever the CEO is unavailable. In some cases, this man is more brutal than the CEO and is the most respected and widely feared man in the gang. His power over what happens on the streets is almost unlimited.

"The third is like the Chief Financial Officer, or CFO. He is responsible for ensuring that the cash is collected, laundered, and dispersed to wherever it needs to go. And a great majority of that will be funneled back to the cartels that provide the lifeblood of the gangs—the drugs." Turning back to face the teams, he told them, "Now there's the big dog on the street. The cartel. The gangs are merely the foot soldiers who distribute the product that enriches the producers. It is estimated that over 90 percent of the drugs within the United States pass through the city of Chicago. Without Chicago, it would be another city, and we'll get into that shortly. But for now, we'll worry about Chicago since they or some other entity with ties to the city are paying Black Water, and they are only concerned with solving their problems. Just bear in mind that the cartel will not take this lying down. Their financial interests are tied to whatever city can provide access to their drugs. And for them, the flow of drugs must never stop."

Chapter 9

"The next gang is the Vice Lords," O continued as the screen changed. "Also all black and mostly West Side but has tentacles pretty much citywide, as does the Gangster Disciples. They number about thirty thousand also." O waited for everyone to select the correct folder before continuing, "One unique thing about this gang is that there are many sects beneath them. Some are the Conservative Vice Lords or CVLs, the Traveling Vice Lords or TVLs, and the Four-Corner Hustlers. Their organization is somewhat different since each of these subgroups has their own hierarchy but still falls beneath the Vice Lords, although they do exercise some autonomy.

"Now the next gang, the Almighty Latin Kings, is somewhat different since they are primarily Mexican, Latino, or Puerto Rican. Membership in Chicago is about fifty thousand. They do have some blacks, but the top remains Hispanic," O told them as the screen changed again.

"There are some unique rivalries between them and the other four gangs that are primarily black. This strain between the gangs may be able to be exploited, but the basic plan remains the same for each gang. The Latin Kings also have some legitimate business dealings," O remarked as he prepared to change the screen. "Most of the gangs do, but some have a more extensive business portfolio than others. We'll discuss some of that when we get into the CFO's area of responsibility and how they move the massive amounts of cash that the drug operations generate.

"Next, we have the Almighty Black P Stones." O said glancing at the new screen. "One of the oldest gangs in Chicago, it started back in the 1960s. One of its most famous members is Jeff Fort, who has been locked up since the 1970s. Nationwide, it has over one hundred thousand members but only about twenty thousand in Chicago.

"And finally, the Black Disciples. One of the top gangs, they also have about thirty thousand current members. And as their name suggests, all black, with some history going back to a more political base, much as the Black Panthers. Now as you have probably noted, there are four all-black gangs and one mainly Hispanic gang. There is some interaction among the gangs, even what can only be described as a council of sorts that meet annually to discuss things like territory or whether or not to allow Meth into the city.

That's not to say that there isn't any Meth. It's just that it's more uncontrolled and very small in comparison. Plus, it has no connection to the cartel, and they don't care if Meth is on the streets. It could become an issue if it starts interfering with their drug operations but very unlikely since the cartel has no fingers in the production end."

The screen returned to the first screen with the names of each gang as O said, "As you've noticed, each of you has a folder on each gang. However, you'll also note, if you haven't already, that the folder for the particular gang you've been assigned is much more extensive. And even more so within the gang assignments regarding the individuals your team is targeting.

"The Vice Lords are being treated the same as the other gangs regardless of the sects beneath them. It was originally planned to target each of these sects, but since they will probably fragment into separate and almost ineffectual gangs, the decision was to just eliminate the top three of the Vice Lords."

The people at each table flipped through their individual assignments as O continued, "Now I'll admit that I've always favored a more extensive plan. I advocated for using the cartel model of eliminating each of the individuals we've targeted, but I included every family member or close friendship, to include every man, woman, or child. Brutal? Yes." O paused for a couple of seconds to let the enormity of his plan to sink in and continued, "It works extremely well for the cartels. However, I recognize the impact of such a massive operation and the political impact. The public would never stand for any organization operating in such a manner within the United States."

"Maybe they would finally come together politically to rid the United States of the cartel and its ties to the gangs and drugs, but more than likely, they would decry such brutality for a couple of days until another liberal bleeding heart newscast about the deplorable conditions within certain segments of our society," he continued, getting more animated. "Blaming the violence on people's impoverished condition is pure horseshit. Look at the enormous wealth some of the most brutal and cruel of them have accrued. It's about power, control, and getting even richer. I've spent years dealing with these animals, and you'll never solve the problem with another government attempt at placation or handout. It may appear to be humane, but it's more akin to putting your hands over your ears and going, 'La La La La' when you don't to hear something. Like the truth."

Jim leaned close to Gene and asked, "Is he always so tight-lipped about how he truly thinks about certain issues?"

"You should have been here over the last year while we were developing this plan," Gene answered, smiling. "O is only on loan to us from the CPD and has spent the majority of his over twenty years as a member of their elite anti–gang-and-drug task forces. I guess years of watching what happens on the streets on a daily basis has given him a very different perspective.”

“I can understand that,” Jim agreed. “Sort of like the way life in the jungle in ’Nam turned mild-mannered farm boys into harbingers of death who would decapitate heads and collect the enemies’ ears to make necklaces?”

“Speaking from personal experience?” Gene asked knowingly.

“I knew some people like that,” Jim said, nodding and smiling. “More than I’d like to admit. But yeah, I’ve seen that attitude develop after seeing what life in the mud is really like. Especially when the enemy would set babies on mines, hoping some hapless Marine would pick him up. What’s worse? Killing the enemy and taking his ears or killing your children just to kill your enemy?”

Chapter 10

"Okay," O said after looking around. "Let's take ten minutes for you to use the facilities or refresh your drinks. Please don't take much more time than that since we still have some major issues to discuss."

Jim flipped through the folders in front of him and remarked to Gene, "It appears that all my folders are basic. I mean, there's no folder on the gang or individual I'm supposed to be assigned. Has Black Water finally made a mistake?"

"Not a chance," Gene answered. "I was the final authority on who comprised each team and who they were assigned to eliminate."

"Then why don't I have an assignment?" Jim asked. "I have the basics but no specifics."

"That will come later," Gene said, standing up. "For now, just assume that you'll be given a target that can't be discussed with the rest of the teams. Also, you'll be receiving a list of each team's members and their specific targets."

"Because?" Jim asked standing.

"First, you're being 'promoted,' if that's how you want to view it," Gene said as they started for the doors that led to the hall.

"Promoted," Jim mused as they headed toward the men's restroom. "Does that include my own car, driver, and private jet?"

"You wish," Gene said, smiling. "It's something we need to discuss because it's specific only to this assignment. But there's time to talk about that on the way to pick up Jennifer this evening."

Selecting a urinal several down from Gene, Jim looked around and remarked, "Okay. I'm promoted to something that obviously has no benefits. And it's only temporary. Sounds like I'm being set up for the fall guy in case this outlandish scheme fails to produce the desired results or, even worse, in case it does and the fallout becomes too toxic for the company."

"Now you know I'd never do that," Gene said, heading for the wash basins. "Regardless of the outcome, I'll be the one to take any criticism. You know me well enough that I'd never let one of my men or women get blamed for my failures."

"I know," Jim said, turning on the water to wash his hands. "You've always been 100 percent behind your people, and we always knew it. I've seen too many commanders try to pass the blame onto some subordinate. I've always detested those leaders who lead from behind and are too willing to sacrifice their people to cover their own asses."

"As I said, we'll discuss the dubious promotion while we drive to Alexandria," Gene said as he headed out of the door. "But we need to discuss your specific target here without the rest of the teams knowing who it is."

"When will we get to that?" Jim asked as they entered the briefing room.

"Probably tomorrow," Gene told him as they picked up their glasses from their table. "For now, I just want you to get a good overview of the operation and see if you've spotted any flaws or have any recommendations to improve it. I believe that the next speaker will have some additional details that will give you a little insight as to one of the key elements.”

“And I still don’t have a partner,” Jim remarked as they returned to their table.

“You’ll have a partner,” Gene answered as they took their seats. “There’s still a small obstacle to overcome to get the one I think is best suited for this mission. But it should be resolved by tonight. She should be here when we start tomorrow if the company managed to do their job.”

“From my experience, the company always does their jobs,” Jim remarked as O stepped up to the podium.

“Yes, they do,” agreed Gene as everyone turned their attention to another man standing beside O.

Chapter 11

"Okay. Let's keep this moving, and maybe we'll be able to cover everything and get out of here at a reasonable hour this evening," O said as he turned toward the other man by the podium. "I'd like to introduce a gentleman we'll simply call Larry M. Larry has numerous ties to the agencies down in St. Louis that have basically the same problems as we have in Chicago, although to a lesser degree. So, I'll let him tell you about their issues and how it ties in with our assignment."

The man stepped onto the podium, and a map of St. Louis, Missouri, showed up on the screen.

"Good afternoon, everybody," Larry said, looking down at the teams assembled before him. "As O said, we have a minor problem down in St. Louis compared to what Chicago is facing. However, we envision the issues will soon be exacerbated if this plan works and Chicago becomes the least attractive city for the cartels. As has been mentioned, the drug problem won't just go away. And we have information that St. Louis will almost certainly become the next Chicago."

Glancing at the map, he said, "We already know that some of the gangs in St. Louis are vying to become the central distribution point for drugs coming into the United States. As you can see, we have the railroad system, rivers, and interstate highways that will allow the same advantages to the cartels for distribution as Chicago has. The gangs there aren't quite as extensive as in Chicago, but several have close ties to the Gangster Disciples and the Vice Lords. As a matter of fact, there are sects of the Vice Lords within the St. Louis area. They are primarily located in East St. Louis, which is actually in Illinois, but if what our informants say is even close to the truth, they have aspirations of becoming just as powerful as the parent organization in Chicago.

"We're sure that they are actively involved in discussions with certain individuals from the various cartels regarding expanding their influence. They have broached the idea that they would be a better location for the distribution than Chicago. They've sent several high-level members down to South America to demonstrate their sincerity and to demonstrate the obvious benefits of St. Louis over Chicago. So far, the leadership in Chicago doesn't know that one of their so-called chapters is trying to do an end run around them. We're not sure how much longer the treachery will go unnoticed. That's why now is a crucial time for this operation. The elimination of the major players in Chicago will embolden the St. Louis Vice Lords and will also force the cartels to move their hub. And since they have the inside track, the St. Louis Vice Lords sect will most likely be the logical choice."

O stepped back up to the microphone and said, "Now one of the reasons we're bringing Larry and his folks on board is because we plan on using those same Vice Lords from St. Louis to take the fall for all the assassinations in Chicago. We've already identified fifteen or twenty members whose DNA is on file with several agencies, and we've developed background data on them just as we have on the individuals in your folders.

"These members will be identified as the killers based on your teams planting the DNA and ties to the guns involved. We've developed a plan to have these certain individuals out of the St. Louis area during the Chicago operation so that they will have no alibi or be able to proclaim their innocence to their own gangs. And to answer the unasked question"—O smiled—"their bodies will be located in Chicago following the teams' missions. The obvious inference will be that the St. Louis Vice Lords decided to mount an offensive to take over the distribution from their associates and their rivals. This will certainly demonstrate to the cartels that they have the power and capabilities to fulfill the role of controlling the distribution. Now that's a broad-brush look at the ties between Chicago and St. Louis. I'll let Larry give you a quick look at where they are in the planning and what they'll need to ensure the coordination between the teams in St. Louis and those operating in Chicago."

"Pretty simple," Larry said, stepping back up. "All we really need in the way of coordination is regarding the timing. We certainly don't want our boys dying before their time. Even a cursory autopsy would prove that they couldn't have been involved. And we need to have them removed from the St. Louis area with at least enough time to travel to Chicago and perform their missions. We do plan on executing them in St. Louis. It's only about three hundred miles, and we can drive that in a little over four hours. The bodies will be in a temperature-controlled truck so that the small amount of time won't be an issue since we expect it to be a couple of hours before the CPD can get them and your real targets on the slab. Even a field exam by the on-call forensic pathologist won't be accurate enough to give credence to the slight time of death issues."

"That fact, along with the DNA on the victims, will be sufficient to conclude that it was a gang rivalry," O said, stepping up beside Larry. "And the firearms you teams will be issued have been used in St. Louis and will be found in possession of our unwilling accomplices. That should seal the direction any official investigation will take.

"Okay, we'll take about an hour for each of you teams to take a more informed look at your specific assignments, have something to eat, and come back with suggestions or anything you believe we've either missed or where we need to do more research. The overall objective is to cripple the main gangs in Chicago and make damn sure that you guys and the organization are never associated in any manner to this act of unnecessary and brutal violence upon the poor disadvantaged members of our society."

Chapter 12

Jim had gotten a sandwich and a small salad from the buffet table during the break and was sitting alone since Gene had told him that there were a couple of issues he needed to take care of. He was almost finished eating when Gene returned with both Larry and O.

"Jim, I'd like to introduce you to these two gentlemen," Gene announced as Jim stood. "Larry, this is Jim Lashley."

The two shook hands as Gene said, "Jim's been with Black Water for almost fifteen years. He joined us when he was flying F-4s in the Marine Reserves after Vietnam. O, this is the man who'll be coordinating all the teams once we activate the operation."

Jim shook O's hand as Gene continued, "Jim was involved with Dark Water operations, the international enforcement arm of Black Water, until he retired from the Marines and joined American Airlines as a pilot. Now we use him mainly with the domestic side, Muddy Water, since his duties with American take him around the United States."

"Nice to meet both of you," Jim said as Gene motioned for them all to sit down. "I'm a little surprised that Gene didn't tell me about having to coordinate this operation until now."

"I told you that you were getting a promotion," Gene said, smiling as he picked up his glass of tea. "Well, this is it."

Jim shook his head and asked, "O, what's your background?"

"First Marines," O told him. "I joined in '76 and was trained as a Mortarman and Machine Gunner and stationed at Twentynine Palms. After that, I joined the CPD and worked the streets for about five years before I was assigned to the Drug-and-Gang task force. I've been there ever since."

"Sounds good," Jim said, nodding. "Except the part about Twentynine Palms. I passed close to the base when I was driving through the area on I-10. Pretty desolate."

"That, it was," O agreed. "But there was plenty of room to practice all sorts of artillery without disturbing the civilians."

"I'm sure," Jim agreed. "We'll have to get together for a beer later and compare notes. What about you, Larry?"

"Air Force," Larry answered. "I was a mechanic on the F-106 with the 318th Fighter Interceptor Squadron at McChord Air Force Base from '78 until '81. After my enlistment was up, I moved back to St. Louis and joined the police. Sort of like O, I spent a few years on the streets and finally wound up in the anti–drug-and-gang business. Over the years, O and I have had several joint operations. Mainly because of the Vice Lords since the St. Louis sect is closely tied with the ones in Chicago."

"You Air Force guys," Jim said, smiling. "Always sleeping in a nice warm bed, with shiny shoes and a well-stocked club to have a cold beer at the end of your eight-hour shift. And living in the Pacific Northwest must have been difficult too."

"Brutal," Larry said, laughing. "I'll admit that we had it pretty plush compared to O's time in the desert and especially your time in 'Nam. Gene gave us a mini brief on you back when we were just beginning to put this operation together."

"I guess we'll let you join us Marines for a beer," Jim told him, smiling. "We'll let just about anybody *buy* us a drink."

"We can all have a drink later," Gene told them. "But for now, we need to take care of a little company business since they're the ones paying our salary. O will be your contact point in Chicago if you have any questions regarding the operation there." Gene said looking from Jim to O. "We, the company, will be funneling all the intelligence to him on where the targets are as we begin executing the final phase. Since he is intimately familiar with the area, he'll also be available to redirect our teams to their targets should there be a need."

Looking at Larry, Gene continued, "Larry will be almost completely autonomous except for coordination on the timing of the teams that will be operating in St. Louis. All the updates from the dedicated satellite information will flow directly to him. It is crucial that we don't activate the Chicago teams until the teams down there have completed their assignments."

"How much time will you need once you start your operation?" Jim asked Larry.

"Well, it shouldn't take more than thirty to forty-five minutes to gather our targets and the four hours I mentioned to get them to Chicago," Larry answered. "So, once I'm given the go-ahead, I can ensure delivery to anywhere between Joliet and Justice just off 294 within five hours."

"What about on the Chicago side?" Jim asked, looking at O. "How much time do you estimate from the execution order to have Chicago teams complete their assignments?"

"If every target is where we anticipate, based on the research we've done over the last year, thirty minutes," O answered.

"What is the best window to ensure everyone is where we expect?" Jim asked.

"Between two o'clock in the morning and four," Gene answered. "We need you to be in Chicago by ten o'clock the night we give the order. That will give you plenty of time to recheck all the teams with O and Larry. If you're satisfied that everything is in place, then you'll give the final order."

"If we have to abort on the first night, how will that impact the plan?" Jim asked.

"Not much," Gene answered as both O and Larry nodded. "All our assets are extremely flexible. Your schedule is probably the most restricting. That and another factor that I'll discuss with you later."

"Looks like the natives are getting restless," O remarked, looking around. "I better get back up onstage and see if they've got any questions."

Chapter 13

Larry and O returned to the front of the room and waited for everyone to look toward them before O spoke.

"Well, you've had a few minutes to review your assignments. Are there any questions regarding the overall operation?"

"How accurate is your information regarding my—and I'm sure others have the same question—targets?" came the question from one of the tables.

As he saw other people nodding, O answered, "About 97 percent. As I mentioned earlier, we've been monitoring your targets and the others associated with their gang for over a year." Referring to a new slide on the screen behind him, he continued, "As you can see here, we've tracked every individual twenty-four hours a day. We've had a geosynchronous satellite over both Chicago and St. Louis for the entire period. Additionally, there have been teams verifying the data through personal reconnaissance. The only reason we have a 3 percent uncertainty is that everybody occasionally has some variance to their normal routine. But the period selected has the greatest probability of being accurate."

"What happens if our target just happens to be in a different location?" came another question.

"On the day of our operation, we'll be following each of the targets through both satellite and personal surveillance," O assured them. "If there appears to be some deviation from the expected locations, we'll be providing the specific team with minute-by-minute updates of the target's location."

"And if there are nontargeted personnel at the revised location?" someone asked.

"That's up to the discretion of the team," O replied. "If you have to eliminate the other people, it's up to you. We've gamed this hundreds of times, and one of the factors we've looked at is bystanders. The consensus is that any additional personnel most likely have some tie to the target's activities. Especially given the time frame of the operation."

"You mentioned using guns with ties to St. Louis," someone else asked. "When will we be given them?"

Larry stepped up to the podium and answered, "As soon as the company selects the first probable date. I've gathered twenty weapons in St. Louis that have been used in different crimes over the last year but were never turned over to St. Louis PD."

"You mentioned targeting more individuals than the three we're assigned. What do we do with them?" another team member asked.

"You will be provided an extremely detailed folder on each one of those targets I initially identified," O told them. "That folder will include every piece of information the company gathered, along with high-definition photographs, of the exact movements of each individual. Those folders will be left beside the body of the head of each gang. The company believes that just knowing how detailed we were in gathering information and that they could be next will provide them with the same incentive to get out of the gang or drug business."

"And if it doesn't?" the same person asked.

"Then we already have enough information to launch a second wave against any gang that doesn't seem to take our not-so-subtle warning," O answered. "The company and I came to this compromise, and they assured me that the satellites and other methods of tracking would stay in place until we see the results of the first strike."

"Sounds like you really want a more aggressive approach," someone from the back remarked.

"Not necessarily," O told them. "I've just seen how the cartels and some of the gangs operate when they want to leave a lasting impression and prove their willingness to do whatever is necessary to prevent interference with their operations. I'm all in favor of keeping the violence down to a minimum, but I've got my doubts on this operation. However, the door remains open if we need to revisit the problem. Just remember, the amount of money each gang will lose is enormous. I'm afraid that the next man down the chain of command will want to step up and try to take charge. If that happens, we'll be back here soon, and more drastic measures may prove to be necessary.

"Now if there are no further questions, we'll adjourn for the day. Please make sure you bring your folders back tomorrow morning. If there are any issues you need to bring up, feel free to do so. Any suggestions will be appreciated. Good evening."

Chapter 14

Jim gathered up all the folders from his table, while Gene went to talk to O and Larry. Still a little concerned about who his target would turn out to be, he watched the various people from the other teams talking before leaving the room.

As Gene approached, he asked, "Are you staying in Alexandria tonight, or are you coming back here?"

"I've got a room at the Alexandrian, same as you," Gene told him as he gathered his notes from the table. "I figure we'll need the drive back here tomorrow to discuss anything you think of tonight."

"Sounds good," Jim remarked as they headed for the door. "I'm sort of curious about why my target wasn't discussed."

"Very sensitive issue," Gene told him as they headed down the hall. "There are only a handful of people who know about it, and everything about his elimination must appear to be from natural causes."

"Sounds like most of the assignments I've had since I left the Marines," Jim said as they left the building and headed for Gene's waiting Suburban.

"One of the reasons the company keeps your assignments in the 'natural causes' category is that you seem to have a special talent for that sort of work," Gene said as their driver held the doors open. Once inside, Gene handed Jim a thick folder and added, "Start reading. I've got to review my notes and get ready to call the office when we get to Alexandria."

For the next twenty minutes, Jim read through the material and waited until Gene appeared to be finished reading his notes before saying, "You've got to be kidding me."

Gene set his notes aside and said, "Nope. We, the company and a few of the people who are aware of that man's operations, think that he and his people are one of the main reasons that the city has had such a difficult time catching the upper-level people in the five gangs we're targeting."

"How did someone so high in the CPD get so deeply involved?" Jim asked, looking at a picture of a captain of the police department.

"We're not sure," Gene admitted, shaking his head. "Probably the same way most people get involved with things that they hope will never be discovered. We think that he was recruited back when he was just a normal street cop. What we don't know is if he was turned just for the money or if one of the gangs had information on him."

"How did you discover him?" Jim asked as he read the biography of Capt. Robert Nelson.

"There were rumors floating around the department for years," Gene answered. "But there was never a name or any actual proof. Then when we were setting up the operation a year ago, there were a couple of instances when Captain Nelson was seen in the wrong location. So, to eliminate him from any suspicion, we began surveying him along with the other targets. That's when we discovered that he had accounts in overseas banks that couldn't be explained. Then we began watching a few of the patrolmen who seemed to be interacting with him more often than we thought necessary."

"What are you doing about those people?" Jim asked, wondering just how many people within the CPD were involved.

"They'll be removed once the operation is complete," Gene told him. "There aren't really that many people, and it's being left to the city to clean its own house. Not sure if you know it, but dirty cops seem to have a problem with making the wrong traffic stop or attempting to serve a warrant on the wrong people."

"Sort of like fragging back in 'Nam," Jim said, nodding.

"Fragging has been around long before 'Nam," Gene told him. "Although it's usually been used against some superior officer or noncommissioned officer whose ineptness is putting the troops in peril, it's also been used by the lowest grunt to get rid of someone who is endangering the rest of them."

"I've heard of it being used against cops who turn on their brothers," Jim remarked as he thought about the implications to the CPD if this information became public.

"Definitely," Gene agreed. "Did you ever see the movie *Serpico*?"

"Yeah," Jim answered. "I remember seeing it right after my last tour in 'Nam. I think Jennifer and I had just moved to Mesquite."

"Sounds about right," Gene told him. "I always wondered if we had some problems like that down at the lower levels in the Marines. Maybe some kid who saw his Sergeant doing something that he disagreed with, so the Sergeant put him on point every time the mission looked a little dicey."

"I don't know," Jim said as he sat back and thought about his two tours as an enlisted Marine in Vietnam. "I'd hate to think it happened, but I know a lot of the guys who were there for their second tours really had some issues with those who came to the Corps instead of doing jail time. It would be very easy to just say that Joe Blow was always taking chances out in the field and that it finally caught up with him.”

“Well, Marines are people with the same problems as everybody else,” Gene said as they pulled into the hotel. “I’ll meet you and Jennifer in the lobby in an hour if she’s ready by then.”

“I’ll try to make sure she is,” Jim said, smiling. “If not, I’ll call your room.”

Chapter 15

An hour later, Gene was waiting in the lobby, talking on the phone, when Jim and Jennifer came walking from the elevator. Holding up one finger, Gene quickly finished his call and smiled at them, saying, "I hope you don't mind, but I just ordered for all of us."

"That's fine with me," Jennifer said, taking Gene's hand as he stood. "I'm sure you know better than us what's good at all the restaurants around here."

"Not necessarily so," Gene told her as he led the way to the front doors. "But I've taken so many people to the Chart House that I'm pretty familiar with their menu. And having been around you two for so many years, I sort of know your various tastes."

"As long as you're picking up the bill, I guess you get the opportunity to select the meal," Jim said, smiling as Gene's Suburban pulled to a stop in front of them. "And I'm pretty sure you'll find a way to expense this to the company."

"Speaking of the company," Jennifer asked as she slid across the seat in the rear, "how often do you think I can come with Jim when you guys get together here?"

"Depends," Gene said, laughing. "But just remember that Jim doesn't always get a private jet and that he normally stays down at Quantico."

"That's true," Jim said as they sped toward the Potomac. "I don't think you'd be nearly as happy with the accommodations on a Marine base."

"I think I can put up with anything," Jennifer said as she watched the historic scenery of Old Town slide by. "Regardless of what you think, I'm still a Marine's wife, and I've already demonstrated that I can live with just about anything that Jim needs to do."

"I've no doubt about that," Gene said as they arrived at the Chart House restaurant. "I'm pretty sure that just day-to-day living with Jim is as close to a living hell as any woman should be forced to survive."

"Thanks so much," Jim said, smiling as they entered the restaurant. "I always thought of living with me as paradise for the lucky lady who won my heart."

"Oh, it is," Jennifer joked as the maître d' led them toward the patio. "Life with you has always been like a princess's fairy tale. I'm just glad I didn't have to keep kissing frogs trying to find my prince."

"So now I'm just another frog," Jim remarked as they were seated at a table close to the railing separating the patio from the river. "But I have to say that this is a nice view. I'm glad it's not raining."

"I can't take credit for that," Gene said as a waiter approached with a bottle of Duckhorn Vineyards Merlot and three glasses.

"Now that surprises me," Jennifer joked as a taste of the wine was poured for her. "I thought Marine Generals were tantamount to God himself, and we all know that God controls everything."

"We do leave some of the minor details to him," Gene said, winking at Jim.

After taking a small sip of the wine, she nodded and continued, "If the rest of the meal is as good as this, I'll let you take credit for everything. Including the weather."

Waiting as the waiter poured everyone a glass, Gene smiled and said, "I think you'll find that everything here is beyond reproach. Now why don't you tell Jim and I what you spent your day doing while we were slaving over hot papers?"

"Just wandering around," Jennifer said as a dish of shrimp, crab, avocado, and mango arrived. "There's so much history within mere steps of the hotel that I was surprised when I noticed how late the time was. I think I could spend a month just walking around here."

"The biggest thing to me is how well-preserved the area is," Gene remarked as they took samplings of the dish. "Some of our old historic cities—and I'll use Baltimore as an example— have become blight ridden and too dangerous to really enjoy. Beautiful old buildings falling down. Block after block of burned-out buildings where people sit around with nothing to do. I think it's shameful that the governments of these cities don't do something to restore what could be a Mecca for tourism."

"I'll stay out of that conversation," Jim said as a plate of grilled halibut with pico de gallo made with avocado, jalapeno, tomato, cilantro, and lime was set in front of him.

"You don't have to say anything," Jennifer retorted as her dinner of blackened swordfish covered with lump crab, asparagus, and béarnaise sauce arrived. "I bet Gene knows your political leanings as well as I. And I'm not sure if the other diners here want to hear about it."

"I think we should stay away from any conversation that would distract from our meals while we enjoy watching the boats out on the Potomac," Gene said as his baked mahi-mahi with lemon shallot butter, seasoned vegetables, and coconut ginger rice was placed in front of him.

"Should we talk about what you and Jim are doing up here?" Jennifer asked as she looked from Jim to Gene and took another sip of wine.

"Maybe we should just stick to discussing what you saw during your wanderings around Old Town," Jim suggested. "That's much more interesting than listening to Gene and I talk about reviewing statistics on crime and issues regarding solving the world's problems."

"I agree," Gene diplomatically said, nodding. "What do you plan for tomorrow?"

Chapter 16

After Gene told Jim and Jennifer good night back at the hotel, they decided to go for a short walk before going up to their room. Leaving the hotel, they headed east along King Street.

"What time are you and Gene going back to Quantico tomorrow?" Jennifer asked as they approached North Royal Street.

"We'll leave the hotel about seven o'clock," Jim answered as he admired the buildings along the street.

"What time do you think you'll get back?" she asked crossing Royal Street.

"Depends," Jim answered. "I'm hoping that we'll get everything done by noon, but it could last until late afternoon. Sort of like today."

"Does that mean that we'll get to stay here another day?" Jennifer asked as they crossed King Street into Market Square.

"Maybe," Jim told her as they walked along the sidewalk. "If we don't finish until late afternoon, we'll probably stay another night."

"What if you finish by noon? Can we stay another night anyway?" she asked.

"I'm pretty sure we can," Jim told her. "Do you want to stay another night?"

Stopping and putting her arms around Jim's neck, she said, "Yes. Especially if I get some time alone with you."

Jim put his arms around her waist and softly whispered in her ear, "If that's what you want. Even if I have to pay for the extra night in the hotel and arrange for the flight home, I want you to be happy. I know we haven't had much vacation time for a few years now, but we'll have this weekend."

Jennifer kissed him on the lips and stepped back, looking into his eyes before saying, "You know, I still remember the first time you came into our restaurant. You were the sexiest man I had ever seen. And you've gotten even sexier over these last fifteen years."

"And you were the most beautiful woman I'd ever met," Jim said, smiling at her. "Even though you smelled like french fries and onions."

"What do you expect when you come into a burger joint?" she replied, laughing at the memories. "A maître d' like tonight?"

"I expected a cheeseburger and fries," Jim told her, taking both her hands. "But what I got was the most amazing woman in the world."

"It sure took you long enough to realize that," Jennifer said, squeezing his hands. "I thought you'd never have the cojones to ask me."

"And what do you think now?" Jim asked, feeling the familiar stirrings that always happened when he realized that he was still deeply attracted to Jennifer.

"I think we better get back to our room before we embarrass these poor folks who are just out for an evening stroll," Jennifer said as she turned back toward the hotel.

"I don't mind embarrassing a few strangers," Jim said grinning.

"I think you'll like what I have in mind better than street sex," Jennifer said, leaning over and kissing him on the cheek.

"Just what do you have in mind?" Jim asked as they retraced their steps.

"A quick shower together, maybe an hour of just playing before we get serious, and then another hour of making you the happiest man in the world," she answered as they approached the hotel.

"That does sound better than a park bench quickie," Jim told her as they headed for the elevators. "But could you wait until room service leaves?"

"Room service?" she asked. "Why do we need room service?"

"I'm getting an order of french fries," Jim said, laughing as the elevator doors closed. "That smell and being naked with you is the most erotic thing I can think of."

Chapter 17

The next morning, Jim rose early and was ready to go downstairs when Jennifer sat up in bed, asking, "Are you sure you don't want to take a few more minutes with your wife before you go?"

"As good as that sounds, if I don't meet Gene and get to Quantico this morning, we sure won't get finished by noon," Jim said as he stepped to the side of the bed to kiss her goodbye. "But you go have fun, and I'll try to call you when I know how long we'll be working," he continued heading for the door.

"Don't forget to talk to Gene about us staying if you're finished today," Jennifer reminded him as she got out of bed.

"I won't forget," Jim said, stepping into the hall. "Love you."

Gene was waiting in the lobby when Jim exited the elevator and quickly stood to meet him on the way to the door.

"Everything good?" Jim asked as they saw their car approaching.

"Pretty much," Gene said, opening the door of the car. "How about you?"

"Good," Jim said, walking around to the other side of the car. "I've got a couple of questions though."

"Such as?" Gene asked as they headed south to Quantico.

"First and most important, Jennifer wants to stay another day even if we finish today," Jim said, seeing Gene smile knowingly.

"Not a problem," Gene told him. "I sort of expected that. Now what's number two and not nearly as important?"

"Let's start with the elimination of the top three of each gang," Jim answered. "Why don't we keep the financial guy or CFO alive and see if we can get some information out of him regarding where their money is and how they launder it?"

"Worth considering," Gene said, nodding. "What else?"

"Those folders with the details of the lives of the people we aren't going to eliminate," Jim continued. "I think if we leave them with the bodies, it will suggest a more organized approach than a mere gang hit. Especially if the CPD gets the folders. They'll know that someone with more extensive assets is involved."

"What do you suggest we do with all that information?" Gene asked. "We spent a lot of time and money compiling it."

"First off, we definitely show the CFO in great detail what we have on his family and friends," Jim answered. "And we let him see that we have folders on the others. Maybe he'll get the hint and tell everyone else that they're being closely watched and that a hit could happen any minute if the drug activity resumes."

"Okay, I'll give that to the company and see what they think," Gene said, nodding. "Anything else?"

"I don't know how you had planned on the actual hits, but I think it needs to be in front of the CFO," Jim added. "That way, there's no doubt about his future if he doesn't cooperate."

"Sort of like how some of the chopper pilots operated in 'Nam," Gene said. "Grab three or four of the villagers and ask a question of one of them. If they didn't answer or lied, toss them out about a hundred feet off the ground. By the time a couple of them had been thrown out, the next guy was willing to give you his grandmother."

"Not saying I approved of that," Jim said, looking at Gene. "But since we're going to eliminate these people anyway, why not use the act itself to help us take down the organization?"

"That could take some major revisions to the plan," Gene admitted as they continued south on I-95. "We'll get with Larry and O before the briefing starts and see what they think."

"I just thought there were some issues that could be handled better," Jim told him. "I know you guys have spent a lot of time setting this up, and I hate to be the one to throw a wrench into the works."

"No," Gene said, shaking his head at Jim. "That's why I brought you in. Sometimes a plan gets headed down a road, and numerous small changes take place. Nobody stops to look at where it's headed and suggests starting all over if it's gotten off track. A fresh view never hurts."

"I guess that justifies my promotion," Jim said, laughing. "Now I'm sure that a personal jet and unlimited expense account will follow suit."

"I do so enjoy your uninhibited sense of humor," Gene said as they pulled up to the facility's first set of gates. "And your imagination is beyond comprehension."

Chapter 18

As soon as they entered the briefing room, Gene told Jim to grab something to eat and go back to the table where they had been yesterday. After getting a plate of fruit, a Cinnabon, and a cup of coffee, Jim opened his folder on the CPD Captain.

Reviewing the material, he started thinking about ways to eliminate the man without raising any suspicions about his involvement with the gangs and drugs. He knew that if the man died on the same night that the other people were eliminated, it would provide speculation regardless of the method used. If the company had been directed to make it appear to be unquestionably natural causes, it would have to be done either before or after the mass assassination.

The problem with that was if Captain Nelson was eliminated before the hit, it might cause ripples within the gangs that would negate the year's work of predicting the target's movements and locations on the night of the operation. If he waited until after the primary operation, Captain Nelson would most likely be spooked and extremely wary of any attempt to get close enough to execute any covert operation that would mimic natural causes.

Deep in thought, Jim almost didn't notice when Gene arrived at the table with Larry and O.

As they placed their plates and coffee cups down, Gene said, "Larry and O think you are probably onto a good idea."

As they were taking their seats, Jim closed the folder on Captain Nelson and said, "I hope you guys don't think I walked in here to take away from all the hard work you have done."

"Not at all," O said, shaking his head. "I've seen the lowest street cop come up with a better plan after all of us on the task force had spent months planning a raid. Sometimes it's the guy who's never seen the plan who notices the most obvious flaw."

"I agree," Larry said, stabbing a piece of cantaloupe with his fork. "I think bringing all our targets to a central location will reduce the number of St. Louis gang members we need to *recruit*. I can imagine that instead of fifteen to twenty, we can get by with five or so."

"Do you think you can reduce the numbers by that much?" Gene asked. "That's pretty optimistic. I'd feel better if we stuck with the original plan on your end."

"Here's why I think the reduction is a better solution," Larry countered. "It was going to be difficult to get twenty members within the time frame we had to work with. Not impossible but much simpler with fewer people. And since we're going to have the Chicago gang members in one location, it's entirely possible that the fewer Vice Lords from St. Louis could kidnap the ten Chicago leaders and do a St. Valentine's Day type of massacre."

"That would also make it easier to get rid of the St. Louis members," O added, nodding. "We could even engineer a *traffic accident* that would result in all the men perishing in the fiery crash since five men could fit into a single car."

"And since they are all together in the car, an autopsy on the charred remains would be unable to accurately determine the time of death," Larry told them. "They would have the guns that can be tied to the assassinations, and DNA will identify the bodies. That will tie them to the St. Louis Vice Lords."

"Okay," Gene said, convinced that the proposal had merit. "I guess we can postpone the rest of this session until the company can game the new scenario and see if there are any modifications we need to make in the plans to kidnap the financial guys."

"Good," O said as he took a bite of his pecan roll. "I've got to give the company credit for bringing Jim in. I just wish he had gotten involved back at the start."

"If I'd been here during the initial planning, I'd probably have been satisfied with the original plan," Jim told him, shaking his head. "Like you mentioned a few minutes ago, sometimes it's the newbie who sees an opportunity. Most of the time planners become so enthralled with their efforts that they can't see the flaws."

"Sort of like me and my last girlfriend," Larry said, laughing. "I was initially so enthralled with her looks that I couldn't see that she had the brains of a slice of cantaloupe."

"I see that you're still attracted to cantaloupe though," Gene said, laughing as Larry was taking another piece of cantaloupe from his plate.

Larry put his fork down, shaking his head and saying, "Suddenly, I'm not so hungry. Maybe we better get up front and let everybody know that they can head home and wait for us to come back in a few days."

Chapter 19

"Did you call Jennifer?" Gene asked as they were heading back to Alexandria.

"I called the room and left a message at the desk," Jim answered. "She'll get it when she checks. And given how interested she is in staying another day, I'll bet she's checking every thirty minutes."

"Probably," Gene agreed. "If you don't think she'll mind, I'll make dinner arrangements for tonight. But if you guys want to be alone, that's all right too."

"I'm sure she'll be happy to have you join us," Jim told him. "You know she's been asking about coming with me again, so she'll have no objection."

"Good," Gene said, nodding. "I'll call another restaurant on the Potomac called the Blackwall Hitch. I think she'll like it. How about for seven o'clock?"

"That's fine," Jim answered. "Now there's something I need to run by you regarding our special target."

"What's that?" Gene asked, dialing the restaurant's number from the Suburban.

"I'll wait until you finish," Jim said. "It's a little detailed, and I have several questions."

After hanging up, Gene said, "Okay, what's your first question?"

"Have you ever heard of a parasite named *Naegleria fowleri*?" Jim asked.

"Nigeria what?" Gene asked.

"Not Nigeria. *Naegleria*," Jim said, chuckling. "Sounds close but way different."

"Okay, to answer your question, I don't think I've ever heard of whatever it is you're talking about," Gene responded. "Should I have?"

"Probably not by its scientific name," Jim told him. "But you may have heard about a certain brain-eating amoeba."

"Yeah, I've read about it. Lives in warmwater areas and enters the brain though the nasal cavities or something like that," Gene said, nodding. "What's that got to do with your target?"

"I've been thinking that if I remove the Captain too early, as in even one day before the other teams execute their missions, the gangs may radically change their patterns," Jim told him. "And if I wait as much as one day after the teams complete their assignments, he may start taking extraordinary precautions that would make my job much more difficult."

Gene thought for a minute before saying, "I can see that. But how does this brain-eating thing enter into the equation?"

"I need to do a little more research on it," Jim answered. "But if I remember correctly, it takes about five days for the amoeba to cause any symptoms and about five days from then until the victim dies."

"How do you plan on getting Captain Nelson to be in any water that would have the amoeba?" Gene asked.

"Doesn't necessarily have to be in a particular body of water," Jim informed him. "It's been discovered in ordinary tap water, such as if somebody used it in one of those nasal irrigation systems. It has also turned up at least once on a slip and slide a family used in their backyard."

"Okay, I get your point. But the question remains the same. How do you get him to the amoeba?" Gene asked.

"I plan on bringing the amoeba to him," Jim said, smiling. "But that's where I need the company's research division."

"What do you need of them?" Gene asked, wondering how plausible this idea might be.

"I need for them to find a way to weaponize the amoeba," Jim answered. "I'd suggest a powdered form, although a concentrated solution in liquid form would probably work."

"Okay, how do you plan on delivering it? Shove it up his nose?" Gene asked.

"More or less," Jim admitted. "Sort of like we did in Baltimore. But it will take a major distraction and something to temporarily incapacitate him for a few seconds."

"Sounds like you need the lab to do two things," Gene said. "Weaponize the amoeba and find a drug that will give you a few seconds to administer it."

"Precisely," Jim admitted. "But it meets all my parameters for timing. The only thing I'm having a problem with is how to get near enough to him to give me the opportunity to get the amoeba into his nose."

"What if I told you that we already have an asset close to Capt. Robert Nelson?" Gene said, smiling.

"What do you mean?" Jim asked, not surprised that the company was well into some operation involving the Captain.

"Do you remember the lady who just happened to be at Dunnahoe's Crapshoot in Baltimore?" Gene asked.

"Of course," Jim said, nodding. "Good-looking lady named Valerie, I believe."

"That's her," Gene confirmed. "And I'm not surprised that you remembered her. A very stunning woman."

"Are you saying that she's in Chicago?" Jim asked.

"Been there for almost a month," Gene answered. "Her job is much like it was in Baltimore. Get close to the target and keep him interested while we decide what we're going to do."

"Is she my partner on this operation?" Jim asked, wondering how the chemistry between them would be.

"No, she never gets involved with the actual assassination," Gene answered. "But she can be invaluable in getting you close enough for you to do whatever is needed."

"Then who is going to be my partner?" Jim asked as they approached the hotel.

"Jewell," Gene answered. "You two work very well together, and I trust you and her won't let anything get in the way of the mission."

"You know I'd never let anything do that," Jim said as they pulled in front of the hotel.

"I know," Gene said, opening his door. "I'm more talking about you two not getting involved with each other. Now let's see if Jennifer has managed to get your message and how long we need before getting ready for dinner."

Chapter 20

After they were dropped off at the Blackwall Hitch restaurant, Gene said, "I reserved an outside table, if that's all right with you."

"That sounds great," Jennifer answered as they walked in. "I do enjoy watching the boats on the river, and we can always sit inside when we're back in Texas."

"Good for me," Jim agreed as the maître d' led them toward one of the outside patios.

"I'm going to suggest Kim Crawford Unoaked Chardonnay," Gene said, nodding to the maître d'.

"No Merlot?" Jennifer asked, taking her seat.

"I think you'll like this wine," Gene told her as he sat. "Especially if you order what I'm about to suggest."

"I'm fine with you ordering," Jim said, looking out toward the Potomac. "I'm just glad to be sitting here with the love of my life and a very dear friend."

Jennifer reached across the table to take Jim's hand and said, "I too am glad to be here with the love of my life and a very dear friend."

"Thank you both," Gene said, smiling. "I'm always happy to be with you guys. If I could pick my family, I'd certainly include you two." As their waiter brought the wine, Gene looked at him and said, "We're ready to order, sir."

"Certainly," the waiter said as he set a glass in front of each of them. Then looking at Jennifer, he asked, "What would the lady like this evening?"

"The gentleman will be ordering for all of us," she answered, smiling.

The waiter nodded and simply said, "Very well. What does the gentleman wish to order?"

"The lady would like the Maryland crab cakes. The other gentleman will have the Day Boat sea scallops and saffron risotto. And I would like the crab-stuffed rockfish," Gene said, picking up his glass of wine. As the waiter turned to leave, Gene raised his glass and toasted, "To a lasting friendship."

"Indeed," Jim said as he tapped his glass to both Gene's and Jennifer's.

"And a wonderful friendship, it is," Jennifer said as her glass clinked with the others. After taking a small sip, she asked, "Since you came back so early today, I assume that you finished your job and we'll take the jet back home tomorrow."

"Not really," Gene said, setting his glass on the table. "We had to discontinue the conversation because of a slight flaw Jim pointed out."

"Really?" Jennifer asked, looking at Jim. "Does that mean you'll have to come back again?"

"Yes," Gene answered. "I've got to do some follow-up with the company and the customers to see if they agree with Jim's suggestions. If so, we'll do some additional research and then try to bring everybody back again."

"How long do you think that will take?" she asked.

"I'm hoping that we can have everything ironed out by next weekend," Gene said as the waiter came back to the table with another bottle of the Chardonnay.

"Compliments of the house, sir," he said, setting the bottle down. "I'll be right back with your dinners."

"Does that mean I'll get to come back with Jim?" Jennifer asked anxiously.

Smiling, Gene answered, "Most likely, if he agrees."

"Oh, he'll agree," Jennifer said, smiling at Jim. "Won't you?"

"Nothing I'd like better," Jim told her. "I just need to take a look at my flying schedule to make sure I can make it next week."

"I'm pretty sure you aren't flying," Jennifer told him. "We had talked about going up to Lake Texoma for the weekend."

"That's right," Jim agreed, knowing that Gene had already looked at his schedule also. "So, I guess we'll be back here for another little vacation."

"Jennifer may get a vacation," Gene told them. "But since we've had to revise our operational plans, you'll be lucky to get home in time for dinner. You may even have to spend a night or two at the base so we can make up for the time you cost the company with your observations of our last plan."

"You wouldn't do that," Jennifer said, frowning at Gene. "I'm looking forward to more nights like this."

"Don't worry," Gene told her, laughing. "I'm enjoying the evenings as much as you. We'll both be here unless something monumental arises."

"Good. But if I keep eating like this, I'll need to go shopping again before we come back," Jennifer said as their meals were delivered. "I've never eaten so much good food in just two days."

"As if you need an excuse to go clothes shopping," Jim joked as he picked up a piece of scallop. "But I agree about the food. I could definitely get used to this, but I'm sure my uniforms would need to be let out a little."

"Just don't think it will always be like this," Gene said as he took a bite of his rockfish. "And to answer your unasked question, all three of us will be taking the plane back to Mesquite tomorrow. Please be ready to leave by nine o'clock."

"We'll be ready," Jennifer assured him, smiling. "And we'll be glad to come back next week in the plane again."

"We'll see," Gene said, looking at Jim and shaking his head. "I think we've created a monster."

"You invited her," Jim reminded him. "I'm just along for the ride at this point."

Chapter 21

Jim had returned from his normal scheduled trip the following Thursday morning when he received a call just after Jennifer had left for work.

"Got anything going on this morning?" Gene asked as Jim answered the phone.

"Not really," Jim told him. "What do you have in mind?"

"Lunch with some friends," Gene told him. "How about if I come by in about forty-five minutes and we'll head down to your favorite restaurant?"

"Sounds good to me," Jim replied. "Who are the 'some friends'?"

"I'll let that be a surprise," Gene told him, laughing. "I think you'll enjoy it."

Jim hung up and returned to watching the news while he drank his coffee. Shaking his head at how Gene enjoyed his little mysteries, he decided to take a quick shower and shave before they arrived. He had barely finished dressing when the doorbell rang. As he opened the door, he was surprised to see Jewell standing there, smiling at him.

"Now that's not the reception I expected from you," Jewell said as Jim looked past her to the black Suburban. "I sort of thought you'd say something nice like 'You look wonderful' or 'I'm so glad to see you again.' Not that blank stare like you just did. What's the matter, Jim? Is my beauty so stunning that you're speechless?"

Jim shook his head and answered, "No. I'm just a little surprised that Gene sent you to the door. But I guess I'm not that surprised either. He likes his little games. Anyway, I'm guessing that time is of the essence and that I need to come with you right now."

"Pretty much," Jewell said as Jim pulled the door shut behind him as they headed to the Suburban. "Val and I have to get back to Chicago this afternoon, and Gene says he needs to be in Quantico as soon as possible after we see if his plan will work."

"Val?" Jim asked, smiling as they approached the car. "Now that is a surprise."

Jewell stopped just before they reached the car and said, "Why, Jim, if I didn't know better, I'd think that you're happier to see her than you are me. But I know that can't be true. I've been your dream girl since we met on the flight so many years ago."

"Of course not," Jim said, opening the rear door. "You'll always be my dream. I'm just surprised that she's here."

"Sure," Jewell told him as she got in the back seat with Val. "I've known you too long not to know the way you think."

"You remember Valerie," Gene said as Jim slid into the front seat.

"Of course," Jim said as he shut the door. "Baltimore, I believe. How are you, Val?"

"Good," Val replied. "It's been a while. How have you been?"

"Good as well," Jim told her as Gene headed for the restaurant. "Gene said something about you being involved with this operation. It's good to see you again."

"You as well," Val replied. "Gene asked me to see if I could help you guys with a little problem in Chicago. So I've been up there for a little over a month. I like Chicago all right, but I prefer being home in Atlanta."

"We'll see if we can't get you back home in the next week or two," Gene said as they pulled into the parking lot at Venice Pizza. "First, though, we need to see if we can't coordinate you guys for this operation."

Once seated in the vacant back area, Jim asked, "How's the lab doing on the amoeba stuff?"

"Pretty good," Gene told him as the waitress arrived with menus and glasses of water. "A few minor problems that we hope to have resolved in a couple of days if what we're going to work on today seems feasible." As soon as the waitress had taken their orders and left, Gene continued, "We're able to freeze-dry the amoeba and make it a powder. Then once it contacts moisture and any temperature above about eighty degrees Fahrenheit, it becomes active again."

"What about delivery?" Jim asked.

"Pretty much like the solution we used in Baltimore," Jewell answered. "Except we have to get the material directly into the target's nose instead of on his food. That brings up the point you made back in Quantico. We have to provide a window of opportunity for you to perform the operation without our man realizing what's happening and also to not remember that anything out of the ordinary took place."

"That's where I come in," Val told him. "My job is to make sure that Robert is completely unaware that something other than a normal dinner with me happened."

"And that brings us to today," Gene said as their meals arrived. "And the coordination among the three of you is paramount. Not to mention the problem should the material be inadvertently contacted by either of you, so we have to get this right."

Chapter 22

"Okay," Gene told them as soon as the waitress had gone. "Let's take a look at how we're going to make this work. First off, we need to slightly incapacitate Captain Nelson. To do this, it has to be relatively fast acting, unnoticeable, and of short duration. Now the lab has developed a mixture that I believe will work." Gene looked at each of them. "I'm going to get a bit technical here, so you'll know what you're dealing with. The first ingredient is the *Atropa belladonna* root. It's part of the nightshade family, which includes potatoes, tomatoes, and tobacco. The active ingredient is atropine. As a matter of history, in ancient Rome, the wife of Emperor Claudius used it to terminate their marriage vows." Gene smiled slightly. "And Livia, the wife of Emperor Augustus, was rumored to have used it also."

"Thank goodness we only die financially when we get divorced today," Jim remarked.

"Oh, I wouldn't be so sure of that," Jewell said, laughing. "It's better to get everything instead of half. Can we get a little extra of this mixture when the operation is over?"

"I haven't given you the entire mixture yet," Gene said as they bantered. "But you should also know that the antidote is physostigmine. I included this little bit of information in the event either of you should ingest any of the mix.

"Another tidbit about the belladonna root. Macbeth of Scotland used it to poison the troops of Harold Harefoot, King of England, during a truce. The soldiers were so incapacitated that they couldn't stand and had to retreat to their ships. This is pretty powerful stuff."

"What's it mixed with?" Jim asked. "Because by itself, we're going to have a little problem with Robert still being conscious when we try to deliver the amoeba."

"I'm getting to that," Gene rebuked him. "The second part of the mix is Rohypnol flunitrazepam, more commonly known as a roofie."

"Why do we need both?" Val asked. "Isn't the roofie known as the date rape drug?"

"Yes, it is," Gene answered. "The belladonna is there to add confusion and hallucinations. It's almost as fast acting as the roofie, but it's longer lasting. And the tests we ran show that it adds to the effects of the roofie. And we plan on neutralizing the roofie when we administer the amoeba."

"How does that work?" Jim asked. "Are we going to give him a shot?"

"No," Gene explained. "The antidote for the roofie is flumazenil, and it's administered nasally, the same as you'll administer the amoeba."

"What about the timing?" Jewell asked.

"The belladonna is relatively quick acting," Gene said. "And as I said, it's about the same as the roofie. About twenty to thirty minutes from administration. And as I said, we plan on neutralizing the roofie when we give him the amoeba. The antidote will counteract the roofie, and the effects should be gone within one to two minutes. But the confusion of the belladonna will last much longer."

"When do I give him the amoeba and roofie antidote?" Jim asked.

"That's up to Val," Gene said, nodding at her. "She'll be beside him at the restaurant and is in the best position to know when he's unresponsive. That's when you will step to her table and use a syringe to give him the amoeba and the antidote for the roofie."

"How am I going to get him to take the roofie and stuff?" Val asked.

"That part is easy," Gene told her. "We have a waiter who will pour your wine, and Robert's glass will already have a few drops of the mix. It's clear and tasteless. The reason for telling you about the mix and the antidotes is just in case you should get the wrong glass."

"Who is going to give me the antidote?" Val asked, surprised that the possibility of a mistake existed.

"Jewell," Gene assured her. "She'll have some roofie antidote and that for the belladonna in her purse just in case. But the waiter is fully aware of the importance of getting the contaminated glass to Robert. He's been a member of our organization for several years and has never made a mistake. But we always have a plan B."

"Or a way out," Jim said as he shook his head. "What's that plan?"

"If something happens between the time the waiter pours the wine and the time he hands you the first glass, which is his normal routine," Gene told them, "then you have the option of dropping your glass if you suspect something is wrong. Or if the waiter signals you. Just don't drink even a sip from Robert's glass."

Chapter 23

"Now even if you should ingest some of the mix and we can't give you the antidote, it's not fatal," Gene told Val. "You'll be disoriented for a period, but it'll wear off. However"—he looked at each of them—"the same can't be said for the amoeba that's mixed in the powder with the roofie antidote. If any amount—and I stress this—of the amoeba gets into your nasal passage, it is fatal. There is no known antidote."

"How can we guarantee that none of us comes in contact with it?" Jewell asked. "How are we supposed to administer it and ensure that none of it affects any of us?"

"We've looked at that extensively," Gene assured them. "First, I'll explain how the *bug* will be handled up to the point of giving it to Robert. It will be stored in a small 3 cc syringe like this one." Gene opened the briefcase he had brought in and laid a syringe on the table. "The mix will be loaded at the lab under the strictest protocol, and the syringe will be sterilized more thoroughly than anything that the Center for Disease Control can imagine."

"What about it escaping before we need it?" Jim asked. "If it's *ready to use*, as it must be, how do you prevent a single micron of that crap from leaking? I've used syringes enough to know that the smallest movement of the plunger can expel some of the contents.”

“That’s true,” Gene countered. “But there’s a very thin flexible membrane within the syringe that was inserted before the mix. That membrane will be ruptured when sufficient force is exerted on the plunger. Before that, it’s impossible for anything to escape. We tested this repeatedly and determined the exact force needed to break the membrane yet not required so much that the mix would be forced out overly aggressively. We also placed the membrane almost halfway down the cylinder so that the first movement will expel just a small amount of air.”

“What if he moves his head?” Jewell asked. “Or if he sneezes? What about where that stuff goes then?”

“Good question,” Gene told her. “We’ve thought of that and have developed a procedure that will prevent any of the mix from escaping into the air.” Pulling a baggie from the briefcase, he laid it on the table next to the syringe. “This contains a napkin exactly like the ones at the restaurant. However, it’s been dampened with a chemical that will kill the amoeba. The real reason we’re here today is to practice using both the syringe and the napkin to make sure that none of this nasty stuff gets loose to affect you or anyone other than the intended target.”

“Okay, what’s the plan?” Jim asked, picking up the syringe. “Who does what?”

“We believe that having Val use the napkin is the most logical,” Gene explained to Jim. “She’ll have it in her purse and will place it in her lap when she first notices that Captain Nelson appears to become disoriented. Then when she gives you the signal that it’s time to give him the mix, she’ll have it ready to cover his nose as you step over to put the tip of the syringe in.”

“What about me?” Jewell asked. “What am I supposed to do while Jim’s giving him the mix and Val’s covering his nose?”

"As always, you'll be a distraction," Gene said, smiling at her. "As soon as Val gives Jim the signal, you'll wait for our waiter to approach with a tray of drinks. When he's close and looking at you, you'll get up suddenly and bump into him as he's passing behind your chair. Since you're sitting farther from Val and Robert, you'll cause anyone who happens to be looking in the vicinity to focus on you and the waiter as Jim and Val perform the operation. Now ideally, this shouldn't take more than five to ten seconds," Gene said as he put ten more syringes on the table. "Each of these has the exact membrane inside and requires the identical pressure required to break it as the one you'll be using. First, we'll start with Jim seeing just how much pressure is required," Gene said covering the syringes with his napkin as the waitress came around the corner.

Chapter 24

As soon as the waitress left them, Gene handed Jim one of the syringes, saying, "What we're after is just to break the membrane without any of the powder coming out. It's not that much pressure, so go slowly until you feel a slight change."

Jim held the syringe between his first two fingers and applied pressure with his thumb. Watching the plunger slowly slide into the cylinder, he was mildly surprised when it suddenly gave way.

"Good," Gene said, taking the syringe and handing him another. "Try it one more time."

This time, Jim pushed the plunger in quickly and watched as it stopped just before any powder exited the open end of the syringe. "Just a little awkward, but it takes less pressure than I thought," Jim told them, handing the syringe back to Gene.

"Yeah," Gene said, picking up another syringe. "But the tip has to be up to get it in his nose. Now if you're happy with it, I'll let Jewell try it."

"Why me?" Jewell asked. "I thought I was just there to distract the customers."

"That's true," Gene said, handing her a syringe. "But we can't just give up if something happens to prevent Jim from doing it. I don't expect it, but this is plan B."

Jewell took the syringe, mimicking Jim's motion, and pressed the plunger. A slight amount of powder shot from the tip, surprising her. "Wow," she said. "That's not supposed to happen, is it?"

"No," Gene told her, grinning. "That's why we're here practicing with baking powder instead of the nasty bug you'll be working with in Chicago. Try it again."

The next attempt was successful, and Jewell asked for one more before being satisfied that she could handle the job if necessary.

"Now let's work on the coordination," Gene said as he retrieved a purse from his briefcase. "Val, you'll have this purse with the napkin inside. Our lab built in a special compartment that is virtually sealed when the zipper is closed. We prefer for you to open it after Robert takes his first sip of wine," he said opening the compartment and showing her how it was constructed. "We left the napkin in the open for thirty minutes at the lab, and it was still sufficiently wet to absorb the entire amount of powder we used. Anyway, try to delay for at least fifteen minutes, but if you get a good chance to take it out unobserved a little before that, go ahead."

Val took the purse and held it in her lap as she looked across the table at Jim. "Jim won't be sitting at our table, will he?" she asked as she slipped her hand into the compartment of the purse.

"No, but we'll set the stage for that as soon as you're comfortable with how you plan on removing the napkin," Gene said, looking back from Jim to her.

"You mean like this?" Val said, smiling as she laid the napkin on the table.

"Exactly," Gene replied. "I'm guessing that you're happy with that part of the operation. So, I want Jim to take the seat at the table just to my right. You'll be sitting on the same side as I am so you can see Val, who's going to be just to my left." As Jim moved to the assigned seat, Gene continued, "Jewell, please take the chair directly across the table from Jim. I'm playing the part of Robert, so you'll be looking directly at me if you glance to your right. Use your peripheral vision as much as possible because we don't want you to distract Robert."

"Wouldn't that help Val?" Jewell asked as she took her seat across the table from Jim.

"No," Gene told her. "If Robert thinks anyone is watching him, it could result in him getting nervous. We want him to be completely unaware that anybody has any interest in him other than Val."

"Okay," Jewell said. "What direction will the waiter come from when I'm supposed to bump into him?"

"He'll come from your left," Gene answered. "You can expect to see him just a few minutes before Val and Robert get their wine. And, Val, the waiter will be standing beside the doors leading into the kitchen area, waiting for you to signal him to head back toward your table. Jewell, just be looking for Val to look up toward where the waiter will be standing. Matter of fact, you can look over there to make sure you know where he is and can watch him approach.".

"Now let's give this a first shot," Gene said looking at everybody. "I'll give a running commentary that should approximate the timing, except I'll shorten the time from drinking the wine to the desired effects."

Chapter 25

"Okay, I've just taken a sip of the wine," Gene stated. "So we can expect nothing for maybe fifteen minutes. There may be some early indications that Robert is having some difficulty concentrating in the next five to ten minutes, so Val will be paying close attention. You may even notice some slight slurring in his speech. Val, by now, you should have the napkin out of the purse if possible." He looked at her and continued, "If you don't get a chance, you shouldn't have a problem getting it ready before Jim steps over to administer the powder. Now let's assume that Robert is noticeably affected." Gene said looking at Jim. "Val is going to make sure the napkin is opened and in her left hand."

"Why my left hand?" Val asked.

"Because you'll need to turn to your right, and it would be awkward to try to cover his face with your right hand," Gene explained. "So, turn slightly, put your right hand on his—*my*—shoulder, and be ready to cover Jim's hand as he puts the syringe by my nose. Jim, Val has just given you the signal, and the waiter is approaching Jewell." Gene said looking at them. "Quietly slide your chair back and step over to my right-hand side. Jewell, as the waiter gets within a couple of feet or when Jim gets out of his chair, you get up and knock the tray out of the waiter's hands. Jim, put the syringe against my nose using your right hand and put your left hand on my right shoulder. Val, as he leans over with the syringe, you use the napkin to completely cover the syringe and Jim's hand."

As Jewell rose and turned to her left, Jim stood and leaned over to Gene, putting his left hand on his shoulder as instructed. As he put the syringe against Gene's nose, Val covered it with the napkin.

As she was putting the napkin over his nose, Gene told Val, "Keep the napkin over my nose until you feel Jim's hand start to move away. Jim, hold onto the syringe lightly and let Val take it from your hand. Val, wrap the napkin completely around the syringe and Jim's hand, wiping his fingers as much as you can. Then put it into the compartment of the purse and zip it shut with your right hand. Make sure you leave it alone until we can take it back to the lab. We don't want to take any chances of there being some residual amoeba anywhere for you to come in contact with."

"Now the only other thing is that Jim will be wearing a nitrile glove on his right hand." Gene continued looking at him. "If you don't press too forcefully on the plunger, none of the powder should leave the Captain's nose. However, if it does for any reason, the glove will prevent it from getting on your skin."

"And Val will wipe my hand with the napkin to remove anything that may have escaped," Jim said, nodding.

"Exactly, and the napkin will neutralize any amoeba that might get on her left hand," Gene confirmed. "And then you'll go directly to the men's room to put the glove in a baggie we'll supply for the operation. It'll contain a mixture exactly like on the napkin. Just make sure you don't touch anything with your right hand until you remove the glove. And be sure to remove it by the wristband, turning it inside out."

"Guys, this is a very dangerous part of the operation," Gene said as they retook their seats. "I almost cancelled this because of the possibility of one of you getting even a single microbe of the amoeba on your skin. I've been assured that it can't harm you unless it enters your noses. It's in a powder form and needs moisture and at least eighty degrees to activate. That and all the other precautions such as the napkin and glove will reduce the risk to almost nonexistent. But you must exercise extreme caution with this nasty little bug. I can't stress enough that you're risking your lives if you don't follow the protocol exactly. Once the syringe is used, it must be still considered deadly. The same is true of the glove you'll be wearing, Jim. The smallest amount of the amoeba in your nose will kill you. And if you touch anything after you use the syringe with the glove still on, you're taking a chance on leaving some of the amoeba behind for some innocent person to contact it. That's unacceptable. Now let's look at the timing of when we want to perform our little dinner party. We think five or six days before the main operation would be about right. What do you guys think?"

"When do you plan on having everything ready in Chicago and St. Louis?" Jim asked.

"Two weeks," Gene answered. "St. Louis says they can be ready on their end with a couple of days' notice. Chicago has a Black Water–owned building where we will bring everyone. Mr. O said they needed a couple more days to set it up for our operation and some other issues regarding the teams that will now be bringing their *guests* to the party."

"Val," Jim said, looking at her, "do you think you can get Robert to take you to some water park or lake within the next week or so?"

"Probably," she answered. "We've already discussed going to Great Wolf Lodge some weekend. Will that work?"

"What's your angle?" Gene asked Jim.

"I know that this amoeba has been found in public water systems such as at a house. But if we can tie him to a water park like Great Wolf, it provides us with another possible location for the contamination," Jim explained. "I'm just looking at another way to make this appear to be more feasible."

"That'll probably result in shutting down Great Wolf for a while," Gene said, considering the idea. "But it does lend some additional plausibility to it."

"I'll make sure we go there," Val said, nodding. "Not that I relish another day with him, but I knew the job when I joined Black Water."

"Okay, let's run through this again," Gene said after a moment to let everyone think about what Val had just told them. "I want this to be flawless before we leave here today. If any of you thinks this is too risky or has a better idea, we still have a few days to make any changes."

Chapter 26

"What's your schedule like next month?" Gene asked Jim as they were driving back to his house.

"I've got two nights in Chicago each week," Jim answered. "The first day is DFW to Phoenix (PHX), back to DFW, and then to ORD. The next day, it's just ORD to DFW and back. Then one leg home."

"What time do you get to ORD?" Gene then asked.

"About four o'clock in the afternoon the first day and then noon on the next," Jim told him.

"Okay," Gene said, nodding. "We'll plan on our first—and hopefully only—shot at Robert on your first trip next month. What day is it?"

"It's on the fourth," Jim said. "Then back in Chicago again on the fifth."

"That should work just fine," Gene said, looking at Jewell. "What's your schedule?"

"I'm doing nothing but Dallas turns," Jewell said. "I'm not exactly sure what days right now, but I know I can always trade for pretty much any day you need since there are several every day."

"Okay, we'll set it up for the fourth," Gene told them. "That gives us about a week to firm up the plan with Mr. O and let him coordinate with Larry M."

"What about the restaurant in Chicago?" Jim asked.

"The Cite restaurant," Gene answered. "It's one of Captain Nelson's favorites, and it just so happens that we were able to get our gentleman employed there."

"How did you arrange that?" Jewell asked, knowing which restaurant they were discussing.

"Once we discovered what the Captain was up to with the gangs and drugs, we put people in positions in several restaurants and other businesses where he frequents," Gene explained. "The man at Cite has been there for over six months. That's about the average for him."

"I'm guessing that he's a full-time Black Water employee and that the waiter job is just a cover," Jim remarked.

"Aren't we all?" Val asked, laughing.

"I guess it depends on how you look at it," Jim said, smiling. "I'm either a full-time airline pilot who works part-time for Black Water, in this case Muddy Water, or I'm a full-time Black Water employee who works as an airline pilot for cover."

"Which one takes the most of your time?" Gene asked, knowing the answer. "And which one pays you the most?"

"That would be American Airlines," Jim answered. "But some months, it seems that it's Black Water."

"I guess I'm definitely a full-time Black Water lady," Val told them. "Even though I'm sort of like the waiter, I spend most of my time trying to get close to the subjects and usually get by just saying that I'm self-unemployed."

"Doesn't that lead to more questions?" Jewell asked her.

"Not necessarily," she replied. "Usually, the men are more interested in when I can spend time with them than what I do in the meantime. If it ever does come up, I'm recently divorced and taking some time off to determine what direction the rest of my life will take once I deplete my divorce settlement."

"That sounds like so many of the women I know in Chicago," Jewell told her. "I think half the women I meet at the gym or anywhere else are recently divorced or wanting to be."

"Then it's probably a very believable story," Jim said, shaking his head. "And I hear a lot of the same stories from our flight attendants."

"Don't forget about the pilots," Jewell argued. "They're either divorced or working on it. At least, that's the story they tell us."

"Let's get back to the operation," Gene finally said. "We need to meet one more time before the fourth. I'm going to talk to O when I get back and we'll shoot for somewhere around the first. Is that good for everyone?"

"Good for me," Val told them. "I'm pretty much available any day until this is over."

"Good for me too," Jewell acknowledged. "I've got the first two days of next month off."

"I'm pretty sure I'm supposed to be flying my last trip of this month and getting back on the first," Jim said.

"I'll get with the company and see if they can't help out a little bit," Gene said as they approached Jim's house.

"You mean the way I always seem to get displaced for training or something when you need me?" Jim asked as they came to a stop.

"Pure coincidence," Gene said, smiling as Jim opened his door. "Pure coincidence."

Chapter 27

The following morning, just after Jennifer left for work, Jim got a call from crew scheduling at the airlines telling him that they needed his upcoming trip to qualify a new Captain. He acknowledged the call and his removal from the trip. Just moments after Jim hung up, the phone rang again.

Answering, he heard Gene saying, "I guess you can make it this weekend."

"It appears that the tentacles of Black Water reach across the nation," Jim told him. "And I'm certain that it was a *pure coincidence*."

"Stranger things have happened," Gene said with a smile. "Now let's discuss your trip back up here."

"I guess you want me there on the first," Jim told him.

"No, I want you here on the thirty-first," Gene corrected him. "I want Jewell and Val here on the first, and you need to still be here."

"What's happening on those days?" Jim asked.

"A revisit of the first meeting with all the teams, Mr. O, and Larry," Gene answered. "We need to review all the changes to the original plan and make sure the timing for everything is solid."

"Okay," Jim said. "Now you know that Jennifer is going to want to come with me. Have you factored that into the program?"

"Yes, I knew she'd want to come back," Gene answered. "I've already reserved the same rooms for you guys and made arrangements for dinner both nights."

"How will we be getting there?" Jim asked. "Commercial or your jet out of Love Field?"

"Same as before," Gene assured him. "I looked at commercial into Reagan International, but it involved too much wasted time traveling down to Quantico and didn't provide the flexibility I want."

"Jennifer will be happy about that," Jim said, smiling. "She thinks this is the way we should always travel now. I guess the free passes we get from the airlines aren't good enough for her now. Flying standby isn't attractive since she's discovered private jets."

"Unfortunately, she's about to discover that coming with you is a rarity also," Gene told him. "But for now, we'll pamper her a little bit."

"I guess you know she'll blame me for any time she doesn't get to come with me," Jim said.

"I do know that," Gene answered. "But I'm sure you can convince her that it's not always an option. Now there's another issue we need to discuss when you get here."

"What's that?" Jim asked.

"I can't discuss it over the phone, and I don't have time to come down there right now," Gene informed him. "However, when we finish this call, I think you'll find a package on your front steps that will provide the details. You need to look at all the material and be ready to discuss it when you arrive."

"Is it something to do with this operation?" Jim asked, walking over to the front door.

"No," Gene told him. "Just go ahead and read it and then destroy the material. I think you'll understand everything you need to know, and I'll answer any questions you have when you get here. Until then, just see if you can find any problems with our proposal."

"Okay," Jim said. "I'll see you Friday."

As soon as he hung up, Jim opened the door and saw a large manila envelope just outside the door. Picking it up, he looked up and down the street to see if anyone was watching. Initially not seeing anything out of the ordinary, he finally noticed a small white Ford pickup parked in a driveway a block down that was facing away from the garage. Stepping back into the house, he waited a couple of seconds after closing the door and then opened it just enough to look down the street and saw the pickup leaving.

Black Water, Jim thought as he shut the door.

Refilling his coffee, he took his cup and the envelope to the table, anxious to see what Gene had been talking about. Opening the envelope, he saw several photos of a man who appeared to be in his mid-thirties.

I've seen this guy, Jim thought, studying the pictures. *He's been in the local news several times over the last month or so.*

Putting the pictures down, he started reading the narrative that had accompanied the photos. As soon as he read the name, he knew who the guy was.

"Leonard Blair," Jim said to the empty room. "You're the slimy asshole who got caught spying on little girls at the school where you're one of the janitors."

Reading about the investigation and trial where Leonard was found not guilty because of tainted evidence gathered by the police, Jim recalled the outrage of the community about how the investigation had been bungled and how Blair had been turned loose without even a slap on the wrist.

The following pages described what Leonard had been doing since being freed without even having to register as a sex offender. The description of how the court had prohibited the police from *harassing* him as they tried to perform surveillance was hard to understand. But it was obvious from the material Jim was reading that someone had contacted Black Water, and they were doing what the police were prohibited from doing.

The last few pages described what information the company had and how they planned on resolving the issue. The bottom line was that Black Water had been contracted to eliminate Mr. Leonard Blair.

Jim laid the material on the table and leaned back in his chair, understanding what mission the company was assigning him. The thought of calling Gene back crossed his mind but was dismissed almost immediately. He knew that Gene couldn't discuss it over the phone, and he really didn't know himself what he wanted to do about it.

Taking the material into his office, he fed each sheet into the shredder and then gathered the narrow strips from the trash can. Carrying the pieces to the grille sitting just outside the back door, he poured charcoal lighter fluid over the pile of paper and tossed a match on it. Watching the flames dancing, he thought again about the decisions he had made since joining the company after his experiences in Vietnam.

Opening the door and going back inside, Jim again thought about how cheap life could be.

Chapter 28

On Friday morning, Jennifer was showering when Jim woke up.

"Did you start the coffee?" Jim asked as he climbed out of bed.

"Yes," she answered from the shower. "And I put some cinnamon rolls in the oven. They should be ready in about ten minutes. Please check on them."

"Sure," Jim answered, heading for the kitchen. "I'll grab some coffee and shower as soon as you get out." Just as he was pouring his cup, the phone rang. "Hello," he said as he looked into the oven at the rolls.

"Good morning, Jim," Gene told him. "Any problems with a slightly earlier departure from Love Field?"

"How much earlier?" Jim asked, taking a sip of his coffee.

"About an hour," Gene answered. "I need for the plane to pick up Larry in St. Louis before you get here. Is that going to be a problem?"

Jim looked at the clock on the stove and answered, "Shouldn't be. That still gives us about an hour and a half to get to the airport. It'll rush Jennifer a little, but that's the price of a free private jet."

"Okay," Gene said before hanging up. "I'll see you when you get here. And I'll have some additional information on the *Lenny* operation when we get together."

Jim hung up and headed for the bedroom, carrying his cup. "You need to hurry," he said as he approached the adjoining bathroom door. "Gene just called, and we need to be at the airport an hour earlier."

"Why?" Jennifer asked as she reached out of the shower for a towel.

"We'll be going to St. Louis before we get to Virginia," Jim told her as he watched her dry off. A familiar feeling coursed through his groin as he looked at her, and he suggested, "Do you think you could give me a hand with my shower?"

"Maybe," she said, smiling. "If I didn't have to be ready so quick. You'll just have to wash your own back."

"I wasn't worried about my back," Jim said, setting his coffee on the counter beside the sink.

"I know exactly what you're talking about," Jennifer said as she grabbed another towel and wrapped it around her hair. "You just take care of yourself while I try to rush and get ready in time for the flight. You'd think that they'd call and ask if we could leave early. This is getting to be very inconvenient."

Shaking his head, Jim pulled his shorts off and tossed them in the hamper, saying, "I'll certainly bring that up with Gene when we get there. How dare they?"

After showering and shaving, Jim dressed and tossed a clean pair of jeans in his suitcase along with enough clean socks, underwear, and knit shirts for the anticipated three days. Anything beyond that would require a quick trip to the laundromat or shopping.

"Why are we going to St. Louis before we go to Virginia?" Jennifer asked as she tried to decide which clothes she wanted to take.

"We're picking up another guy," Jim answered as he shut his suitcase. "You need to hurry up and pick what you're taking. I'll be back for your suitcase as soon as I load mine."

"I guess that means no Mile High Club for this trip," Jennifer said, smiling as she folded her selection and put it in the suitcase.

"Well, there's still the trip from Love Field to St. Louis," Jim joked as he headed out of the bedroom. "There's plenty of time since you couldn't *wash my back* this morning."

Half an hour later, they were parked at the terminal, waiting for the jet to arrive. Watching the planes from Southwest taking off and landing, Jennifer remarked, "This is so much better than waiting in line and being stuffed in with a bunch of strangers."

"Speaking of that," Jim said, "you know that most of the time, you won't be able to come with me. And even if you do, it's more than likely on American or some other airline."

"I know," she answered with a slight smile. "But I'll always be ready to go if you want me to."

"What about your job?" Jim asked as they saw their jet approaching the ramp outside.

"I think they can spare me for a day or two every now and then," Jennifer said as Jim got up to get their suitcases.

Waiting for the jet to park, Jim opened the door and held it for Jennifer, saying, "Maybe you should have that discussion with your boss when we get back. He may have other ideas about how many days he can spare you before he decides that he can do without you entirely."

"He's already told me that if I need a day off every so often to just ask," Jennifer told him as they watched the pilot coming down the steps from the jet.

"Hi, folks. Is there any more luggage?" the pilot asked, approaching them.

"Nope," Jim said as he shook hands. "Light load this time."

"Okay. Then let's get you guys aboard, and we'll be on our way," he said, grabbing one of the suitcases. "We'll refuel in St. Louis when we pick up the other guy. Until then, y'all just sit back and enjoy the ride."

Chapter 29

After stopping to pick up Larry in St. Louis, the flight continued uneventfully to Quantico. Gene met the plane as it taxied to the terminal and had a staff car waiting to take Jennifer to Alexandria while he went with Jim and Larry to Black Water Headquarters. After they cleared security and found their seats in the conference room, Larry headed to the podium, where O was waiting.

As soon as he left, Gene asked, "How'd the flight go?"

"Fine," Jim answered. "I was initially a little worried that Jennifer would ask some embarrassing questions of Larry, but she almost completely ignored him."

"I briefed Larry ahead of time, just in case she got curious," Gene told him. "His cover story was to be that he's a computer analyst and isn't involved with any of the company's projects that you're working on."

"Speaking of projects, what do you want me to do regarding Leonard?" Jim asked.

"Eliminate him," Gene responded matter-of-factly. "I thought that was made pretty clear in the materials you were given."

"I gathered that," Jim pointed out. "But how did we or, more correctly, the company get involved with an issue that has nothing to do with national security or anything remotely connected to our usual activities?"

"First, I don't know exactly why the company takes on every contract," Gene lectured Jim. "This decision was made well above my pay grade. But I do have a little background on Mr. Blair that may alleviate some of your concerns. Leonard Blair was active long before the bungled investigation in the Dallas–Fort Worth area. He's been placed at several previous locations where young girls, usually nine or ten years old, have gone missing."

"Why wasn't that part of the story on the news or in the papers?" Jim asked.

"Since there were never any charges and certainly no convictions, he has a right to privacy, and none of what we know but can't prove can ever be used against him in any court," Gene told him. "And it also means that no news outlet will be allowed to broadcast or print anything that could be prejudicial to Mr. Leonard Blair."

"I understand all that," Jim argued. "But why isn't this just a police matter? I'm not entirely comfortable with this assignment."

"You didn't seem to mind getting involved with a certain gentleman who was bothering Jennifer a few months ago," Gene reminded Jim. "And that man did nothing other than make unwanted sexual advances against your wife."

"But I didn't kill him," Jim retorted.

"No, but he wasn't involved in the disappearances of any young girls either," Gene emphasized. "More importantly, the problem was resolved when he was fired. Now back to Leonard. The company got involved a few weeks ago, found that our boy seems to like young girls, and traced his employment history. That's where they discovered the missing girls I told you about, following the news story and the lack of charges in the Dallas area. Leonard made the mistake of zeroing in on a certain young girl at the school where he currently works. That girl noticed a man behaving rather oddly and told her father. He did some investigating and determined that it was Leonard."

"Why didn't he go to the police?" Jim asked.

"He did," Gene confirmed. "But since the police had already been ordered to refrain from any form of *harassment*, their options were limited. That brings us to the key to the assignment. The father just happens to be closely associated with Black Water." Gene waited for a few seconds before continuing, "So it parallels your situation where you wanted to take some action yourself instead of letting the company act. In this case, because the father's activities have been officially recorded and he would be immediately suspected, the decision was made to ensure he was completely clear of any actions taken by the company."

"That's where I come in," Jim said, nodding. "But is it really necessary to eliminate him? Can't we do something a little less dramatic?"

"That was discussed ad nauseam," Gene answered. "Just think about what you would do if it was your child. Or if you knew that someone was going to do harm to Jennifer. The man has caused unbearable pain to too many families as it is. The law seems powerless to prevent him from further activities. And I'm sure you agree that he must be stopped before another child disappears."

"So I'm elected," Jim said, resolved to the assignment.

"Yes," Gene said, nodding. "I understand some of your reluctance, but sometimes it falls to someone like you to do what needs to be done when all other efforts have failed. Especially when a child's life is at stake."

Jim sat staring at Gene for a few seconds before finally saying, "Not a problem. Has the company developed a plan, or do I need to do that on my own?"

"The company has a plan, but you're free to develop your own if you don't like theirs," Gene told him. "But it needs to be cleared through them. Just remember, they have infinitely more resources that you. I'll make sure you get a copy of their work and rationale when you get home. Until then, let's concentrate on the Chicago problem."

Chapter 30

"Okay, everybody," Mr. O said as he took the stage with Larry. "Let's please grab a seat and take a quick look at the changes the company has recommended since our last meeting." Waiting until everyone had taken their seats, he continued, "I think you'll see that very few actual changes have been made to your individual assignments. You're still responsible for the initial three targets, but you'll be bringing them to a central location."

He put an overhead view of a large warehouse on the screen and said, "This facility is where each individual will be brought and, for lack of a better word, interrogated. There are separate rooms for each of the five gangs and three restraining chairs for the top three whom we designated as the CEO, the COO, and the CFO."

"The CEO and the COO will be questioned as if they had a chance of survival, but they will never leave the building. At least not standing. Since all three are together, the execution of the first two should make the CFO very compliant," he remarked. "That and a little informational package that you'll show him should convince him that he only has one chance at saving his own life as well as that of his family members and friends whose lives will be detailed in the package."

He waited until everyone had a chance to look at the details within each team's packages and said, "As you can see, the company spent considerable time and expense to follow all of the CFO's immediate family as well as numerous other relatives with whom he maintains a close relationship."

"What about the St. Louis gang members?" one of the team members asked. "Are they going to be at the same facility?"

Mr. O stepped aside as Larry answered, "Only one. He will be placed in one of the rooms to provide another layer of misdirection about who committed the assassinations. The others will be found in a wrecked and burned van somewhere between Chicago and St. Louis per the initial plan."

Mr. O stepped back to the microphone and clarified, "The guns used to eliminate the Chicago people will remain as we initially told you. There will be another gun that will be linked to Chicago, and it will be the one that fired the round that killed the St. Louis member we'll leave in the room. The CEO of the Chicago Vice Lords will be the one who supposedly fired the gun, and it will be found in his hand."

"How do you plan for him to have shot the man who killed his COO?" Jim asked as he looked at the picture of the warehouse. "It seems that it would be difficult for him to have been strapped into a chair and sat watching his friend be shot and then be able to kill the man who is pointing a gun at him."

Larry looked at Mr. O for a second and answered, "That does present a different perspective that we need to consider. Any suggestions?"

"Just shoot him in the face when you get him in the room," Jim answered. "Let him lie on the floor while you finish with the other two. Then put the gun in his hand that shot the St. Louis guy, and the assumption will be that he shot the man as they entered the room. Following that, another member of the St. Louis gang shot him. Then the gun that shot the CEO will be found with the members who died in the crash as they attempted to return to St. Louis."

Waiting to see if anybody had anything else to add, Larry whispered to Mr. O and then told the audience, "That works for us. What about you guys who are assigned the Vice Lords?"

A man from one of the tables answered, "Works for us too. What do we do with the CFO once we're done?"

"Once you're satisfied that he's given you all the information about the location of their financial assets and that he fully comprehends the consequences of any future activity on him, his family, and his friends, take the package from him and leave the room," Mr. O said. "We'll have another asset take him from the room and drop him in a very remote location. If you determine that he is being uncooperative or likely to resume his activities, his body will be left with the other two.

"One thing I'm sure you've noticed. All your teams will be in white nondescript vans. It will be completely sanitized after you leave the warehouse and return to the hotel where you'll be staying. Once you get to the hotel, leave the van in the parking lot with the keys in it and go to your rooms. We have people who will be waiting, and they'll take care of any *residue* that may have found its way into the van.

"Okay, unless there are any questions or suggestions, we'll break for the day, and you can take a closer look at the revisions in your folders. We'll meet back here tomorrow morning and finalize the plans for the operation. Please get your teams together this evening or tonight and make sure there are no areas where we might need some tweaking. Until tomorrow, have a pleasant evening."

"One quick question about the location," Jim said. "How did the St. Louis people get access to this particular warehouse?"

Mr. O stepped back to the microphone and answered, "Records will show that it has been leased by the Chicago Vice Lords for several years and was thought to be part of their distribution system. There will be traces of various drugs throughout the facility. Now anything else?"

Chapter 31

As they headed toward Arlington to meet with Jennifer and go to dinner, Jim carefully read the information regarding Leonard and his background and what the company had discovered. Leonard had been employed at several schools where children had either gone missing or reports of sexual abuse had occurred. Unfortunately, Leonard had escaped every attempt to lawfully prosecute him. The only result was that he was removed from his position as custodian at the schools and that each school had been prevented from informing any other school regarding employment of their suspicions or any investigations into Leonard's activities.

For several years, he had been allowed to move freely about the state and continue his perverted activities. The latest incident where he had been caught but released because of irregularities in the investigation was just another example of where criminal activity continued unabated because of minor infractions in the process of bringing them to justice.

"What has the company done up to now?" Jim asked as he put the folder on the seat between them.

"He's been under constant surveillance, and his home and car have been bugged with both video and voice transmitters," Gene answered. "Additionally, there are tracking devices in his car and one inserted into his wallet when one of our teams acting as local police stopped him at one of the toy stores in the Galleria Mall in Dallas. We have also planted a camera in the girl's bathroom where he works. It has his fingerprints and DNA on it and will be discovered shortly after he is eliminated.

"The major thing we discovered while watching him is that he has a severe asthma problem. He requires daily doses of pirbuterol and uses an inhaler produced by Maxair. We've replicated the inhaler and replaced the pirbuterol with a tincture of *Gelsemium elegans*, commonly known as heartbreak grass. It causes paralysis of the spinal cord, leading to almost complete loss of muscular power and eventual asphyxia. The variety we'll be using grows in Vietnam, China, and other Asian countries.

"As background, Conan Doyle experimented with various doses back in the 1870s and had to stop after taking twelve milliliters. We're using over two hundred milliliters in a single dose of his inhaler. Since he's been diagnosed with asthma and takes a prescription for relief, death from asphyxia won't be that abnormal. Especially since we may just have some input into where the autopsy will be done and who'll do it.

"Your part of the operation will be to simply replace his inhaler with ours, and you'll have at least twenty minutes plus the time he's in the bookstore to do it if you leave your house when he heads for the bookstore. It's about the same distance from your house to his as it is from his house to the bookstore. The biggest issue we've yet to resolve is what excuse you give Jennifer for your sudden need to leave your house when you get notified to take the action. That's something that you'll need to work out."

"I'll think of something for that," Jim told him. "Now what about replacing his original inhaler after he uses ours?"

"We'll be monitoring him with the cameras we installed and will send a team in to make sure Leonard has taken his final breath, and they will take ours and replace his prescription inhaler," Gene answered. "Then the team will remove everything we installed in the house and the car. We anticipate it will more than likely be a day or two before his body is discovered after he doesn't show up for work. That's also when the bathroom camera will be *discovered.*"

"Why don't you use the same team to make the swap?" Jim asked. "It seems that it would be simple for the same people who bugged his house to do everything."

"It comes down to repeated exposure," Gene explained. "Having the same people returning to the same residence time after time is more likely to be remembered than several different people who are only seen once."

"I agree," Jim said after thinking about it for a few seconds. "When will you get me the replacement inhaler?"

"It will be in the glove box of the car that we'll leave for you," Gene answered. "You certainly don't want to drive the 'Vette," Gene added, laughing. "And we don't need your truck to show up on any cameras between your house and his. There's a Walmart between your house and his located on Samuell Boulevard. I'd suggest that you leave your truck there and take the car."

"That sounds good," Jim said, nodding. "I'll use going there as an excuse, and given the time involved, I can logically explain why it took the time it did."

"Good," Gene said as they pulled into the hotel. "I'll get you the information on the car after you get home. Now let's take Jennifer out for dinner and leave Leonard Blair's upcoming demise until after you get back to Texas."

Chapter 32

"Tell Jennifer that we'll be going to The Warehouse Restaurant this evening," Gene told Jim as the valet took the keys to the Suburban. "It's got some great dishes and a very relaxed atmosphere."

"What type of food?" Jim asked as they entered the lobby and headed for the elevators.

"Steak and seafood," Gene answered. "Let's meet in the lobby in an hour. By the way, Jewell and Val will be here around noon tomorrow, and we can tie up any loose ends before everybody heads home. They will also be flying with you and be dropped off at Chicago before you and Jennifer head to Dallas."

"Is that really a good idea?" Jim asked. "Having both of them with Jennifer for that long could lead to some uncomfortable conversations."

"Both of them know you're married, and they know how to handle themselves around the spouses of other members," Gene assured him. "Plus, I think it's time that Jewell met Jennifer. Maybe that will resolve any doubts about where your loyalties lie. I know that nothing has happened between you two yet, but

I also know there've been some harbored feelings, at least on her part, and I've seen some interest in you as well."

"What's their cover story?" Jim asked as the elevator arrived at their floor.

"They're also computer analysts for Black Water," Gene told him. "If Jennifer gets too curious, they're roommates and going home to Chicago to see their families. I wouldn't worry about it if I were you."

"What if Jennifer asks them about Larry?" Jim asked, stepping off the elevator.

"They've never heard of him," Gene assured him. "The computer section at Black Water is enormous. Sort of like you not knowing every pilot at American."

"You're putting me in a potentially difficult situation," Jim said as they neared their rooms. "I think I'd rather face a dozen armed opponents than face Jennifer if she gets even the slightest hint that I would have any interest in either of them."

"Then I'd suggest that you put on your best poker face and read a magazine on the leg to Chicago," Gene said, chuckling. "Be in the lobby in an hour, please."

"Anybody here?" Jim asked as he opened the door to his room.

"Back here!" Jennifer called from the bathroom. "What's on the agenda for tonight?"

"Dinner with Gene," Jim said as he kissed her on the cheek. "Casual dress, steak and seafood, probably a glass of wine or two."

"How casual?" Jennifer asked as she checked her makeup again. "Jeans casual or cocktail-dress casual?"

"I'd say pants-and-blouse casual," Jim answered as he took fresh towels from the rack. "I'll wear jeans and a knit shirt, but first, I need to take a quick shower."

"Go ahead," Jennifer told him as she stood with the towel wrapped around her. "I'll go look through my clothes to see if there's anything I want to wear."

"I'd say it's a little late to be deciding that you don't want to wear what you brought," Jim said as he stripped down and turned on the shower. "We need to meet Gene in the lobby in an hour."

"I did find a cute outfit shopping this afternoon," she informed him as she opened a package that was on the bed. "I think I'll wear it tonight."

"I think you keep looking at these trips as an excuse to enhance your wardrobe," Jim told her, shaking his head. "I don't know why you even bother to pack any clothes if you're going to buy something new every time we come here."

"What'd you say?" Jennifer asked as he stepped into the shower.

"Nothing," Jim answered. "I'm just glad you found something to wear."

Gene was waiting for them when they stepped off the elevator and said, "Pretty dress, Jennifer. Is it new?"

"Oh, it's just something that caught my eye today while I was waiting for you guys to get here," she answered. "Maybe I can find something better for dinner tomorrow night."

"We'll be leaving tomorrow afternoon," Jim said as they reached the waiting car. "And we'll be going through Chicago to drop off a couple of people."

"Oh, well," she said as she slid across the backseat. "I guess I'll have to wait until the next trip to do any more shopping."

Jim looked at Gene and shook his head, saying, "I'm not sure when that will be. We'll finish this project tomorrow, at least my part of it."

"Jim's right," Gene agreed. "You guys get to go home while I try to get the company to agree to all his suggestions. There'll be a car picking you up around two o'clock tomorrow and bringing you to Quantico for the trip home."

"Who are the people going to Chicago on our airplane?" Jennifer asked as they pulled away from the hotel.

"Just a couple of ladies who work in the computer section at the headquarters who are going to Chicago for a few days to visit their families," Gene answered, smiling. "I think you'll like them. And it's really nice of you to let them share *your* airplane."

Chapter 33

As they entered the restaurant, Gene quietly spoke to the maître d', who led them to a table near the rear a moment later.

As they took their seats, a waiter arrived with a bottle of Joseph Phelps Chardonnay, saying, "I believe this is the wine you ordered, sir."

Gene looked at the label and answered, "Yes. Please pour a glass for the lady to taste." As the waiter was opening the bottle, Gene continued, "If you don't mind, I'll order for us. They have some of the most unique seafood dishes on the East Coast, and I've tried most of them."

"Certainly," Jennifer said as she took a sip of the wine. "And this is excellent also."

"I think we'll all three start with a cup of the She-Crab soup," Gene told the waiter as soon as he had poured a glass of wine for each of them. "The lady will have the stuffed flounder *tchoupitoulas* with roasted potatoes. The gentleman would like the shellfish baked in parchment with potatoes, and I'll take the Crawfish-Crab Imperial and roasted potatoes as well."

"Excellent choices," the waiter said as he bowed slightly and left quietly.

"To another wonderful evening with friends," Gene said, raising his glass. "May we be granted many more like it."

"Indeed," Jennifer said as she tapped her glass to Gene's and Jim's. "I know we can never repay you for your incredible hospitality, but you must come visit and let me cook dinner for us some evening."

"Nothing I'd like better," Gene said with a slight nod. "I've got some business down there later this month. Perhaps I can convince the company to let me stay an extra day so I'm not rushed to get back."

"Just give me a couple of days' notice, and I'll make us a meal that I think you'll find as good as anything here on the coast," she said as Jim nodded.

"Just don't expect any fish," Jim added. "There's a place called the Crowd Cow that sells Japanese Wagyu ribeye steaks that'll melt in your mouth."

"I've heard that they're fantastic," Jennifer agreed. "And I've got a recipe for roasted asparagus with hollandaise sauce that goes so well with the mesquite-smoked steaks."

"Sounds wonderful to me," Gene said as their soup arrived. "I'll bring the wine."

"You know you're always welcome," Jennifer assured him as she dipped her spoon in the soup for a taste. "Wow! This is really good. Just what is in she-crab soup?"

"I don't have a clue about everything that goes in it," Gene answered, smiling. "I just know it's good, and I have it every time I'm up here."

"Maybe it's made from just the female crabs," Jim joked as he took another spoonful.

"Sometimes," Gene informed them. "Crabbing rules usually prohibit keeping the females. And only males of a certain size can be harvested. But true she-crab soup is made with the female. And the roe is what really makes it special. Most of the time, you get he-crab soup. But here, it's true she-crab."

"That makes perfect sense," Jennifer said as she spooned the last of the soup from her cup. "Since one male can breed with any number of females, as long as there's just one male left, we'll always have crabs."

"Same with cattle, sheep, or any other animal," Gene said as he finished his soup. "Man is about the only mammal that tries to restrict their natural breeding habits."

"Not in every culture," Jim added. "Sometimes it's expected for a man to have several wives."

"And sometimes a man just wants several different women," Jennifer argued. "And he certainly doesn't want them for the children they can provide."

"You aren't referring to a certain gentleman named Charlie who used to work where you do, are you?" Gene asked.

"You know about that?" Jennifer asked as the waiter was removing their empty soup cups.

"Somewhat," Gene said as his plate was placed in front of him. "Jim sort of mentioned a little issue with him, and I did a little research into his past."

"Just how much did you tell him?" Jennifer asked Jim.

"Only that someone was causing you a problem and his name," Jim answered as his meal arrived. "I just wanted to know a little more about him, and Gene had access to the information."

"Let's not get bogged down in something that I helped Jim with," Gene said, trying to redirect the conversation. "The company has enormous capabilities to research just about anything or anybody. I just thought I could save Jim a lot of work that might not uncover what I could find. Call it a favor for two of my favorite people."

Jennifer looked at Gene and knew that he would always be part of their lives and realized that she could never break the ties that bound Jim and Gene. More importantly, she couldn't imagine not having him in her life either. "In that case, I'm happy that you could be there to help my husband. Thank you."

"I'll always be there for you guys," Gene said as he poured their glasses full of wine. "You're family to me. Now let's enjoy our meals, and I'll consider that Wagyu steak you promised as returning the favor."

"Agreed," Jim said, hoisting his glass to Gene and Jennifer. "But a mere steak is not enough to cover all the *favors* you've done for us."

"Especially providing me with my own private jet," Jennifer joked as she gave a slight bow to Gene. "But we need to talk about all these people you keep asking us to take with us."

Gene just shook his head as he took the first bite of his meal. "Yeah, we need to do that," he said, smiling and looking at Jim. "We should definitely discuss it someday."

Chapter 34

Gene was waiting for Jim in the lobby early the next morning and told him, "Jewell was involved in an accident this morning on her way to the airport. Not sure yet how bad it is, but I've sent the jet to pick up another lady to take her place. I hope to find out more when we get to Quantico."

"What about Val?" Jim asked. "Was she with Jewell, or is she still coming?"

"She'll be here around noon as far as I know right now," Gene answered. "And so should the other lady."

"I hate to hear that about Jewell," Jim said, shaking his head as they left the lobby. "I hope this doesn't affect our operation, but my real concern is about her."

"Yeah, I know," Gene said somberly. "For now, I'm just hoping for the best."

When they got to the waiting Suburban, the driver surprised them with a treat of Cinnabons and a carafe of coffee. "Good morning, gentlemen," he said as he held the rear door open for them. "I hope you'll enjoy the rolls and coffee since there're some minor delays heading to Quantico today."

"Anything we should be concerned about?" Gene asked as he slid across the rear seat.

"There was an accident involving an eighteen-wheeler early this morning, and the traffic reports have said to expect up to an hour delay," he answered as Jim got in the car. "Maybe we'll be lucky and they'll have the wreckage cleared by the time we get there."

"Thank you for the rolls and coffee anyway," Jim said as the driver started to shut the door. "I hope you have some in the front for yourself."

"I do," he answered, shutting the door. "But I'll only eat them if we're stopped in line somewhere. I wouldn't take a chance on having to slam on the brakes and drop a Cinnabon."

As they pulled away from the hotel, Gene asked, "Do you have any more questions about the Leonard assignment?"

"Just a few regarding the details," Jim answered after swallowing the bite of a Cinnabon he had taken.

"Such as?" Gene asked, taking a bite of his.

"First, the car. I'm assuming that it's a nondescript white something," Jim said, taking a sip of coffee. "And that the plates are current, not listed on some police report as stolen, and that every light, turn signal, or other code has been complied with."

"Of course," Gene said, shaking his head. "Anything else?"

"Are you providing a driver's license under some name other than my own should I be stopped?" Jim continued. "Are there some minor disguises that match the driver's license picture? Is there a phone in the car where you can contact me if there's a change after I leave the Walmart parking lot? Is there a key to his house? Just a few minor details that I think need to make sure are covered."

"You are a stickler for details," Gene said, smiling. "I guess that's why I trust you on these little assignments. You seem to have an eye for the minutiae that most people only think about when they discover that they've forgotten something that could jeopardize the operation."

"After seeing what happened to our guys in Vietnam because some Colonel overlooked some *minor* details, such as lack of cover for a reconnaissance mission, I tend to recheck everything," Jim said, knowing that Gene would understand better than anyone what missing little details could cause.

"Not a problem," Gene told him. "As I said, I knew you were a stickler for the minutiae. So yes, there's a wig, a baseball cap, and a pair of nonprescription black-framed glasses. There's a driver's license in the glove box along with the inhaler. The picture on the license is a photoshopped picture of you as you should look with the wig. The name on the license was run through every known system that tracks wanted people and is clean. The key to the house is on the key ring that will be in the ignition of the car. Everything about the car will be checked again before it's delivered to Walmart. Satisfied?"

"I guess," Jim said, grinning as he took another bite of his roll. "I guess you're almost as anal as I am sometimes."

"Sometimes even more so," Gene said, smiling back. "You didn't ask, but there's an insurance card in the glove box along with your fake driver's license. Getting sloppy in your old age?"

"Could be," Jim answered. "I'm just glad that I've got you to look after my best interests. I'm still a little concerned about the phone in case something happens."

"Glove box. And yes, the battery is fully charged," Gene said, almost laughing. "You just don't give up. How frustrating that must be for Jennifer. I can't imagine having you around twenty-four hours a day checking everything. How many pieces of toilet paper are left on the roll in the guest bath? Are any of the expiration dates on the canned goods about to be exceeded? Do we have another carton of milk because the one in the refrigerator will expire tomorrow? Maddening. Simply maddening. Poor lady. Now I'm sure I need to provide every little convenience, like the private jet, to her just to try to make up for your Obsessive Compulsive Disorder."

"I think she overlooks my minor faults because of my extreme good looks and charming personality," Jim said as they passed the wreckage of the truck and increased their speed toward Quantico.

"Minor faults, my ass," Gene said, looking at his watch. "All I can say is that the lady is approaching sainthood. But it looks like we'll be there in plenty of time for this morning's meeting. Anything else you've thought of regarding the Chicago operation?"

"No," Jim answered after a moment. "I just want to be sure the operation regarding Nelson goes smoothly. I'm a little concerned regarding the new lady."

"Both ladies should be there after we take our lunch break," Gene told him. "Hopefully, there won't be any real issues that the company may have discovered or changes we need to review, and you can have as much time as you need this afternoon to work with them. And I'll try to coordinate the date of the fourth to resolve the Captain issue as soon as I can synchronize your schedules."

Chapter 35

As they approached the first gate to enter the compound, it slid open, and the guard approached the Suburban as the gate closed behind them.

Rolling his window down, Gene asked, "Anything wrong?"

"No, sir," the guard answered, looking at his ID. "But I just got word that you need to call your office as soon as you get inside."

"Thanks," Gene told him as the second gate in front of the car started to slide open.

"Wonder what that's about," Jim mused as they headed for the reserved parking area.

"Guess I'll find out as soon as we get inside," Gene said as they parked and exited the car. "I'll go check while you head down to the briefing. You can bring me up to speed when I get there."

"Not a problem," Jim told him as they cleared the security for entrance into the building. "Anything you want me to tell Mr. O or Larry?"

"No," Gene answered as he headed down one of the halls leading away from the lobby. "If they ask, I'll be there in a few minutes."

Jim headed in the opposite direction toward the briefing room and saw the table with his name in the same area as before. Glancing around to see who was already there, he headed to the tables along the wall to see what was available for a buffet breakfast this morning. Filling a plate with some fruit, scrambled eggs, and a couple of pieces of sausage, he put a spoonful of Picante on the eggs and grabbed a glass of orange juice. After putting everything on the table, he returned to get a cup of coffee and a carafe for later. He had barely sat down when Gene came in and walked to the table.

"Got some bad news," he said as he looked at Jim's plate and decided that he was hungry also.

"What's that?" Jim asked, standing up.

"Jewell's accident was pretty bad," Gene said, shaking his head.

"Will she be all right?" Jim asked as he followed Gene to the buffet table.

"Not sure yet," Gene said as he replicated Jim's selections. "Maybe we'll know something by the end of the day."

"That's not good," Jim said as he got a danish before they returned to the table. "Are you sure we can't wait until we know how long she'll be unavailable?"

"We can't wait," Gene said as they took their seats. "We've got to get this operation rolling, and the first part depends on eliminating the Captain. That part must be our priority for right now."

"Do you think the new lady can get up to speed fast enough to prevent any further delays?" Jim asked as they ate their breakfast.

"Shouldn't be a problem," Gene said as the room began to fill. "Jewell was there primarily as a distraction anyway. And the lady I have coming is perfectly capable of being a distraction."

"I thought Jewell was also the plan B to administer the amoeba in case something happens to me," Jim remarked. "Is there a new plan B?"

"It's still pretty much the same thing," Gene answered. "But let's not get too carried away with the *what-if*s until we see if you're satisfied with her replacement."

"Understand," Jim said as a man in a beige knit shirt with a Black Water emblem approached the table.

"Thanks," Gene said as the man whispered quietly and then walked away. "I guess we have our answer now."

"What's that?" Jim asked, finishing his eggs.

"First, Jewell's still in the emergency room, and we won't know anything further until she's out of there," Gene told him. "And it will probably be much later before there's any chance of finding out her long-term prognosis."

"That's horrible," Jim said, thinking about their long-running close relationship. "I certainly hope she's going to be all right."

"We all hope so," Gene said. "She's been with the company longer than you have, and I know you guys have been friends since you came back from your second tour in Vietnam."

"Yeah," Jim said reflectively. "We've been close friends. I'm sure she'll be back soon. She's a pretty tough little lady."

"That, she is," Gene agreed. "Now we'll have to get her replacement ready before you guys leave this afternoon. If either you or Val have any doubts about the coordination among you three, we'll either stay another day or meet in Mesquite in a few days after your next trip."

"Sounds good to me," Jim said, accepting the fact that it was necessary to put any thoughts about Jewell aside for now. "What's the new lady's name?"

"Marie Laveau," Gene answered. "She's been with the company about five years and has been involved in several operations like this. Very capable and a fast study. I think you'll be impressed."

"That name sounds familiar," Jim said. "Have I ever worked with her?"

"No, I don't think so," Gene answered. "You're probably thinking of the song by Bobby Bare. I think it was popular about the same time you were coming back from your last assignment flying F-4s pilot in 'Nam."

"That's it," Jim said, smiling. "I just hope she's not a voodoo lady like in the song. I agree that she'd be a major distraction but probably too much so."

"No relation to the object of the song and certainly not any physical resemblance," Gene said, smiling. "She'll be here shortly, and you'll get a chance to judge for yourself. Now it looks like Mr. O is about ready to get this meeting started."

Chapter 36

"Good morning, everybody," Mr. O said as he stepped up to the microphone. "I hope everyone had a good evening and is enjoying breakfast. But we need to cover a lot of material in a short time, so please pay attention and hold any questions or comments until the end. First, there's a slight modification to the plan on kidnapping the top three from each gang.

"It was brought to our attention that it just might be impossible to bring one or more of the individuals to the central location. Attempting to get each one could be too time-consuming and jeopardize the operation. So, at the discretion of the team leaders, if getting any single individual to the location appears to be a major factor, eliminate him using one of the St. Louis guns. If you can bring his body, do so. If not, get the other two, and we'll worry about it later."

Pausing to let that sink in, he continued, "The only individual we really want alive at the facility is the CFO. But even he is expendable. We'll find another way to get the information we need. Bottom line, time is more critical than any single one of our targets being brought in alive. If you have any reservations about making the decision, I'll contact Mr. Lashley, who'll give you the authorization or approve additional time."

Jim looked at Gene and asked, "When was this discussed?"

"When we were revising the plan to accommodate your suggestions," Gene told him. "You knew that you were going to be the final authority. We just added a minor adjustment to your responsibilities. You're in a better position to know how the operation is progressing and can give any of the teams a little more time to bring someone in if it can be accomplished within the time frame."

"You could have said something earlier," Jim complained. "I thought that my role with this phase of the operation was to just give the go-ahead to the teams."

"And it still is," Gene explained. "Just like planning an air strike back in 'Nam. You've got to allow some wiggle room for the late tanker for refueling or the Forward Air Controller (FAC) whose plane couldn't get to the target on time. You've got to make quick decisions sometimes to salvage a mission. It could be as simple as increasing your airspeed by a little or remaining on the tanker until the FAC gets on target. It's your decision as to when to get the teams to the final destination. Nobody else has the overall view and can watch it unfold to make the critical decisions that will determine the outcome. That's why you got promoted."

Realizing that Gene was right, Jim simply nodded and said, "Not a problem."

Larry had just joined O at the podium and said, "We have managed to get a tainted weapon for each member of the teams. However, it would be extremely beneficial if only one gun was used by the teams. Since we're only bringing five St. Louis gang members, we need to be cautious that there aren't too many weapons found with their bodies or that a weapon not discovered with them can be determined to be the real cause of death. If you must use a weapon at any point, try not to use any of the others and make sure it's the one left behind."

"That's not to say that if it's a matter of getting one of your team members hurt, you can't use any or all the weapons," O added. "Just make sure we know which ones were used. It could always be assumed that one or more of the St. Louis gang members were carrying more than one weapon."

"Exactly," Larry told them, nodding. "And make sure you leave anything regarding this operation in the room with the bodies. We don't need anything floating around when we finish."

"That's right," O added. "We have a team that will sanitize the facility when everyone has left. They will destroy anything that can be used to nullify our attempt to place the blame on the St. Louis guys. They'll also make sure that all the guns are accounted for and that any not fired or left with the charred bodies in the van will be returned to St. Louis. As of now, we plan to implement the operation on the eleventh. We have about a two-day window, but anything past the twelfth will probably cause major issues. Maybe even postponing the entire operation. If any of you think you'll have problems with that, please let me know today. If a situation arises that can't be resolved, we can replace a team member, but that could have an adverse impact on the efficiency of the team. And especially if it's the leader of the team, we could have serious issues." Looking at Larry to see if he had anything to add, O said, "If you have any questions or comments, now is the time."

Watching everybody at the tables shake their heads. He told them, "Good. If anything comes up over the next few days, make sure to notify General Barker. You'll all receive final instructions regarding hotels, vehicles, and other necessary items or adjustments to the schedule from the company no later than the sixth. So once again, if there's nothing else, thank you for your attention this morning, and good luck with your assignments."

Chapter 37

Just as everyone was leaving the room, Val walked in and spotted Gene and Jim talking. When she got to them, she asked, "Did you hear about Jewell?"

"Yes," Gene told her. "She's still in the emergency room, and it will be later this afternoon before we'll get any more information."

"This is horrible," Val said. "She was supposed to be on the plane with me, and I finally called headquarters when I didn't see her right before the flight left. They told me that she had been badly injured in the crash and for me to come on anyway."

"I know," Gene said as he put a hand on her shoulder. "And I'm sure this is really tough on you since you two have become good friends. But rest assured that the company will do everything possible to take care of her."

"How's this going to affect the operation regarding Captain Nelson?" she asked. "I'm not sure that we can pull it off without her."

"There's another one of our people on their way right now," Gene answered, looking at his watch. "I sent the jet to New Orleans to get her when I heard about Jewell this morning. She should be here anytime now. I want you and Jim to get with her and see if we can salvage it.”

“Does she have any experience in this sort of operation?” Val asked.

“Definitely,” Gene answered. “She’s been with us five years or so and has participated in several identical operations. I think you’ll find her to be extremely competent. Otherwise, I wouldn’t have sent for her. This part of the operation couldn’t happen without the three of you. And elimination of the Captain is integral to the overall operation.”

A diminutive dark-haired lady approached them and said, “Hello, General. Thanks for sending the jet. How can I help you?”

Turning, Gene said, “Marie. So glad you could make it on such short notice. Let me introduce you to your team members. This is Val, and she’ll be the dinner guest of our target.”

Val held out her hand. “Good to meet you, Marie,” Val said, shaking her hand.

“You too, Val,” Marie said, looking at her.

“And this is Jim,” Gene said as the ladies finished their quick but obvious appraisal of each other.

“Nice to meet you,” Jim said, extending his hand.

“You too, Jim,” Marie responded as she accepted his hand. “Now what’s our mission, and what’s my role?”

“Let’s head over to the corner where it’s a little more private,” Gene said, leading them away from the few people left in the room. Selecting a table the farthest from the door, Gene motioned for them to take a seat. “Now the operation involves administering a chemical mix to a CPD Captain who has close ties to the gang and drug problems. Your role will be to purely distract anyone who may be paying attention to you guys while Jim and Val give him the actual chemical.”

"Is that all?" Marie asked. "That's a pretty minor part. Are you sure you even need me?"

"Well, that's not quite all," Gene continued. "It's probably only a minor part if everything else goes well. But you'll also be carrying an antidote for the chemicals used to prepare him for the thing that actually kills him."

"What's the antidote for?" Marie asked.

"It's in case Val gets the chemical instead of the Captain," Gene answered. "It's basically a roofie, and it'll be delivered in a wine glass by one of the waiters. It's highly unlikely but possible that Val could get the wrong glass. The antidote is there for her."

"What's the real tool for the assassination?" she then asked. "And am I carrying the antidote for it?"

"The real *tool*, as you call it, is an extremely deadly amoeba," Gene told her seriously. "I can't stress how deadly this little organism is. There is no antidote for it, but you won't have any contact with it either."

Marie looked from Val to Jim, shaking her head, and replied, "I guess I'm glad all I am is a distraction. I really don't envy anyone who has to handle something like that."

"The company has taken several safeguards," Jim said as he noticed how dark brown and bright her eyes were. "We have a couple of techniques to try to prevent even a micron of this stuff from going anywhere except up the Captain's nose."

"Now that's the basics," Gene told Marie. "What we wanted you here for today is so that you three can practice the coordination and you'll be able to see your exact role. And please feel free to mention anything you notice that might enhance the mission or might cause a problem."

"Certainly," Marie told him. "When do we start?"

"As soon as one of my assistants gets here," Gene told her. "He was supposed to be watching for you and bring my briefcase that contains duplicates of everything you guys will have at the actual restaurant."

Just as he was finished talking, a man in a black knit shirt and khaki pants walked up, carrying a hand-tooled leather briefcase.

"Sorry I'm late," he said, handing it to Gene.

"Right on time," Gene said, smiling as he laid the briefcase on the table. "Thanks." He opened the case and removed several syringes and napkins that were duplicates of the ones they would have at the restaurant and like the ones Jim and Val had practiced with back in Mesquite. "I'll let Jim and Val explain and demonstrate what they're going to do," Gene told Marie. "You'll be sitting across the table from Jim like you're his dinner date. I'll be the target. And we can run through this until you and they are satisfied that you're ready. Now unless there are any questions, we'll get started."

For the next hour, Jim and Val practiced on Gene as Marie watched and mimed her bumping into the nonexistent waiter.

When they were happy with their efforts, Marie said, "Pretty simple. Shouldn't be a problem. And it looks like Jim and Val have been practicing before."

"Yes," Jim said as he stood up. "We went through this several times with Jewell. But it never hurts to do it again."

"What now?" Marie asked, looking at Gene.

"I'll have the jet take you back to New Orleans, unless you want to stay overnight," Gene answered.

"What about me?" Val asked. "Same offer to Chicago?"

"Yes," Gene told her. "If both of you want to stay overnight, I'll arrange for a hotel, and you two can get to know each other. That might be the best thing we can do this late in the program. What do you say?"

"Sounds good to me," Val said, smiling at Marie. "Since she's got my antidote, I'd like to get to know her better."

"Me too," Marie said. "I didn't have any plans for this evening in New Orleans anyway. Is the company buying us dinner tonight?"

"Of course," Gene said, knowing that the two of them would spend hours probing for each other's secrets. "First-class hotel, and the restaurant there is super. It'll all be charged to the company. Now there will be tickets for your flights home when you get to the hotel. And unless there are any questions or comments, we'll all head out, and you can expect your final instructions in a few days." After everybody shook their heads, Gene said, "Well, Jim, I guess we better head to Alexandria. Good evening, ladies. I'll see you guys later."

Chapter 38

On the drive up to Alexandria, Gene asked, "Do you have any questions regarding our problem down in Dallas?"

"Not really," Jim answered. "Has the company determined when we need to proceed?"

"Yes," Gene told him. "We need to take care of this on Monday."
"You're talking about two days from now," Jim responded. "What's the rush?"

"Let's look at your schedule," Gene explained. "Tomorrow you and Jennifer fly home. By the way, you'll be going commercial. The tickets will be at the hotel desk when you check out tomorrow morning."

"What time is our flight?" Jim asked, knowing that Jennifer would be disappointed that they wouldn't be on the private jet.

"About one thirty," Gene answered. "I didn't want to rush you guys."

"That's fine," Jim said. "You were talking about my schedule."

"Yeah," Gene said, nodding. "You're flying a trip starting Tuesday. That night, you'll be taking care of our police Captain with Val and Marie. You'll get home on Thursday. I want

Friday, Saturday, and Sunday open in case we need to get you back up here regarding the operation scheduled for the eleventh. We could wait until all these things are over, but the company wants the Leonard thing completed as quickly as we can. That pretty much means Monday. Is there a problem with that?"

"No," Jim answered. "Pretty simple. I'm assuming that everything is in place or will be by that evening."

"Most assuredly," Gene said, nodding. "He's still under constant surveillance, and the car will be ready and in the Walmart parking lot by noon on Monday. The only thing that may impact our plan is if he doesn't go out that night. If we have to postpone, the plan is to reschedule for Thursday after you get back from your trip."

"All right," Jim agreed as they approached the hotel. "Are you going to be in Chicago for the operation with Val and Marie?"

"Yes," Gene assured him. "I'll be at the hotel when you get in. Marie and I will have rooms there also. There will be a message at the desk when you check in telling you where we are. Give me a call when you get to your room, and I'll have any updates for you."

"Will Val be there too?" Jim asked.

"No, she's been living in an apartment in Chicago for the last couple of months," Gene explained. "Robert would find it strange if all of a sudden, she was at a hotel. But we'll be in phone contact up until everybody leaves for the restaurant."

"How will Marie and I get to the restaurant?" Jim asked.

"We've got a taxi reserved for you," Gene told him. "It's sort of on loan and will be waiting to bring you back from the restaurant after you take care of Captain Nelson."

"What about the syringe?" Jim asked.

"I'll give it to you when you and Marie are ready to leave," Gene answered. "I'm picking it up at the lab that morning before I leave Quantico, and I don't want that potential catastrophe out of my sight until I hand it to you."

"I understand," Jim agreed. "And I'll make sure that none of the little bug gets loose after I empty it. There's always a little residue left in a syringe, but I'll do the same thing I used to do when I gave my horses a penicillin shot."

"What's that?" Gene asked as they got out of the car.

"Well, first off, the shot had to be IM or intramuscular," Jim answered. "If even a miniscule amount gets into the bloodstream, it causes a violent reaction. The best technique is to draw the plunger back after inserting it. If there's no blood, then you know you aren't in a vein. But you also need to draw the plunger back as you remove the needle because you probably went through some small veins inserted it. You'll be coming back through them as you remove the needle. And even a small drop on the tip of the needle will wind up in the vein, and within seconds, you'll have a real problem."

"So you're saying that you'll pull the plunger back after you empty it in Nelson's nose," Gene said as they neared the elevator.

"Exactly," Jim answered as the doors opened. "I'll pull it about halfway back to make sure I suck any residue from the end back into the syringe. Hopefully, any mucus from his nostril will provide an addition sealant to the end of the syringe before Val takes it with the napkin."

"Good idea," Gene said as they rode the elevator to their floor. "Now let's meet in the lobby in an hour, and I'll take you guys out to dinner."

Chapter 39

"Good evening, General," Jennifer said as she and Jim stepped out of the elevator. "Where are we going tonight?"

"Ernie's Crab House," Gene told her as he kissed her cheek. "It's a short walk from here, but I'll guarantee you that the food is excellent."

"A little stroll sounds good," Jim said as they followed Gene out of the hotel. "I've been sitting in either the Suburban or the conference room all day. I think my legs have forgotten that they're supposed to take me wherever I need to go."

"And I've been sitting right there beside you," Gene reminded him as they headed down the street. "Jennifer's probably the only one of us who got any exercise today."

"I did manage to visit a few stores," Jennifer said, smiling. "There are some very nice shops up here that carry a very different style from what I usually find in Texas."

"I guess that means they don't carry much of a selection of jeans and boots," Jim said, laughing. "But I'll bet that there are some stores in Dallas that carry all the latest fashions. Maybe not in Fort Worth, but Dallas seems to think of itself as the premier city in Texas for any fashion or social issues."

"That may be true," Jennifer said as they crossed a street. "At least they don't have herds of cattle roaming down the streets."

"Now that's only a couple of times a day on the North Side," Jim reminded her. "It's all for the tourists, and they aren't roaming. A few longhorn cattle walking down the same street for a couple of blocks time after time is not a herd."

"Still, I like shopping in Dallas better," Jennifer told him. "Maybe if Fort Worth didn't always call itself Cow Town."

"Isn't their motto 'Where the West Begins'?" Gene asked.

"Yeah, it is," Jim answered as they saw Ernie's Crab House. "They constantly try to separate themselves from their snooty cousin, Dallas."

"Still a little of the Old West attitude, is there?" Gene asked as he held the door to the restaurant open.

"Of course," Jim said, nodding at the maître d'. "Especially up on the North Side. Some of the old saloons are rumored to have been there during the cattle drives. One even boasts of having been a former brothel owned by Buffalo Bill Cody."

"Really?" Gene remarked as the maître d' led them to a table near the rear. "Why am I not surprised that you'd know that?"

"Yeah," Jennifer added as she took her seat. "How do you know that?"

"It's just that some of our pilots actually live over in that part of the Metroplex," Jim answered. "And lots of them go to Fort Worth for dinner, movies, dancing, or just somewhere to have a few beers."

"Have you ever been there?" she asked as the menus were passed around.

"No, but it's not a house of ill repute now," Jim told her as he opened his menu. "It's just another saloon down on Exchange Avenue. There are several old ones down there. The White Elephant Saloon is supposed to be where some sheriff from Fort Worth got into a gunfight with the owner of the saloon. Although it was originally in an area known as Hell's Half Acre, it was moved down to Exchange and still boasts about some of its history. But the so-called Red Light District is long gone."

"You're always a fount of trivia," Gene said as he nodded at their waiter. "But let's see if we can elevate our conversation somewhat above Old West gunfights and brothels. I'm going to suggest that we have the Crab Feast for three and coleslaw on the side."

"That sounds good to me," Jim said, looking at Jennifer.

"Me too," she said, closing her menu. "And I think I'd like a glass of tea."

"That's the answer then," Gene told the waiter. "And I'll have tea also. Jim?"

"Tea sounds good," he answered. "Unsweet, of course. With lemon."

"What time do we need to be at the airport tomorrow?" Jennifer asked as they waited.

"Probably around noon," Gene answered. "Did Jim tell you that you're flying out of Alexandria?"

"No," Jennifer told him. "Is the jet coming up here to get us?"

"No," Gene said. "You're going commercial. The tickets will be at the hotel front desk tomorrow morning."

"What happened to the jet?" Jennifer asked with disappointment clearly on her face.

"I have other needs for it tomorrow," Gene told her as the waiter came back with their meals. "And I'm sorry that I couldn't get you first-class seats on the flight home, but you'll be home by five o'clock."

"Well, I guess it's all right this time," Jennifer complained. "But I sure hope we get the private jet for the next trip."

Jim looked at Gene and just shook his head.

Chapter 40

On Monday morning, after Jennifer left for work, Jim was making sure his suitcase was packed for his trip on Tuesday. He was pretty happy with how things had gone regarding the plan to eliminate Captain Nelson but now needed to get back to the day-to-day life of an airline pilot.

Once satisfied that he had sufficient clean socks, underwear, and regulation white shirts, he rechecked his off-duty clothes—tennis shoes, jeans, and T-shirts along with a sweater or jacket depending on the weather at the overnight cities—making sure the shave kit had a fresh razor, deodorant, and enough toothpaste left in the tube for four days if any delays arose once away from DFW.

He knew that the company would provide him with a suit for the visit to the restaurant where he and Val would complete the mission regarding Nelson. He also knew that the company would destroy it after he returned to the hotel just in case some of the amoeba had wandered onto the jacket or pants. If there was a single worry about this mission, it was handling the deadly combination and not knowing if he had somehow managed to infect either himself or one of the others.

Taking a cup of coffee into the living room, he was watching the local news when the phone rang.

As soon as he answered, he heard Gene saying, "I've got some not-so-good news about Jewell."

"How is she?" Jim asked, turning the sound down on the TV.

"She's in intensive care," Gene answered. "The accident was caused by a loaded cement truck that blew a tire just as it was passing her. It swerved violently into her and crushed the car against the concrete wall that runs along the road. They had to cut her out of the car, and she almost didn't make it to the hospital. Too many broken bones to mention, but the major immediate concern is internal injuries."

"Do you know how long she'll be in intensive care or when she can have visitors?" Jim asked as his level of concern elevated.

"We sent one of our doctors to see what the company needed to do to ensure that she is getting the very best treatment, and he thinks it will be at least a month," Gene answered. "And then it's going to be a long road to recovery."

"Any guess at when she'll be able to go back to work flying or with the company?" Jim asked.

"Not at this time," Gene said. "Our doctor has very low expectations as to whether or not she'll ever go back to flying. The Federal Aviation Administration has numerous rules about physical requirements, as does American Airlines."

"I know," Jim agreed. "What's the company's plan if she can't return to work?"

"Since she was technically on duty with the company, even though it wasn't directly involved with an operation, she'll be provided with a retirement package," Gene told him. "It's normally about 3 percent of your annual salary for each year you've been with the company. And the company will also cover any and all health costs associated with the accident for the rest of her life."

"That's good," Jim agreed. "But I know that she'd rather be doing her job instead of sitting around. Her love of the job, especially the flying, was one of her biggest motivators. I'd hate to see her lose the company job as well if the FAA won't release her to return to flying."

"I know," Gene told him. "I'll be watching her progress closely, and if at all possible, I'll have her back on the job here. It may only be a desk job, but it'll keep her involved."

"I'm sure she'd like that," Jim agreed. "She needs to feel as if she's part of the organization. Even though flying was her number-one love, she relished these little excursions into the more adrenaline-fueled parts of the missions."

"It does become addictive," Gene admitted. "The field work is always the most exciting part of our mission. And speaking of field work, are you ready for tonight's mission with Leonard?"

"Certainly," Jim answered. "I plan on telling Jennifer that I'm going out for some ice cream to give me an excuse to leave. What time do you expect him to leave his house?"

"It's normally been around seven or eight o'clock," Gene answered. "His routine is to go home, stop and get either something to eat before he gets there or some frozen meal, and then drive to the bookstore if he hasn't been there in a few days."

"When was the last time he went?" Jim asked.

"Last Friday," Gene said. "We fully expect him to go tonight. I'm guessing it will be in the same time frame, and we'll call you as soon as he's observed leaving his house."

"What if Jennifer answers the phone?" Jim asked.

"The caller will identify himself as somebody from crew scheduling and will ask for you to call a number that's only one digit away from the real one," Gene answered. "When you call, you'll be updated on his activities and advised to head toward his house. Just try not to delay too long if Jennifer answers the phone. The time window is pretty broad, but five or ten minutes' delay in returning the call could have a serious impact on the assignment."

"Understood," Jim agreed. "I'll make sure that I'm close to the phone after six o'clock, and even if I'm in the bathroom or something, I'll hear it ring. Jennifer knows to always tell me immediately when the airline calls. Sometimes just a couple of minutes' delay getting back to the schedulers can result in losing a trip or missing out on getting paid for a trip you don't have to fly."

"Good," Gene told him. "I'll expect a call when you leave Leonard's house. The phone in the car is preset to dial my number if you press 1 three times."

"Sounds good," Jim said, nodding. "With a little luck, Mr. Leonard Blair will be sleeping peacefully for the rest of his short life by nine or ten o'clock tonight."

"That's the plan," Gene concurred before hanging up. "Just let me know when you're done."

Chapter 41

About four thirty that afternoon, Jim called Jennifer at work and told her that he was going to go to Venice Pizza and get a Sicilian-style pizza called "The Works" for tonight's dinner. Knowing that she'd be home shortly after five, he decided that with the pizza, there would be few dishes to do, and if the call came to head for Leonard's house, he would be able to leave any time after about six or six thirty.

Calling ahead to place the order, he knew that it would take about twenty minutes for them to bake the pizza. That would be about the time needed to drive there. Given another twenty minutes to get home, he would be home just before Jennifer arrived. That would be plenty of time to set the table and have everything ready.

It was almost five fifteen when Jim got back with the pizza, and Jennifer's car was already in the garage. Carrying it in, he announced, "Pizza man!"

Jennifer turned from the sink, smiling, and said, "Boy, Venice Pizza has sunk to new lows with their delivery boys. I guess they're trying to help the chronically unemployable."

"I'm trying to work my way through modeling school," Jim said as he set the still-warm pizza on the table. "I hope to someday be a centerfold for *GQ Magazine*."

"Maybe you should save your money," Jennifer joked. "I don't think they use knuckle-dragging Neanderthals in their commercials."

"You're talking about the former me," Jim said as he put his arms around her. "Just this weekend, I demonstrated the inner gentleman every evening when we went out to dinner."

Jennifer put her arms around his neck and whispered, "Yes, you did. And I just want you to remember how much more fun your little excursions to Virginia or wherever you go to meet Gene would be if I was there."

"Oh, I'll remember," Jim told her, kissing her cheek. "And I know you will always want to go. But it may not always work out that way. For now, why don't we enjoy the pizza before it gets cold?"

They had just finished eating and Jennifer was putting almost half of the pizza in the refrigerator when the phone rang.

"I'll get it," Jim said as he put the plates in the sink. Hearing that Leonard had just left his house, Jim hung up and said, "Telemarketer. I told him we didn't need aluminum siding for the house. I wish there was some way to stop companies from calling after five o'clock or something."

"They can be a pain," Jennifer said, rinsing their plates. "I'm just glad that I don't have their job. I'd hate to know that I was being a pain in the butt to everybody whom I called and that they were probably cussing me after they slammed the phone down."

"Me too," Jim said as he opened the freezer. "Don't we have any ice cream?"

"I guess not," Jennifer answered. "I think you ate the last of it before we went to Virginia."

"Well, that just won't do," Jim said, closing the freezer door. "Having a scrumptious meal like we just enjoyed and not having a delicious dessert reduces it from dining to mere eating."

Jennifer laughed and remarked, "So that would be fine dining if you had what? A bowl of ice cream? And you deny your knuckle-dragging ways."

"Even a caveman likes ice cream," Jim said, mimicking an apelike walk toward her. "Me want ice cream!"

"I guess you need to take your club and scour the forest for it then," Jennifer joked as she rubbed his head. "What kind do you plan on getting?"

"Blue Bell Pistachio Almond," Jim said, pulling her to him. "Is that all right with you?"

"How about Rocky Road?" Jennifer asked, rubbing his nose with hers.

"How about both?" Jim said as he took his arms from around her waist. "I think it's Blue Bell season, and the limit is two."

"Want me to go with you?" Jennifer asked as he started for the door.

"Not necessary," Jim answered, knowing that going shopping for ice cream this late was something she wouldn't want to do. "Not unless you want to."

"No, I need to do a load of laundry. You go ahead. Just don't be too late with my Rocky Road," she told him. "I'll see you when you get back."

Chapter 42

Jim left the house and headed northwest on Galloway Avenue. Reaching U.S. 80, he headed west and glanced at his watch. He had only spent three or four minutes after the phone call, but he wanted to make sure he had sufficient time to get to Leonard's house and replace the inhaler before the little pervert got back home.

Making sure that he wasn't speeding, he finally reached the exit for St. Francis Avenue. Heading south on St. Francis, he then turned east on Samuell Boulevard. Less than a mile from there, he saw the Walmart on the north side of the road.

Pulling into the first entry, he started looking for the white Chevrolet that the phone call had said would be waiting about a hundred yards from the main entrance and several parking spots from any other cars. Seeing a lone white car that sat almost conspicuously by itself, he slowed as he drove behind it. Seeing that the license plate matched the numbers he had been given, he drove to the closest shopping cart return area and parked his truck.

Looking around as he got out of his truck, he didn't see anything that looked out of place. With lots of cars parked between his location and the store, he started walking toward the Chevrolet. Several cars passed him as he walked toward it, but he blended in with the other shoppers returning to their cars.

Opening the driver's door, he noticed that the dome light had been disabled. Shutting the door, he reached over and opened the glove box and took out the keys, phone, and inhaler. After laying the phone and inhaler on the seat beside him, he started the car and pulled out of the parking lot. Back on Samuell Boulevard, he went back to join U.S. 67 heading west.

According to the map, he should be at Leonard's house in less than fifteen minutes. The traffic was reasonable for Dallas because of the lateness of the day, and Jim didn't see any problem making it to Leonard's house within the time frame he had been given.

Less than ten minutes from when he had left the Walmart parking lot, he took the exit for North Munger Boulevard. Leonard's house was just a mile or so north on Bryan Street. Turning right onto Bryan, he spotted the house in the middle of the first block.

Seeing nobody in the adjacent yards or driveways, Jim pulled to the curb in front of the house and looked for signs of anyone inside. The information he had gotten assured him that Leonard lived alone, and he would have gotten a call if anything had changed.

Taking the keys and the inhaler, he walked up the sidewalk and made one final glance in both directions before inserting the key in the doorknob. Holding his breath, he turned it and felt relief when the door unlocked. After a final glance around, he opened the door and stepped inside. He had been told that Leonard kept the inhaler on a table in the living room beside a brown leather recliner.

Spotting the inhaler, he memorized the exact position of it on the table, picked it up, and verified that the one he had was an exact duplicate. Replacing it with the one he had brought, he put Leonard's in his pocket and turned for the door.

Locking the door from the inside, Jim stepped out and pulled it shut behind him. He was almost to his car when Leonard's car came pulling into the driveway. Turning to face him, Jim wondered just how much Leonard had seen.

"Hi," Jim said, walking over to his car. "Are you a friend of Larry?"

"Who's Larry?" Leonard asked as he got out of his car. "And what are you doing at my house?"

"I was supposed to meet Larry here," Jim answered. "I may be a little early, but I don't mind waiting."

"I don't know any Larry, and I'll ask again, what are you doing at my house?"

"I just told you," Jim said with a puzzled look on his face. "I'm supposed to meet Larry here. He and I are going to dinner with another friend of his. I don't remember his name, Paul or something. I'm not sure."

"There's no Larry here," Leonard said, getting mad. "And there's no Paul or whoever. You're at the wrong house."

Jim cocked his head and said, "I'm sure this is Larry's house. He told me to come north on Munger and turn right on Bryan. Then it would be the third house on the left."

"Did he say to turn right on Bryan Street or Bryan Parkway?" Leonard asked.

Jim paused as if he was thinking and said, "I think it was Bryan Street. But to be honest, it could have been Parkway. All I remember was Bryan."

"This is Bryan Street," Leonard emphasized. "Bryan Parkway is the next street north on Munger."

"I guess I made a mistake," Jim said, shaking his head. "I just saw Bryan and assumed that it was the only one in this area."

"You certainly made a mistake," Leonard said, putting his hands on his hips. "Now I'd appreciate it if you'd leave."

"Not a problem," Jim said, backing away. "I'm sorry if I caused any problems. I just never thought that there would be two Bryans a block apart. Sorry to have bothered you."

Leonard just stared at Jim for a minute and turned toward his house. Jim slowly walked to his car, keeping Leonard in sight until the door to the house closed behind him.

Crap, he thought as he started the car. *That was close.*

Going east on Bryan Street to Hubert Street, he turned left and pulled over. As he grabbed the phone, he noticed a missed call.

Dialing 111, he breathed a sigh of relief and almost immediately heard Gene asking, "What the hell happened?"

"I left the phone in the car," Jim explained. "I assumed that since nobody called me before I got here, Leonard wasn't going to be back so soon."

"Leonard came out of the bookstore much quicker than the team expected," Gene told him. "He was halfway home before anybody noticed. They immediately called you but got no answer."

"Yeah, Leonard got here much quicker than I expected too," Jim agreed. "I guess I should have put the phone in my pocket."

"Probably would have been a good idea," Gene said. "But even then, it would have been dicey. Just a couple of minutes of inattention by the guys who were monitoring him could have been disastrous."

"No shit," Jim said. "Even thirty seconds sooner, and he would have caught me closing his door. That would have been very hard to explain."

"What *did* you tell him?" Gene asked.

"I made up a story about meeting somebody named Larry who lived on Bryan," Jim answered. "It's a good thing that I remembered there were two Bryans side by side. Otherwise,

I'm not sure if I could have provided a plausible excuse for being on his property."

"That was quick thinking," Gene told him. "And the videos showed him glancing around inside, but obviously, he didn't see anything out of place. We'll know in a couple of hours when he uses the inhaler."

"All I can say is that *that* was too close," Jim told him. "I know that I should have been carrying the phone, but I'm hoping that somebody has a word with those guys who were just sitting on their asses while mine was being hung out to dry."

"Rest assured, that has already been taken care of," Gene said. "There are now a couple of ex–Black Water employees in the Dallas area."

"I hate that they lost their jobs," Jim told him. "But it's that very lack of attention to the job, no matter how mundane or boring it seems, that gets people killed."

"I know. I couldn't agree more. But it was a successful operation. And that's what counts," Gene said. "Anyway, I'll see you in Chicago tomorrow night, and we can discuss it further if you feel the need."

"No," Jim said as he pulled away from the curb. "Let's just chalk this one up to a learning experience. Nobody died."

"Not yet," Gene agreed. "But hopefully, in a matter of hours, that won't be true. Anyway, you did what I always expect of you. And I do apologize for the screw-up. Have a good evening."

"You too," Jim said as he hung up and tossed the phone back on the seat as he turned left on Bryan Parkway and headed back to get his truck.

After parking where he had found the car and putting everything back in the glove box, Jim headed into Walmart to get the ice cream that was the reason he had given Jennifer. Once inside, he grabbed a basket and quickly found the frozen food area and ice cream section. Seeing the familiar green tub with a brown trim top, he opened the glass door and selected one of the containers. The beige-and-brown container of Rocky Road was behind the adjoining door, and he put one in his basket. Heading for the checkout section, he stopped and took a Butterfinger off the shelf of impulse-buying items that sat just before the cashier.

After paying, he headed back to where he had left his truck. Approaching it, he noticed that the white Chevrolet was now missing. Not surprised, Jim got into his truck and headed back home. As he pulled into the driveway, he noticed that the entire time from the phone call to now was just over thirty minutes.

Going in the back door, he called out, "It's just me! Me and some ice cream!"

Jennifer walked in as he was putting the two cartons in the freezer and picked up the bag that had held the ice cream. Looking inside, she pulled out the Butterfinger and asked, "And how did this manage to find its way into your bag?"

Jim just smiled and took it from her hand, saying, "It looked lonely there on the shelf as I was checking out. Want some Rocky Road?"

Chapter 43

On Tuesday morning, Jim woke early partly because of having an early sign-in for his flight, partly because of wondering how the operation regarding Captain Nelson would play out without Jewell. Marie seemed competent, but an operation this complicated with a new person still worried him.

As he stepped out of the shower, Jennifer came into the bathroom and asked, "In a rush to leave this morning?"

"No," Jim told her as he admired the way she looked in just an old T-shirt of his. "Just woke up and couldn't get back to sleep. I'll go make some coffee, and we can have a few minutes before I have to leave."

"That sounds good to me," Jennifer said as she brushed against him as he turned to leave. "Unless you want to come back to bed and spend a few minutes there."

"You should have mentioned that before I took my shower," Jim said, putting his arms around her waist. "I don't have time for another shower, and I know just how long a few minutes with you in bed can stretch into."

"You're no fun," Jennifer said as she rubbed her breasts against him. "I can remember when nothing would keep you from wanting a few minutes."

"Make the same offer when I get back," Jim joked as he kissed her cheek and pulled away. "I'll be glad to spend more than a few minutes. You may have to call in sick for the day."

"Promises, promises," Jennifer replied, smiling. "I may just hold you to them this time. What time are you getting home?"

"About noon on Thursday," Jim answered. "Unless there are any problems. But the forecast for the entire week looks good for all my flights."

"In that case, I'll tell my boss that I will be extremely late coming to work Friday," she said, pushing him out of the bathroom. "I'll be out for some coffee and a *few minutes* with my number-one man in a couple of minutes."

"And just who is number two?" Jim asked as he headed for the kitchen.

"I'm afraid that you're not cleared for that information," she answered before shutting the door. "Top Secret, No Foreign Dissemination, Eyes Only, Need to Know clearance is required."

Two hours later, Jim had parked in the employee lot and was boarding the two-car electric train that ran from the parking lot to the terminal. Seeing a Captain hurrying to catch the train, Jim held the door open and waited for the man to get in.

"Thanks," the man said as he set his suitcase on the floor. "I appreciate you holding the door."

"Not a problem," Jim said. "I hate being just a couple of feet from the train as it pulls away."

"Frustrating," the Captain said, nodding. "I'm Rob Sproc."

"Good to meet you, Rob," Jim said, shaking his outstretched hand. "I'm Jim Lashley."

"Where are you headed today?" Rob asked as the train rumbled around the airport.

"Phoenix first, back here, and then to Chicago," Jim answered. "How about you?"

"Same thing," Rob told him, smiling. "Quite a coincidence. Most of the time, I don't meet my FO until I get to the airplane."

"I know," Jim said as the train made its first stop and they waited for a few more people to board. "Occasionally, I'll meet my Captain in operations, but unless I know him, it's just a bunch of people in blue jackets with four stripes hacking away at a computer. And you know, you guys all look the same to us poor FOs."

"That's for sure," Rob said, smiling. "What's your background?"

"Marines," Jim answered. "You?"

"Air Force," Rob told him. "C-141s."

"F-4s," Jim responded. "A few years in the mud before that."

"Retired?" Rob asked as they approached the terminal where they would disembark.

"Yeah," Jim said, bending over to get his suitcase. "Eight years active and the rest in the Reserves."

"No offense, but you look a little older than most of our FOs," Rob told him, getting his suitcase. "But I'm always glad to be flying with anybody with military experience. I've found that the trip seems to go better—fewer worries about skill levels and certainly more to talk about. Civilian pilots don't seem to grasp the big picture and certainly don't have the depth of experience military pilots have."

"No shit," Jim agreed. "I've had some real issues with a couple of the Captains whom I've had to fly with. I have no problem flying with just about anybody, but sometimes it's a struggle to keep my mouth shut."

"Speak your mind with me," Rob said as they headed up the stairs to the terminal. "Don't ever hold back if you see anything that you don't like."

"No problem," Jim told him as they came to the door to operations. "My biggest problem is when I have to fly with a Captain who never buys Cinnabons in the mornings."

Rob almost broke out laughing and said, "I think this is going to be a good month. Even if you were unfortunate enough to have to be a Gyrene."

During the flight briefing, when they got to the airplane, Rob suggested, "Instead of swapping legs to fly, why don't we fly the outbound and inbound legs? That way, neither one of us has to fly every return to DFW."

"Sounds good to me," Jim answered, nodding. "Which leg do you want to fly first?"

"Why don't you fly to Phoenix and back? I'll fly to Chicago and back to DFW tomorrow. Then you fly back to Chicago, and I'll fly the return leg to DFW on Thursday," Rob proposed.

"You're the Captain," Jim said, agreeing. "I'm happy with anything as long as somebody buys Cinnabons."

"Agreed," Rob said, laughing. "How about whoever flies the first flight of the day buys the Cinnabons?"

"Great," Jim said, smiling. "The only problem is that some of the airports don't have Cinnabons. As a matter of fact, none of my legs are from an airport with them."

Rob thought for a moment and shook his head, saying, "Either you're an evil genius or you've played this game before."

"You know us Gyrenes," Jim said, smiling. "We live to take advantage of you Air Force guys."

"Fair enough," Rob said. "Just remember that next week, we swap legs."

"Still great," Jim replied. "Since there are five sequences this month, you'll still be buying more than me. And that includes Cinnabons for the Flight Attendants."

Rob turned his head and muttered, "Son of a bitch. Outsmarted by a frigging Marine."

Chapter 44

After arriving at Chicago just a little before four o'clock, Jim and Rob stood outside the terminal, waiting for the van to take them to the hotel.

"Too bad we don't all stay together like we used to," Rob said, referring to the fact that the flight attendants changed almost every leg.

"I know," Jim agreed. "I liked it better when you got to know them and who the flake was and who you could trust to handle things in the back without constant whining or complaining."

"At least I didn't have to keep a list of their names for each leg," Rob complained as the van arrived. "And the one who served first class always knew how I liked my coffee after the first flight."

"It just felt better to know everybody in the crew," Jim agreed as they loaded their bags. "Now it's like a handful of strangers trying to pretend that there's some connection. Sort of like a dysfunctional family reunion."

"That's a good way to describe it," Rob concurred as they headed for the hotel. "Any plans for this evening?"

"Meeting some friends for dinner," Jim answered. "What about you?"

"Not really," Rob told him. "I've got some paperwork that I brought and then probably dinner and a movie on TV. My wife's parents were visiting over the weekend, and I'm ready for some alone time."

"In-laws can be a little disruptive," Jim said as they approached the hotel.

"Oh, her dad is okay," Rob replied. "But her mother is a busybody know-it-all. No matter what I do or say, she tries to turn it into something she can criticize. I don't know how her dad can stand to be around her. She all but called him a stupid worthless idiot so many times over the weekend that I wanted to ask him if he'd like to go fishing for the rest of their visit. Just to get him away from her."

"That had to be brutal for you," Jim told him as they took their bags from the van and tipped the driver. "I would have had a hard time keeping my mouth shut."

"Trust me," Rob said, nodding. "If my wife hadn't kept giving me her 'don't you dare' look, I'm sure I would have said something that would have caused a major rift in the delicate fabric of our relationship with her family."

"Major rift in the delicate fabric?" Jim smirked as they set their bags in front of the hotel desk to get their rooms. "You are definitely Air Force."

"How would you describe it?" Rob asked, taking his room key. "I guess it would require single-syllable words comprising four or less letters. Probably consisting of repeated vowels. We Air Force gentlemen have an admirable vocabulary, and I momentarily forgot that I was dealing with the primordial ooze that finally morphed into the upright being fondly known as a Marine."

"The few, the proud," Jim said, smiling at the desk clerk. "We warriors will always acknowledge our attributes, which don't include excessive verbiage when a single glare will suffice."

"Suffice? Now there's an anomaly," Rob said, laughing. "Two syllables and only two vowels. Quite an accomplishment for a mud-crawling Marine."

"Do you guys always argue like this?" the desk clerk asked as he handed Jim his key and an envelope. "Some man left this for you, sir."

"This isn't arguing," Rob answered, grinning. "More like friendly harassment. Interservice rivalries are the life blood of the military. But we all serve and won't tolerate anybody who defames any of us."

"Defames," Jim said, picking up his bags. "There he goes again. Silver-tongued smooth talker. He means gives shit to."

"Let me explain it this way," Rob said to the clerk. "Marines land on a five-hundred-foot-long runway and then go to the mess hall to have beer with five thousand smelly sailors. An Air Force pilot lands on a ten-thousand-foot runway and joins fifty beautiful nurses at the Officer's Club for a martini. Who would you rather be? Marine or Air Force?"

"I've seen some of those nurses," Jim said, laughing as they headed for the elevator. "Some of them make a sailor look pretty."

"I've heard that about the Navy," Rob said as they rode the elevator to their floor. "Too many nights at sea together. Sharing the same beds. Everybody starts looking pretty."

"Let's not be too hard on my brother sailors," Jim told him as they got off the elevator. "Even on shore, they have a hard time with the ladies."

"That must be why the base in the Philippines was established," Rob remarked, heading for his room. "I think 90 percent of the Navy guys I've met have Filipino wives."

"And probably 99 percent of them regret it after they get back to the United States," Jim agreed as he stopped in front of his room. "I'll see you in the morning."

"You too," Rob said, opening his door. "Have a good evening."

Chapter 45

As soon as Jim got in his room, he set his bags at the foot of the bed and pulled his uniform jacket off. Tossing it on the bed, he opened the envelope and noticed that the only thing written on the page was a room number on the floor below his.

After hanging his jacket and pants up, he took a pair of jeans and a T-shirt from his suitcase and pulled them on. Next came the tennis shoes. Finally dressed, he opened the door and checked the hall to see if anybody he knew was there. Seeing no one, he hung the Do Not Disturb sign on the outside knob, closed the door, and headed for the stairs at the end of the hall. One floor down, he found the door he needed and knocked quietly.

Opening the door, Gene said, "Come in, Jim."

Stepping inside, Jim saw Marie and Val sitting in the only two chairs in the room.

"Hey, guys," he said as Gene closed the door.

"Have a seat on the bed," Gene said, walking over to the desk. "Slight change of plans."

"I figured something was wrong when I saw Val here," Jim told him. "She was supposed to be at the restaurant in a couple of hours."

"Nothing's really wrong," Gene told him as he sat on the edge of the desk. "But Robert called her an hour or so ago and cancelled their date."

Jim looked at Val and asked, "Has this happened before?"

"Oh yes," she answered. "We've had four or five dates, and he's had to cancel twice."

"Did he give you a reason?" Jim asked.

"Not really," she told him. "Just that something came up. Some raid or emergency that he had to respond to. But he promised me that we'd go tomorrow night."

"So, what now?" Jim asked Gene.

"Well, since we're all here, I thought we'd take the opportunity to run through our operation this evening," he answered. "I'd already made reservations at the restaurant for you and Marie. I also changed Robert and Val's reservation to Nolan and Melinda. Let's just call it a dress rehearsal."

"I guess that would be good. Are you not concerned about Val being there again tomorrow night with Robert?" Jim said, nodding.

"Not really. It's a very popular restaurant," Gene said. "Now you'll find a sports coat, a dress shirt, and a pair of slacks in the closet. Along with a pair of nice shoes and some black socks. Those white socks won't quite cut it unless you're going for the geeky nerd look."

"Val and I will slip into the next room and change also," Marie said as she opened the connecting door. "We'll be ready in a few minutes."

Jim stripped down to his shorts and redressed with the clothes Gene had provided. "I guess you folks at Black Water have a file on me that includes my pants, shirt, and shoe sizes."

"We have a file on you that includes almost everything," Gene answered, smiling as he took a chair. "Just as we do on everybody who works for the company."

"Okay," Jim said, taking the other chair. "What happened to Leonard after I left?"

"He did look around his house pretty thoroughly," Gene told him. "He walked into every room and looked around for several minutes."

"I was worried that he may have seen me closing the door," Jim admitted. "But since he didn't mention it, I figured that at most, he might be suspicious since he more than likely thinks he's under surveillance."

"Not really," Gene explained. "His lawyer filed some complaint several weeks ago to prohibit the police from *harassing* him. So, after a few days of watching for them, he more or less relaxed."

"I guess he didn't know that we were watching also," Jim noted. "And I'm sure Black Water is more adept at clandestine operations than the Dallas Police Department."

"Undoubtedly," Gene agreed. "And I'd bet we have a larger array of toys to monitor everything."

"Oh, I'm sure of that," Jim said. "I doubt if they have the budget for the sophisticated *toys* the company has."

"Even if they had the money, they don't have the clearance to use some of the latest technology that we have access to," Gene told him. "But after a few minutes of looking around, he finally sat down in his recliner and turned the TV on. After an hour or so, he picked up the inhaler and took his usual dose."

"What happened then?" Jim asked.

"Pretty much as we predicted," Gene answered. "At first, he just seemed dizzy. He tried to stand up but sort of fell back into his chair. Then he acted like he had the dry heaves and started jerking back and forth in his chair. Within ten minutes, he kind of arched his back and appeared to be gasping for air."

"Sounds pretty horrific," Jim said. "Not a very nice way to depart this world."

"Not near as horrific as how he treated those little girls," Gene reminded him. "Anyway, the team waited a couple of hours until they saw no further movement and entered the house. They made sure that there was no pulse or breathing and scrubbed each room to remove everything we had planted. Then they verified that there were no further readings from the operations center. After that, they wiped down every surface that you were seen to touch, exchanged the inhalers, and left."

"Now what?" Jim asked.

"We'll wait another day and make a call from the school to the police saying that he's missed the last two days of work," Gene answered. "They'll go to his house and probably see him in his chair through the window. Noting no movement or response to knocking on the door, they'll enter and discover the little pervert dead."

"I believe I remember you saying something about having the autopsy covered too," Jim said.

"Yes, it's taken care of," Gene told him. "And although we didn't do anything regarding the police, I feel sure that they'll close this investigation the second the coroner identifies the case of death as asphyxiation because of severe asthma-related issues."

Chapter 46

"What about Jewell?" Jim asked as Val and Marie came through the connecting door.

"We were talking about her earlier," Gene said as he got up. "Not much different. Still in intensive care. Still no visitation allowed. Not much we can do for now."

"I wish there was something we could do," Jim said as he got out of his chair. "I'm going to miss her. I just hope she can come back to work."

"We all do," Gene told him as he headed for the door. "I've arranged for a limo to take us to the restaurant, and it should be downstairs right now. So, let's head to the restaurant and try to enjoy the evening as well as get a little insight as to what to expect tomorrow."

"I'll keep trying to get in to see her," Val said as they rode the elevator down to the lobby. "I'm sure any friendly face would be welcome."

"I'm sure it would. The Cite restaurant," Gene told the driver as they left the hotel and got in the limo.

"Yes, sir," he answered as the doors closed. "Would you like the lakeshore scenic drive or a direct route?"

"We've got plenty of time," Gene answered. "Let's take the scenic drive."

"Very well, sir," the driver said as they pulled away from the hotel. "Would you like a commentary as we go, or would you prefer privacy?"

"Privacy, please. I've got a lady here who's very familiar with the area. Thanks for asking though." Gene told him as they headed east for the lake. Looking at Jim he added, "You're going to like this drive. Not much like this in Texas."

"No," Jim agreed as they slid through the manmade canyons of buildings. "The poor people who have to live down here seventy stories below the sky have probably never seen the sunset except as it crosses the closest building to the west."

"There's a couple of places where the streets intersect, and you can actually see east to the lake or west far enough to see it," Val said as they approached Lake Shore Drive.

"I just love the term 'with a lake view or ocean view' that realtors use when describing apartments or houses," Jim said as they looked across Lake Michigan. "I flew with a guy who answered an ad for an apartment in Boston that had an ocean view. When he got there, the agent showed him that if he opened one of the windows and leaned out, he could see the ocean between two buildings. It was about five miles away, and there was maybe a three-inch sliver where you could see it."

"But it was an ocean view," Marie said, laughing. "You should see some of the descriptions of property down in New Orleans. The term 'bayou view' more than likely means 'swampland.'"

"It's the same everywhere," Gene added as they approached the Lake Point Tower. "But I think you'll find the view from the Cite is extraordinary. Both of the lake and looking west toward downtown. And the view of the sunset across downtown Chicago with the Sears Tower is spectacular."

"Shall I wait for you?" the driver asked as they pulled up.

"Yes, please," Gene told him. "But we'll be at least an hour before we're ready to go back to the hotel. So, if you'd like to do something while we're eating, that's fine."

"Not a problem, sir," he said as they got out of the limo. "I'll be here when you come back down."

As they approached the elevator, Jim asked Gene, "Have you eaten here before?"

"Several times," Gene answered as he pushed the button for the seventieth floor.

"Such a life," Jim said, watching the floors slide by as they rose to their floor. "Private jets, dining in the finest restaurants around the world, constantly in the company of beautiful ladies. How do I apply for your job?"

"You already did," Gene said, smiling as the elevator doors opened. "The only problem is that there isn't an opening at this time."

"And when does the company expect there to be an opening?" Jim asked as they approached the maître d'.

"Upon my death," Gene said, smiling. "Reservation for Nolan and Melinda?"

"And for Jim and Marie," Jim added. "As far from this gentleman as possible."

"Pardon me, sir?" the maître d' asked.

"Just joking, sir," Jim answered. "We just met in the elevator and were enjoying a pleasant conversation. Adjoining table would be appreciated."

"I believe we can accommodate you, sir," he said as he signaled for a waiter. "Would you prefer a lake view?"

Jim almost broke out laughing and said, "Whatever the gentleman prefers."

"How about a western view since the sun will be setting in a few minutes?" Gene answered.

"Yes, sir," the waiter said as he led them to two adjoining tables and provided menus. "Would you like to start with drinks?"

Gene looked at Val and asked, "What would you like?"

"Do you have Ram's Gate Pinot?" she asked.

"Definitely," he told her as they approached the table. "We have Gap's Crown Vyn, if that would be all right."

"Perfect," Val said as she took the chair Gene was holding for her.

"Could we have a bottle, please?" Gene said, taking the seat to her right.

"Of course. And for you, sir?" he asked Jim as he was pulling out a chair for Marie at the adjoining table.

"I'll trust the lady's taste," he answered as he took the seat across from Marie. "We'd like a bottle also, please."

"Excellent," the waiter told him as he backed away from their tables. "I'll send it right out. I'll be right back to take your dinner orders."

As soon as the waiter was gone, Gene told Jim, "You go through the procedures for Marie, and I'll mimic Robert's most likely actions. We'll start with the point where Robert has already had some of his wine and is becoming disoriented."

As Gene kept his eyes to the left on Val, Jim quietly told Marie, "Start paying a little more attention to Val. As soon as you see her look at me, I'll know that she's ready for me to step over to the table and give Robert the mix. When I start to slide my chair back, you need to look to your left and find the waiter who brought them their wine. He should already be walking toward you with a tray of drinks. Be ready to stand up as he gets almost behind you. If you time it correctly, it will coincide with me getting out of my chair."

As Jim got up, Val took her napkin in her left hand and pretended to wipe Gene's chin. Marie looked to her left and noticed that a waiter was looking at her as she slid her chair back. Jim turned slightly left and put his left hand on Gene's shoulder.

Sitting back down, Jim told Marie, "That's pretty much it. Any questions?"

"I don't think so," she answered. "Do I need to signal the waiter?"

"No," Gene said, looking at her and Jim. "He'll be watching Val and Jim. When he sees her give Jim the signal to approach Robert, he'll head your way."

"You mean he's just going to stand there with a tray of drinks waiting?" Marie asked.

"No," Gene explained. "The tray will be on a table just behind him. We've simulated his role several times, and he knows just about how long it takes for the roofie mix to take effect. He'll be mostly out of sight after he brings the wine, but I assure you, he will be paying attention and knows his job." Noticing their waiter approaching, Gene said, "If everybody is satisfied, we'll order and enjoy our meals. If you want to try it again, we can do so during the meal."

"I'm good," Marie said.

"Me too," Jim said. "And I'm hungry."

"I don't have any problems," Val said. "I think we're as ready as we'll ever be."

"Good," Gene concurred. "Let's just relax for the rest of the evening, and we can discuss anything you may think of tomorrow when we meet again."

Chapter 47

The next morning, Jim was waiting in the lobby when Rob stepped off the elevator.

"Morning," he said, getting up from the sofa. "Ready for another hard day of aviation?"

"Of course," Rob said as he left his room key on the desk and nodded at the clerk. "Good evening?"

"Very good," Jim answered as they walked out to the waiting van to take them to the airport. "Matter of fact, we're going to meet again this afternoon when we get back. What about you?"

"Believe it or not, my wife wants to come to Chicago on our flight back," Rob said as the van pulled away from the hotel. "I think she wants to make up for the misery I had to endure with her mother over the weekend."

"Chicago's a pretty nice town for a night out," Jim said, watching the skyline slide by. "Just be careful where you go. I've heard some pretty scary stories about how in many parts of the city, the gangs are pretty much fearless."

"I know," Rob acknowledged. "I was based up here when I first joined American. I'm well aware of the problems. And it seems that it's gotten worse over the last ten or so years."

"That's what I've heard," Jim said. "But there's a problem in just about every big city. Baltimore is a checkerboard of blight and crime. Even Fort Worth is beginning to have problems with the Hispanic gangs. I grew up in a little town in the Texas panhandle named Muleshoe, and last time I was there, I was told to stay out of downtown after ten or eleven at night. And Muleshoe has only three or four thousand people."

"There doesn't seem to be a solution," Rob said as they approached the airport. "The police seem to be ineffective, the politicians just ramble on about the social injustices that created the problem, and the normal citizen is more worried about what some washed-up actor in Hollywood thinks about it than trying to solve it."

"It is a problem," Jim told him as they retrieved their bags from the back of the van and tipped the driver. "But right now, my biggest concern is if our flight is out of concourse G."

"Why G?" Rob asked as they entered Terminal 3.

"That's where Cinnabon is," Jim said, smiling. "And in case you didn't check, we have four flight attendants on the leg to Dallas."

"I should have known that a Marine can't have an intelligent conversation about a complex issue for more than a few sporadic comments," Rob told him, laughing. "I'll see you at the jet, and yes, I'll have enough Cinnabons for everybody."

"I'll pull the paperwork for you," Jim volunteered. "It'll be at the agent's desk except for the Takeoff Data section. I'll even be so gracious that I'll set up your instruments for you. Don't want you to get sticky stuff on the knobs because I'm sure that an Air Force Officer would never lick his fingers."

"No," Rob said, smiling as he walked away. "We discovered napkins and how to use them for other than blowing our noses."

Jim was standing in the first-class galley area, talking to one of the flight attendants, when Rob stepped into the airplane.

"Good morning," he said, handing her the box of Cinnabons. "I brought something for the crew, but make sure everybody gets one before Jim has a chance to grab them."

"Thanks, Captain," she told him. "Jim said that you volunteered to bring them. That's so nice. Most Captains don't think about us. I'm Lisa. Can I get you anything?"

"Just black coffee," Rob answered as he put his suitcase and kit bag away. "And please just call me Rob."

"Airplane's good," Jim announced as he and Rob got in their seats. "I set the instruments for 28R since that's what they're using this morning."

"Good," Rob said, checking his instruments against the paperwork. "Everything looks good for the trip to DFW, and there are plenty of open seats for my wife to come back with us."

"That's good," Jim said as Lisa handed Rob his coffee. "There's nothing better than when a well-thought-out plan comes together."

"I never said it was well thought out," Rob said, smiling. "I just said that it looks like my wife will be coming with us back to Chicago."

"Maybe she's the one who thought out the plan," Jim said as the gate agent stuck his head in the cockpit door.

"Everybody's on," the agent said. "I'm closing the door a couple of minutes early, if you don't mind."

"That's fine," Rob answered. "If you got all the nonrevenue passengers on, I'm ready to go."

"Everybody who signed up for the flight is on," the agent assured him. "Have a pleasant flight."

"Thanks," Rob said as the agent left. "Before starting engines, checklist, please, Jim."

As Jim started reading the checklist, Lisa stuck her head in the cockpit and said, "Cabin's ready. I'll check back with you once we level off to see if you need anything. And thanks again for the Cinnabons."

Chapter 48

The flight to DFW was smooth and uninterrupted, with no off-course vectors or reduced speed instructions.

Pulling into gate C33 almost fifteen minutes early, Rob told Jim, "I'm going up to check if my wife is on the flight. Do you want me to bring you anything?"

"No. I think that there is a Chili's just across from our gate," Jim answered. "Since we're taking this jet back to ORD, I thought I'd do a quick walk around and run up there and get a glass of tea."

"Then I'll probably see you up there," Rob said, heading up the jet bridge.

Jim finished checking the exterior of the airplane and stepped back in the cockpit to put his flashlight back in his bag. Seeing Lisa sitting in one of the first-class seats, he asked, "Lisa, I'm going up for a glass of tea. Would you like for me to bring you anything?"

"Tea sounds good," she said as she got out of the seat. "I'll go with you."

As they were entering the terminal from the jet bridge, Rob called, "Hey, guys! Come meet my wife!" As they approached,

Rob said, "This is Jim, my FO. And Lisa is our first-class flight attendant. This is my wife, Debbie."

"Hello, Debbie," Jim said, removing his hat. "Very nice to meet you."

"Hi," Lisa said. "Did you get on the flight?"

"Hi," Debbie told Jim and Lisa. "Yes, back in coach."

"At least you're on," Rob chastised her.

"Don't worry," Lisa told her. "I think I can sneak you a drink or a snack from first class if you'd like."

"That's not necessary," Debbie told her.

"Not a problem," Lisa said as she started to leave with Jim. "I'll come back and check on you once we're airborne."

Once they were back on the plane, Rob tossed the paperwork on the console between the seats and said, "No changes to anything. Your leg and your turn to buy Cinnabons tomorrow morning."

"Not a problem," Jim said as he picked up the paperwork. "My wife gives me an allowance that includes up to six Cinnabons per leg."

"You and your Cinnabons," Rob said, shaking his head. "Is that the way you measure success?"

"Oh yes," Jim said, setting up his instruments for the takeoff and departure. "Everything boils down to how many good friends a man has and how many Cinnabons he can share."

"Now that's about as simple of a life goal as you can have," Rob told him. "But I'm betting that there's more to the philosophy than just a Cinnabon."

"Cinnabon is just a metaphor for the good and sweet things in life," Jim explained as he tossed the paperwork back on the console. "And sharing the good things in life with your friends is the most important part of living and makes every day a joy."

"Now I've heard everything," Rob said, noticing that the gate agent was stepping on the plane. "A Marine who uses metaphors. Before starting engines, checklist, please."

The trip back to ORD was routine, and even the usual crowded air in the ORD traffic pattern seemed lighter than normal. Arriving at the gate a few minutes early, Jim started wondering if everything for tonight's operation was going to be completed.

Upon arrival at the hotel, he received the keys to the same room as last night, and once again, there was a message for him. Telling Rob and Debbie that he would see them in the morning, he headed for his room to change. Seeing the same room number for Gene, he headed down the stairs and knocked on the door.

"Come on in," Gene said as he opened the door. "How was the flight?"

"Good," Jim said as he looked around the room. "Is everything ready for tonight?"

"As far as I know," Gene answered. "Val hasn't called to say any different, and Marie is in the other room changing. Your clothes are hanging in the closet, so I guess everything is still on."

"Any news about Jewell?" Jim asked as he changed his jeans, T-shirt, and tennis shoes for the clothes that were in the cleaner's bag.

"Not really," Gene said, shaking his head. "I know you're anxious for some changes, but you have to remember that these things take time. I promise that I'll let you know the minute I know anything. Is there anything that you've thought of since last night?"

"Just wondering how Val's going to get Robert home if he's still disoriented," Jim said as he pulled on the jacket.

"They are getting there in a cab," Gene explained. "We've got another one on loan for the night, and their driver, like yours, is one of us. He'll assist Val in getting Robert into the cab and his house if necessary."

"Good," Jim told him as he checked himself in the mirror. "I figured that you had something in mind, or Val would have brought it up."

"Well, don't you look nice?" Marie told Jim as she came into the room. "I haven't had dinner with such a handsome man since last night."

Jim looked at her and smiled. *Gene was right*, he thought. *She is very distracting.*

"We've got a couple of hours before you need to be at the restaurant," Gene said, watching Jim's reaction to the sight of Marie. "Is there anything you want to go over?"

Marie looked at Jim and shook her head, saying, "No, I don't think so. Yesterday's little dress rehearsal cleared up any questions that I had."

"Me neither," Jim said as he took a seat. "Have you given Marie the antidote?"

"Right here in my purse," she said, smiling.

"And here is the amoeba," Gene said, handing Jim the syringe. "You may not have noticed, but the inside pocket of your jacket is lined with a zippered plastic and cloth that has the same chemical as the napkin that Val will have. If you should accidentally depress the plunger, the damp cloth will neutralize the amoeba. Since we knew that it would be exposed to the air for quite a bit longer than Val's napkin, it's been infused with more than twice the amount of neutralizer and should be good for at least an hour after you unzip it. It was rejuvenated when the jacket came back from the cleaners this afternoon. The glove you'll need is also in the pocket."

"That sounds reasonable," Jim said as he put the syringe in his pocket. "I'll certainly be extremely careful, but I'm glad to know that the little bug we designed for Robert won't get out of my pocket before I want it to."

Chapter 49

Val and Robert were already seated when Jim and Marie were escorted to their table. As they took their seats, Robert gave them a slight nod and returned his attention to Val. Jim saw Val smile slightly at him as Robert was looking away and relaxed slightly. Now that the operation was underway, he felt confident that everybody would do as they had planned.

Marie walked to the far side of the table so that Jim would be seated by Robert as they had practiced. As Jim held her chair, she stole a glance to her left and saw the same waiter as yesterday paying attention without really looking their way.

Jim took his seat and told the waiter, "Could we get a bottle of Napa Valley Darioush, please?"

"Certainly, sir," he answered as he placed the menus beside their plates. "I'll be right back with it."

"Beautiful place, isn't it?" Jim asked Marie as they looked around. "I've heard excellent reviews on their food as well."

"It is," Marie said, smiling. "I just love the view. I've never looked at so many tall buildings like this. I'd love to be up here when there's a low cloud cover and the sun is setting. I've seen time-lapse videos where the clouds are rushing across the sky and the sun makes them gold and pink with tall buildings beneath. Beautiful, but I can only imagine how it would look for real."

Jim glanced quickly at Val and Robert engaged in quiet conversation and noticed that his wine glass was still almost full. Seeing slight lipstick traces on Val's, he assumed that they had toasted and that he had probably taken a sip. Knowing that it could be up to thirty minutes before any disorientation occurred, they would have time to start their meals.

Just as he did the mental calculations as to when Robert would most likely be disoriented enough for him to administer the amoeba, the waiter arrived with their unopened bottle of wine. Displaying a great flourish for effect, the waiter pulled the cork out with an audible pop and proceeded to pour a slight amount in a glass for Marie. Marie sipped, nodding her approval, and the waiter filled her glass and one for Jim.

"Have you selected your meals?" Then he asked, "Or do you need an extra minute or two?"

"I think we're ready," Jim said handing him both menus. "The lady would like the filet mignon, medium rare, and I'd like the Delmonico beef ribeye, also medium rare."

"The filet comes with roasted baby potatoes, baby carrots, and summer truffle with a pear sauce," the waiter said as he wrote their orders. "And the ribeye comes with a pomme purée, asparagus, and cognac peppercorn sauce. Will that be satisfactory?"

"Could we substitute the asparagus for the baby carrots with the filet?" Jim asked, looking at the waiter.

"Of course, sir," he said as he turned to walk away. "Please give us about fifteen minutes to prepare your selection."

Marie noticed Robert reaching for his wine, slightly raised her glass, and said to Jim, "To a lovely evening with a true gentleman."

"And to the beautiful lady who makes every evening lovely," Jim replied as he raised his glass and tipped it slightly toward her.

A few minutes later, Jim noticed that their waiter was coming with their meals and glanced toward Robert. Knowing that the effects of the roofie could become pronounced anytime now, he hoped that the waiter would hurry setting their plates down. Right now was the most critical time for them to be ready to administer the amoeba. Slipping his hand inside his jacket, he unzipped the pocket, removed the nitrile glove, slipped it on, and touched the syringe to ensure that the plunger was still retracted.

As the waiter finished putting their meals on the table, Marie looked at Val and saw her replace the napkin on the table with the one she had pulled from her purse. Knowing that the time was rapidly approaching, she glanced toward where the waiter who would assist her in the distraction had been standing. Not seeing him there, she quickly revised her actions to draw everyone's attention to her.

The waiter had hardly left their table when Robert dropped his fork on the table and appeared to weave slightly in his seat. Val looked at Jim and quickly gave a slight nod. She took the napkin and appeared to be wiping something from Robert's chin as Jim glanced at Marie before he slid his chair slightly back.

Marie took one more glance to her left and still didn't see the waiter coming her way with a tray of drinks. She quickly picked up her wine glass and allowed it to drop, spilling the wine on her dress. Leaping up, she started brushing at the front of her dress and heading toward the restrooms.

Jim got out of his chair as she walked away and pulled the syringe from his pocket. Turning slightly left, he leaned over and put the tip of the syringe a couple of inches up into Robert's right nostril. A quick push of the plunger expelled the amoeba mix, and Jim pulled the plunger back about halfway.

As he started to extract it, Val took her napkin and covered his hand, hiding the syringe and wiping any possible residue from his hand. As Val took the napkin with the syringe hidden inside, Jim headed toward the restrooms as if he was following Marie. A few minutes later, Jim and Marie returned to their table and sat back down.

"I just hope it doesn't stain your dress," Jim said as he picked up his napkin.

"Oh, I'm sure the cleaner can get out any stain," Marie said, brushing at the damp area where the wine had spilled. "Isn't there some home remedy that says to use white wine to remove a red wine stain?"

"I've heard that," Jim said, glancing at Robert and Val. "Should I order a Chardonnay and give it a try?"

"Oh, I think a Sauvignon Blanc would be better," she joked, noticing that Robert was starting to appear normal again. "But I would hate to waste a good wine on a mere dress."

Jim just smiled as he overheard Val ask Robert, "Are you all right? You seemed like something was wrong just a minute ago."

"No, I'm okay," Robert said, slightly shaking his head. "I just felt sort of disoriented there for a second. Maybe the wine. But I feel okay now, I think." He looked around for a second and then sat back, saying, "I don't know what happened, but I still don't feel right. Maybe we better go home."

"That sounds like a good idea," Val said as she stood and signaled for their check. "Let me help you up. I'll take care of the check and get us a cab. I think you just need to get some rest. You've been working too many hours, and the wine just hit you hard."

"You're probably right," Robert said as he struggled to walk straight. "We'll have to try this again some other night."

"I'd love that," Val said, handing the waiter three one-hundred-dollar bills as he presented her with their check. "Let's just get you home, and we'll set another date."

Chapter 50

Jim and Marie watched them leave and looked at each other with relief.

"That could have gone south," Jim finally said. "Where the hell did that waiter go?"

"I don't know," Marie said as the adrenaline subsided in her system. "I almost waited too long."

"You did great," Jim told her. "It may seem like a small thing, but if anybody had seen me working with Robert or how he was acting, it could have been a major incident."

"Well, it's over," Marie said, picking up her wine glass. "I suggest we just relax and enjoy our meal."

Jim looked at her and smiled. "Another good idea. All we can do now is wait to see if the little bug we shoved up his nose does what it's supposed to do."

"So, tell me a little about yourself," Marie said as she took a bite of her filet.

"Not much to tell," Jim said, taking a spear of asparagus from his plate. "Marines, airlines, now here."

"That's a pretty broad-brush approach," Marie said, looking at him. "Okay, I'll start. I'm divorced, no kids. Live in New Orleans by myself. I've been with the company for about five years. When not spilling wine on myself, I have a small dance studio and teach ballet."

"All right," Jim said, putting his fork down and picking up his wine, "I'm married, no children, live in Mesquite, Texas, with my wife, Jennifer, and couldn't dance ballet if my life depended on it."

"How long have you been married?" Marie asked, picking at her food.

"I guess it's been about sixteen years," Jim answered. "How long were you married?"

"Almost ten years," Marie told him. "Probably five of them good."

"What happened?" Jim asked.

"This job," she answered.

"Really? How did this job cause a divorce?" Jim asked, sitting back in his chair.

"He couldn't stand for me to be out on little adventures like this," she explained. "It wasn't that he thought that I'd get hurt or anything. He just absolutely knew that I was involved with someone. When I finally told him about my job, it got even worse."

"How so?" Jim asked, trying to decide if he wanted to finish his meal.

"Now he accused me of having affairs with whom he kept referring to as my *James Bond* men. After the third or fourth time, I finally told him to get out," Marie said, putting her napkin on the table. "You know what? I'm not really hungry, and if it's all right with you, I'd like to go back to the hotel."

"No problem," Jim said, signaling for their check. "I hope I didn't upset you asking about what caused your divorce."

"Oh no," she assured him. "I started the conversation, and believe me, I've rehashed it in my mind so many times, it's like watching an old episode of *Gunsmoke*. I know what Festus is going to say or do in every scene. I just want to get back to the hotel and into my jeans and T-shirt. Time to unwind."

"I'd like to find out what went wrong," Jim told her as he put enough money for their bill and a generous tip in the folder the waiter had placed on the table. "If we had failed tonight, it may have made taking care of our target impossible."

"Maybe I don't need to know," Marie said as they headed for the door. "But why were we using something that could potentially infect one of us when we could have just eliminated him in one of the more traditional ways?"

"We needed to just incapacitate him for a couple of weeks before he actually dies," Jim said as their taxi pulled up. "But he needed to be removed, and if the following operation takes place as planned, he would have disappeared."

"Who was he?" Marie asked as they got in the taxi.

"A rather highly placed officer in the CPD," Jim said quietly as he leaned close. "And a very dirty cop."

Jim sat back and stole a look at Marie's profile as they drove toward the hotel. *Nice perfume*, he thought as his eyes roamed across her face. *Nice everything*, he mused as he turned and looked out at the city.

Chapter 51

As soon as the taxi took them back to the hotel, they hurried to the elevator and repeatedly punched the button for the floor they wanted. Knocking when they arrived, they waited scant seconds before the door opened to Gene talking on the phone.

"All right, but this isn't over. I want you in my office at Quantico tomorrow morning before ten o'clock." Gene hung up the phone and turned to them. "Before you say anything, I know what happened at the restaurant. I'll get into that in a minute." Gene took a chair by the desk and said, "Please sit down."

Once Marie sat in the remaining chair, and Jim was perched on the bed, Gene told them, "First, congratulations on a successful operation. Val called and told me what happened. She got Robert home all right, and he was still pretty disoriented, just as we expected. But as of right now, he suspects nothing. But it may be tomorrow before we know if he remembers or suspects anything"

" Now regarding the waiter . . ." Gene said shaking his head. "It appears that it's one of those unfortunate situations that we couldn't foresee. He was waiting for some sign that the roofie mix was having some effect. But he was also experiencing a severe bout of diarrhea. The options were he could either remain there, waiting for an unknown time and possibly soil himself, or make a quick trip to the men's room. He chose to go to the restroom. I can't say that I wouldn't have made the same choice, but my problem is that he knew ahead of time that he had a gastrointestinal problem. He also knew that his actions were an integral part of the operation. Now he should have apprised us of the situation and let us decide whether or not to replace him. It's not his place to jeopardize the mission without at least alerting us of the situation. That's what's unacceptable."

Marie started to say something, but Gene cut her off, saying, "I know things happen. And I know that everything worked out all right—this time. And it's only because of your quick thinking that the distraction worked. The issue with him is if we can trust him in the future. You have to remember lives are at stake. Let's just say that someone had seen Jim doing something as he was inserting the syringe in Robert's nose. What if that someone had grabbed Jim's arm as he was depressing the plunger? Can you imagine what the result of a deadly amoeba floating around the restaurant would be?"

"He couldn't possibly have known what we were doing," Marie countered.

"Doesn't matter," Gene argued. "He had an assignment. He failed to perform as ordered. He knew there could be a problem, but he took it upon himself to possibly not do as we directed. You may never know what every part of an operation is, but you know that others could be harmed or the company could be harmed by your actions. Anyway, I'll decide what his future with the company is tomorrow after I talk with him."

Both Jim and Marie knew that Gene was right; too much depended on everyone doing their jobs, or the consequences could be dire.

Finally, Jim nodded and said, "I understand. And I'm sure that Val told you how quickly Marie improvised to provide the distraction we needed. You made a great choice in Jewell's replacement."

"Yes, she did," Gene said, looking at Marie. "I've had my eye on her for several years, and there's none better. She's sort of like you, Jim. She can be trusted to go around any obstacle or come up with a solution when most people would still be shaking their heads and wondering what to do. Both of you have that rare ability to think on your feet in the blink of an eye. That's not that common in the real world. And that's what we look for in the people we hire. Now unless you guys have anything to add, I suggest we go to our rooms, think about the operation and what we could have done differently."

Gene stood up and said, "I know Jim needs to get to bed pretty soon because he's flying back to DFW in the morning. And I'll be leaving before the sun comes up to be at Quantico to follow the progress of our Captain, who will be getting very ill in very few days, and figure out what to do about our *shitty* waiter."

Chapter 52

The following morning, Rob and Debbie were sitting in the lobby, drinking coffee, when Jim stepped off the elevator.

Tossing his room key on the desk, he walked over to them and asked, "How was your evening?"

"Good," Rob replied as they stood up. "We went down to the Art Institute of Chicago for a couple of hours and then ended up at a restaurant."

"The museum was unbelievable," Debbie added. "I could have spent all day there and still not seen everything I wanted to see."

"I almost had to cancel dinner plans," Rob agreed as they headed for the courtesy van to take them to the airport.

"Oh, but the dinner was magnificent," Debbie said as they got in the van. "I think I could come back here every trip."

"Chicago does have some great places to see," Jim said as they headed to the airport. "I've been to the Art Institute a couple of times. You're right. You could spend weeks in there and still not see everything."

"I really liked seeing the real paintings of pictures I'd seen in magazines," Debbie remarked. "The pictures were nowhere close to the real thing. I mean, just seeing the colors and the brush strokes. I've bought art books before, but I was shocked at how inadequate they are compared to the real thing."

"That's true. Where did you go for dinner?" Jim asked as they approached ORD.

"Joe's Seafood," Rob answered. "Doesn't sound like much from the name, but it was outstanding."

"Really?" Jim remarked. "What did you have?"

"Florida stone crab claws," Rob told him. "I was surprised to hear that they collect the claws one at a time and then put the crabs back in the water."

"And they were huge!" Debbie exclaimed. "The menu said 'jumbo claws,' and they really were. I could barely eat the three that came on my plate."

"Debbie liked Joe's Mustard Sauce," Rob said as they pulled into the terminal. "It was okay, but I prefer just butter."

"I'm a big fan of Dungeness crab from Washington," Jim said as they were getting their bags from the back of the van. "And I agree with Rob. Just a cup of melted butter, and I can eat a dozen."

"I prefer Dungeness also," Rob agreed. "But it's a real chore to get all the meat out of the little rascals. With the stone crab claws, just crack them open and enjoy."

"Worth every bit of it though," Jim said as he tipped the van driver.

"Hey, looks like we're out of the G concourse again," Rob said, smiling at Jim as they walked into the terminal.

"Is that good or bad?" Debbie asked as they headed for their gate.

"Oh, it's good," Rob said, laughing. "Do you want to tell her, Jim? Or should I?"

"Rob has this perverted sense of humor," Jim answered, looking at Debbie. "He takes great pleasure in having me buy Cinnabons for the crew."

"And this time, you need to get an extra one for Debbie," Rob said, grinning. "In case you didn't look, four flight attendants again."

"It will be my pleasure," Jim said, seeing the Cinnabon kiosk just ahead. "I'll meet you at the gate."

"Tell you what," Rob said before walking away. "I'll do the walk-around this morning. It's been a while since I saw the exterior. All you need to do today is bring Cinnabons and fly to DFW."

When Jim got to the airplane, Rob was still outside, and Debbie was sitting in first class, talking to one of the flight attendants.

"Hey, Jim," the flight attendant said, coming up to meet him. "I'm Julie, and Captain Sproc said you were bringing us some rolls this morning."

"Hi, Julie, and I did bring Cinnabons," Jim told her, handing her the box. "If you'd be so kind as to give one to everybody who wants one."

"My pleasure," she said as she set the box on the counter in the first-class galley. "Would you like anything?"

"Can I get a Mr. & Mrs. T Bloody Mary Mix?" he answered as he put his bags away. "Glass and no ice."

"No problem," she told him as she opened one of the carts used to serve the passengers.

Jim was in his seat, setting up his instruments for the takeoff and departure, when Rob stepped into the cockpit.

"Everything good?" Jim asked without turning his head.

"Perfect," Rob answered, taking his seat. "Weather in DFW is clear, with light winds out of the south. Think you can handle that?"

"Piece of cake," Jim said as he finished and turned in his seat as Julie stuck her head into the cockpit. "Landing to the south will get us in a few minutes early."

"Would you guys like your rolls now?" Julie asked, handing Jim his drink.

"I'll take mine when we level off," Rob told her. "But I'd like a cup of coffee when you get a chance."

"Level off is good for me too," Jim answered, nodding as he poured some of the Bloody Mary mix into the plastic cup.

"Be right back," Julie said, stepping back.

"How was your evening?" Rob asked, watching Jim shake something on his drink.

"Almost boring," Jim lied, thinking back to the almost disastrous affair at dinner. "I should have gone to the museum with you and Debbie."

"What did you just put in your drink?" Rob asked as Jim started to put the small container back in his kit bag.

"Texas Gunpowder," Jim answered, holding it up. "Pure ground jalapeno powder. Want to try it?"

Just then, the gate agent stuck his head in and said, "We're ready to close the door, Captain."

"Get everybody on?" Rob asked, turning in his seat.

"Yes," the agent answered. "And I managed to get your wife a seat in first class."

"Thanks," Rob said. "We'll see you next week."

Julie poked her head in as the agent left and handed Rob his coffee, saying, "We're ready back here, Captain."

"Thanks, Julie," Rob said as she shut the door. "Before starting engines, checklist, please, Jim."

Chapter 53

Jim was on his second cup of coffee and watching TV Friday morning when he saw the newscast about the decision of the local district attorney to declare Leonard Blair's death an accident because of underlying health issues. The demise of the suspected pedophile was openly celebrated in interviews by those whose lives he had adversely impacted. Even several highly placed members of numerous police departments across Texas expressed a notable lack of remorse at his passing.

Still somewhat recalcitrant about his involvement, Jim just hoped that he wasn't asked to participate further in what he could only think of as vigilante vendettas, especially since the impetus for this assignment seemed to stem from a single individual with connections to Black Water. Just as he got up to refill his coffee, the phone rang.

"Good morning," he heard Gene say as he put the receiver to his ear. "I guess you've seen the news about Mr. Blair by now."

"I just finished watching it," Jim answered. "I still have issues with the operation, but I'm also glad that a person like him is no longer a threat to any family with little kids."

"I know," Gene assured him. "Now on to other topics. I called early this morning, and there are no changes in Jewell's condition."

"That's not good," Jim replied. "I was at least hoping that she'd be out of intensive care by now."

"Me too," Gene said. "I also wanted to let you know that the upcoming Chicago operation is 90 percent in place. There are a couple of things left to do in St. Louis, but they're still on schedule in accordance with the plan. The biggest change to the operation is that I'm assigning you an assistant. Our latest gaming with all the variables showed a marked increase in managing all the information."

"What variables are you talking about?" Jim asked.

"Things like being unable to locate any single individual, delays regarding the St. Louis part of the operation, car trouble, or any other of a number of things that can go wrong," Gene explained. "Sort of like the waiter not being in position. We are trying to anticipate the unexpected."

"Okay," Jim said, knowing that keeping track of the five teams in Chicago and the people coming up from St. Louis would be demanding. "I guess I could use the help."

"I know you can," Gene told him. "Especially if there are multiple decision points based on such a fluid environment. Even if everything goes as planned, just having someone to monitor the phones or radios relieves you of some of the time-consuming activities."

"All right. I appreciate you giving me an assistant," Jim agreed. "When will I meet him?"

"It's a her," Gene informed him. "And you've already met her."

"Val?" Jim asked. "Won't she still be involved with monitoring Robert?"

"It's not Val," Gene corrected him. "It'll be Marie."

"That's kind of a surprise," Jim said as her image flashed through his mind.

"Her actions at the restaurant are just another example of how talented she is," Gene informed him. "I wanted someone whom you'd be comfortable with and whom I could depend on to give you any assistance you may need. Further, I wanted someone whom I could trust to step in and take over the operation if something happens to you. I'm assuming that you have no problems with my choice."

"No," Jim answered. "I think she's probably as capable as anyone else I've worked with at the company. And I'm sure you know more about company personnel better than me."

"That doesn't mean that sometimes I don't make mistakes," Gene admitted. "Take the waiter, for example. I selected him because he had shown an aggressive can-do attitude on previous operations. That trait was part of the problem."

"How so?" Jim asked.

"He should have admitted to the company, mainly me, if there was even a slight chance that his condition could impact the operation," Gene explained. "But he decided that he could handle anything. I think part of it was his desire to demonstrate that he was capable of performing any assignment regardless of changing situations."

"Yeah, I saw that in a lot of junior officers," Jim told him. "Type A personalities who refuse to admit their limitations and end up jeopardizing the mission. It's hard to criticize them because we praise those who demonstrate the same attitude and get results."

"Exactly," Gene agreed. "The trick is to keep them on track until they get enough experience to learn that everyone has limitations and occasionally needs help. That doesn't mean that they aren't perfectly capable. It's just that there's only one Superman, and it ain't them."

"I'm assuming that you're referring to me with that Superman comment," Jim joked. "What are you going to do with the waiter?"

"We had a very productive meeting this morning," Gene answered seriously. "He admitted that he almost called in to say he couldn't be there, but he had started taking Imodium that morning, and it seemed to be under control. And I explained what would have happened if there had been an accident with the amoeba. Bottom line, I think he'll prove to be an asset. He knows he made a mistake and feels miserable about it."

"Good," Jim said. "Do you think I need to get with Marie before next week to discuss how we'll operate?"

"I don't believe that's necessary," Gene answered. "But I'll leave the final decision on that up to you. I talked to her about what she would be doing, and she seemed satisfied that there wouldn't be any problems. Like I said, she's a quick study and has proven herself over the years. I'm also using this operation to expose her to a little more of the behind-the-scenes activity that is necessary for the success of any operation."

"All right," Jim reluctantly agreed. "If both of you feel comfortable, I guess I'll wait until we get together in Chicago."

"Good," Gene said. "But if you change your mind or have any questions about her role in this, don't hesitate to give me a call."

"I will," Jim told him. "I guess I'll see you Tuesday evening."

As soon as he had hung up, he started wondering if he hadn't asked about a meeting with Marie because he had concerns about the operation or because the thought of seeing her again was the reason.

Chapter 54

On Saturday morning, Jim was in the driveway, working on his lawnmower, when he heard a car stopping in front of his house. Looking up, he saw the familiar black Suburban that Gene preferred to drive. As the driver's door opened, he stood and started walking toward it.

"General," Jim said as he shook Gene's hand. "What brings you down here today?"

"Something you said Friday that I decided I needed to follow up," he answered.

"What was that?" Jim asked.

"You asked me if I thought that you and Marie should get together before the operation Tuesday," Gene said as he started walking toward the car.

"And you said you didn't think it was necessary," Jim said, following him.

"I've had second thoughts," Gene said as they got to the car. "I decided that Marie didn't have all the background information on the operation that she would need if she was really going to be an asset to you."

"Can't she be briefed on everything?" Jim asked as they leaned against the car.

"Maybe," Gene answered. "But this is not a typical operation. There are so many places where something could go wrong that I'm not comfortable knowing that you had some reservations about her role."

"I do have some reservations about it," Jim admitted. "I thought that we'd resolve them Tuesday afternoon when I get to Chicago."

"I agree that you'll have several hours after you get to the hotel before you have to start paying attention to the operation," Gene said, nodding. "You're getting in around four o'clock, and we've scheduled the abduction of the gang members for two o'clock in the morning. That gives you about ten hours."

"Don't you think that is sufficient time to make sure Marie knows what's going on?" Jim asked.

"Probably," Gene agreed. "But we also need to be monitoring the St. Louis part. Larry has stated that he can have the gang members from St. Louis there in about four hours. That means the oversight needs to be up and running by ten o'clock. Therefore, your time to get Marie completely up to speed is now only five or six hours. Toss in an hour or so for your flight being delayed, trouble getting to the hotel where we'll be operating, or something wrong on the St. Louis end. I'm just concerned that you may not have sufficient time to make sure everything is ready. And remember, this operation is currently active since we've taken step one in eliminating Captain Nelson. If we have to delay more than a few days, he'll probably be dead. And even though it may come across as natural, the gangs will react because they've lost a layer of protection. That could disrupt everything we've been working on for over a year."

"Okay, what's your plan?" Jim asked.

"I want you in Quantico on Monday morning," Gene answered. "I've discussed this with O and Larry, and they concur."

"What does Marie think?" Jim asked.

"She says that she'd be happy to come and agrees that it would help her assist you if she knew more about what was going on," Gene told him.

"Okay," Jim said. "But did you really need to come here to tell me this? Couldn't you have just called?"

"I could have," Gene answered. "But I also know that bringing you back to Quantico when you're scheduled to fly on Tuesday, Wednesday, and Thursday would piss off Jennifer."

"It's going to piss her off whether you call or tell me in person," Jim argued. "Nothing you can say or do will prevent that."

Gene smiled, opened the rear door of the Suburban, and pulled out a cardboard box containing a package wrapped in brown paper and a sack with obvious bottles inside. "If you'll lead the way to the house, I think I may have a way to somewhat smooth the soon-to-be-ruffled feathers of your sweet, forgiving wife," Gene said as he started up the sidewalk.

Chapter 55

Jim opened the front door, leading Gene into the house, and called, "Jennifer, we have a guest!"

"Let's just take this into the kitchen," Gene suggested. "I'm getting tired of carrying it."

"Sure," Jim told him, going through the living room. "I don't know what you've got in the box, but I still don't think whatever it is will make her happy about me going with you again."

"General, what a surprise," Jennifer said as she came through the back door. "What brings you down here so soon?"

"Is that any way to greet an old friend?" Gene replied, setting the box on the table. "Regardless, I'm always glad to see you and Jim. No matter how long or short it's been, it's always a pleasure."

"You know what I meant," she said, kissing him on the cheek. "Of course, it's always good to see you too. All I meant—"

Gene cut her off, saying, "I know what you meant. But you have to forgive an old man his small pleasures, such as teasing you."

"Old man," she scoffed. "I can only hope to be as active and energetic as you are when I'm half your age."

"You *are* half his age," Jim quipped and immediately regretted it. "I mean, you're almost half his age. Or getting close."

Jennifer scowled at him and asked Gene, "Now just what do you have in the box you brought in?"

Gene pulled the brown wrapped package out and walked to the sink, saying, "Remember when you offered to make me a meal that would rival those up in Alexandria? Well, today's the day that I'm taking you up on it. Would you please get me a platter?"

Taking a large turquoise platter from the cabinet, Jennifer set it on the counter as Gene took a ribeye steak from the package and placed it on the platter.

"Oh!" Jennifer exclaimed, looking at the steak. "That's a nice-looking ribeye."

Placing another one beside the first, Gene told her, "You told me about a place down here that had Wagyu beef. Ever since you talked about it and the strange name of the place, Crowd Cow, I've been anxious to try one."

Jim walked over and admired the steaks as Gene put the third one on the platter. "I'm guessing that you had these specially cut."

"I called down this morning before I left Quantico," Gene said, washing his hands. "I told them that I wanted three well-marbled ribeyes cut an inch thick. They told me that their standard ribeye was three quarters of an inch." He pulled the bag from within the box saying, "I thanked him for the information and reiterated that I wanted them cut an inch."

"Looks like you got what you asked for," Jim said, picking up one of the steaks. "This must weigh at least a pound by itself."

"Just a little over," Gene corrected him as he set a bottle of sixteen-year-old A. H. Hirsch Reserve bourbon on the table. "Now I know that you're a huge fan of Jack Daniel's. But I think that you'll really like this. And I'm sure that Jennifer will like this next bottle," Gene said as he took a bottle of 1982 Chateau Mouton Rothschild from the box and set it on the table beside the bourbon. Taking two more bottles out, he smiled and continued, "I thought I'd bring enough for all of us."

Jennifer picked up one of the bottles and said, "This is wonderful, Gene. Where did you find it? I read something about Rothschild wines at a wine tasting I went to a year or so ago."

"A little out-of-the-way liquor store up in Virginia," Gene answered as he took a final bottle out. Setting the ornate box that contained the bottle on the table, he then said, "But this is one of my all-time favorites."

Jim opened it to reveal a bottle of Remy Martin Louis XIII Cognac. "That must be some liquor store," he said, reverently holding the bottle. "And you must have made their month with what you just set on the table. I could have enough Jack to last two years for what you've spent on this."

"If there's one thing in life I've learned," Gene said as Jennifer wrapped her arms around his waist, "it's that you never know what you're missing unless you try it. I've known people who keep saying they are going to try something and die before they do it. I don't care if it's but once in your life. Enjoy the finest that this world has to offer."

"Well, you've certainly brought some of the finest for this meal," Jim told him. "And this will undoubtedly be a far better meal than any we had in Arlington."

"I think this will probably be the best meal I'll ever have," Jennifer said with tears in her eyes. "Not only is it the finest things, but also, it's the finest people. And that's what makes any meal great."

Chapter 56

"Let's go out back and have an early beer," Jim suggested as Jennifer took the steaks to the counter and started putting the wine and liquor away.

"You go ahead," Gene told him. "I need to talk to Jennifer for a second, and then I'll join you."

Jim took two Ziegen Bocks from the refrigerator and headed outside.

"I have a little confession to make," Gene said as Jennifer waited to see why he wanted to talk to her.

"What's that?" she asked.

"First off, you know that I value you and Jim more than anybody else in the world," he said as he motioned for her to have a seat at the table. Taking a chair beside her, he continued, "And I know that sometimes you resent my relationship with him." Pausing to see if Jennifer wanted to say anything, he then told her, "Part of the reason that I came here today was that I need to ask a special favor of you."

"What favor do you need of me?" Jennifer asked, somewhat confused since Gene had never asked for anything.

"I'll get to that in a second," he answered. "But first, I need to explain a little about why I keep getting Jim involved with the things that I do. Since retiring from the Marines, I've been a sort of consultant with a company that provides security and intelligence for several companies and governments around the world. Sometimes I call on Jim to help me decide on what approach to take. His experience in Vietnam and his time working overseas before he retired are invaluable."

"I'll also admit that sometimes I just want the advice of someone who's been in the situation that I'm tasked to provide recommendations on," he said leaning back slightly. "Now I've known Jim for many years, even longer than you've known him. I've learned to trust his instincts, and I've watched him analyze a situation and see details that most people would dismiss. I'm sure you've noticed how anal he can be at times."

"Oh yes," Jennifer told him. "Sometimes it drives me nuts."

"Then you know how he'll pick apart something as mundane as a scene in a movie," Gene said, nodding. "Well, that's just the way his brain works. Who in the world would notice that a cup of coffee on a table in one scene would be slightly turned differently just seconds later in the next one?"

"I know," she agreed. "I've had to put up with 'The fork is missing' or 'That salt shaker isn't supposed to be there' every time we watch TV or go to the movies. You don't know how many times I've had to bite my tongue so that I can just enjoy the show."

"I can only imagine," Gene said, laughing. "You may know the story of how I first met Jim, but you don't know that I had him vetted before that."

"All he's ever said is that his team was pretty much all killed on some hill in Vietnam," Jennifer said. "That, and you helped him get to fly the F-4. He doesn't talk a lot about it."

"Well, lots of the people who were over there try to forget most of what happened," Gene told her, shaking his head. "There were a lot of horrific events, both on our side as well as theirs. But that's part of any war. The point is once I heard about what he did to get his men—or their bodies—back, I started looking into his background before I recommended him for any awards or commendations. It's not common but very embarrassing to give some soldier a high award only to find out that he was less than stellar in his civilian life. That's especially true since we gave some people the choice of prison or Vietnam. We had to take some very unsavory characters."

"Jim did say something about that," Jennifer said. "That's one of the things that he never approved of but had to accept."

"Anyway, you know his background and how he came to be a Marine," Gene continued. "I needed to ensure that I wasn't endorsing a pervert or worse. Bottom line, I found out what you know. Jim's about as honest and a straight shooter as you'll ever meet."

"That, he is," Jennifer agreed. "Sometimes I wish he'd temper his opinions. Especially when he's around people who don't know him. He can be rather judgmental."

"No shit," Gene said, smiling. "That's like saying dry ice is rather cold. But it's that quality that makes him indispensable to   me."
"I've even called him a minutia savant," Jennifer said, laughing.

"That's as accurate of a description as I can think of," Gene said, joining in on the laughter.

"Okay," Jennifer said. "Now what's the favor you need?"

Gene sat back in his chair and told her, "I'm working on a very sensitive operation that has developed a major problem. One of my key members was very seriously injured in an automobile accident, and I've got to replace her immediately. And I don't have time to explain every minute detail of our operation to her replacement. That's where Jim comes in," he added leaning forward. "He's one of the few people I know who can step in and get a firm grasp of what we're doing and also see any flaws that we may need to address. The favor I'm asking is I need Jim in Quantico on Monday." He waited for her to object before continuing. "That means that he'll have to leave with me Sunday night and not get back until late on Monday. And I know that you want him home when he's not flying, and I understand that. Trust me. I know that he wants to be here also. It's easy to tell that he'd rather be here on his days off than hanging out with an old fart like me."

"You said that he'd need to leave with you tomorrow night," Jennifer said, crossing her arms. "Does that mean that you're staying in Dallas tonight?"

"Yes," Gene said, relaxing slightly. "I've got a room at the Double Tree close to Love Field."

Jennifer sat back and thought for a second before saying, "You come here asking me for a favor, yet you get a hotel room instead of wanting to stay here with Jim and me. That's unacceptable. I'll only agree to let Jim go with you if you'll stay here with us."

Gene grinned and told her, "Now I can really see why Jim married you. You're just like him. You speak your mind and don't worry about the consequences. Of course, I'd be honored to spend the night with you guys. I just didn't want to be so bold as to suggest that after I asked you to let me have Jim on one of the days that you thought you could spend with him."

Jennifer rose as Gene did and hugged him, saying, "You can take that sorry knuckle dragger with you anytime you want to. Just promise me that you'll always look out for him."

"That's an easy promise," Gene replied, returning her hug. "I've been looking out for him since I first met him. That's one worry you'll never have. Now let's go join him for a beer."

Chapter 57

"You go ahead," Jennifer told Gene. "I need to run to the store for a few things that I'll need for tonight's dinner."

"Why don't you tell me what you need and Jim and I'll go?" Gene suggested.

"No, I like to look at the vegetables myself before I buy them," Jennifer explained as she looked around for her purse. "It won't take long. All I need is a bunch of asparagus, some baby potatoes, and a few things to make hollandaise sauce and a salad."

"All right," Gene told her, following her to the back door. "But if you need for Jim and me to do anything, just let me know."

She stopped just before opening the door and said, "Gene, you've already done so much for this family. And especially for tonight's dinner. You just go relax with Jim, and I'll take it from here. Except for cooking the steaks. I'd be too scared that I'd burn them or something. I can't wait to try them. I've heard about Wagyu beef, but it's always been way over my budget."

She pulled the door open and said, "Jim, I'm heading to the grocery store. Keep Gene entertained, and you guys try to go easy on the beer. I want both of you completely sober for tonight's dinner."

As Gene came outside, Jim waited until he saw Jennifer walking back through the kitchen before asking, "So how'd that go?"

"Pretty good," Gene answered as he took the unopened beer from Jim. "I don't think you'll have any problem leaving with me tomorrow evening."

"Tomorrow?" Jim asked, almost choking on his beer. "I thought you said Monday."

"I did," Gene replied as he opened the Ziegen Bock. "But I don't want to wait until noon to get you guys together and then have to leave a couple of hours later to get you home so that you can get some sleep before you leave Tuesday. Everybody else will be there tomorrow night. There's a room ready for you, and we'll start Monday morning, about seven o'clock. I'm hoping that we'll be done by two o'clock or so. That gives us plenty of time to get you home."

"And you got Jennifer to agree with this?" Jim asked incredulously.

"Of course," Gene answered, smiling. "I only had to shade the truth a minor amount."

"A minor amount," Jim remarked, shaking his head. "Just what does that mean?"

"It means that I alluded to your skills at seeing flaws in our planning on numerous occasions," Gene answered. "And I mentioned that one of my staff had been in a car accident and that I didn't have time to search for a different replacement for her. So she now knows that you come to Quantico to give me advice on company business."

"And she still knows nothing about the company?" Jim asked. "She knows a little about Black Water since they've been in the news. It wouldn't take too much effort on her part to know what they do."

"I never mentioned the company name," Gene assured him. "But I guess we need to prepare for the inevitable and develop a fictitious company. I'm sure she'll want to know more about it sooner or later."

"More than likely sooner," Jim agreed. "How about Athena Security Consultants?"

"Athena?" Gene asked. "Where did you come up with that name?"

"Ever read Homer's *Odyssey*?" Jim asked.

"Probably," Gene answered. "Years ago. What does that have to do with Athena?"

"The goddess Athena was Odysseus's protectress," Jim explained. "She convinced Zeus to allow Odysseus to go home after the Trojan War. In addition to being a goddess, she could also assume differing identities to allow her to move about unobserved as she assisted him."

Gene merely shook his head and commented, "Always. You *always* come up with some obscure reference to some far-off story or myth and convince me that it's a good idea."

"So does that mean that you think it's a good idea?" Jim asked as he took a drink of his beer.

Gene just looked at him and swallowed almost half of his beer in a single gulp before saying, "Yeah, it's a good idea. A vague reference to an almost forgotten Greek poem that, strangely enough, parallels most of our missions. Only you would remember something from some long-ago literature class."

"That's not why I remembered it," Jim said, finishing his beer. "It was from an episode of *The Simpsons*. Care for another beer?"

"Undoubtedly," Gene said, drinking the last of his. "And if you'll excuse me for a couple of minutes, I've got to go create a long-running history and record of a little-known company called Athena Security Consultants. I'd hate for Jennifer to start questioning my veracity when I'm lying through my teeth."

Chapter 58

On Sunday afternoon, they had just finished lunch when Gene said, "This has been one of the best weekends that I can remember. No work, good food, good friends, and a full night's sleep."

"It's been our pleasure to have you, General," Jennifer replied as she got up to start taking the dishes to the kitchen. "Why don't you and Jim go into the living room and relax while I take care of things in here?"

"Not a chance," Gene said, getting up. "I'll help you, and then we can all go sit."

A few minutes later, as they were quietly watching the local news, Gene asked, "Is there any chance that you might have some ice cream?"

Jim looked at Jennifer and answered, "Yes, I believe that we have some Blue Bell Pistachio Almond. And some Rocky Road if Jennifer didn't eat all of it."

"We have both," Jennifer corrected Jim. "Which would you like?"

"Pistachio Almond," Gene answered. "I keep hoping that Blue Bell will start selling ice cream in Virginia. We have some wonderful ice creams, but somehow Blue Bell is still my favorite. Maybe because it was only available in Texas for so long. It really pisses me off that they would sell it in Oklahoma and not Virginia.”

“I keep telling you,” Jim said as he got up to get them all bowls of ice cream. “Texas has so much more to offer than Virginia. You should convince the company to move its headquarters down here.”

“I wish I could,” Gene said, getting up. “Jennifer, which one would you like?”

“Rocky Road, please,” she answered, smiling about the two of them discussing something as mundane as ice cream.

Returning with heaping bowls, Gene slowly ate his as he reminded Jim, “You know that we need to leave in an hour or so.”

“I know,” Jim said, scooping tiny bits of the green delicacy and letting it melt in his mouth. “It would have been nice if Jennifer could have come with us though.”

“I doubt if she’d like it as much,” Gene said, licking his spoon. “Staying in the compound is not even close to the hotel in Alexandria. Not to mention no shopping and having to eat in the mess hall with the employees.”

“That’s all right,” Jennifer said, getting up to take her bowl to the sink. “I’ll just remind you next time that I didn’t object to you taking my husband away from me on one of his few days off. And I expect for you to send the jet for us the very next time you just can’t do without his presence.”

Jim glanced at Gene as she was leaving and shook his head and asked, “Did you think that you’d get away with just a smooth story and a couple of bottles of wine? You have no idea of how long she’ll play this ace that you gave her.”

“I wouldn’t expect any less,” Gene said as he finished his ice cream. “I’m almost surprised that that’s all she’s asking for.”

“Oh, that’s not all,” Jim said, getting up with his empty bowl. “That’s not near all.”

As they were rinsing their bowls and putting them in the dishwasher, Gene said, "I'm going to pack my bags and make a couple of calls to make sure everybody is still on schedule to get in today."

"I'll be ready in about ten minutes," Jim said as he headed for the bedroom. "If I'm coming back tomorrow afternoon, all I need is a change of underwear and a toothbrush."

"You'll take a clean shirt and your shave kit too," Jennifer said as she followed him. "I don't want you coming home in a stinky shirt and needing a shave when I come to pick you up at the airport. And I'm sure whoever you're going to be working with will appreciate you showering tomorrow morning before you meet them."

"Okay," Jim joked as they walked away. "Give me *eleven* minutes to pack. It's a good thing Jennifer wasn't in the field with us in 'Nam. It would have taken us a week to make sure we had everything necessary for hygiene and appropriate attire before we went into the jungle."

"You're not there now," Jennifer said as she shut the bedroom door behind her. "And I think you need to take an extra few minutes to tell your wife goodbye."

Chapter 59

On the drive to the airport, Gene said, "I just talked to the hospital, and there's still no changes. Like I told you earlier, the biggest problem is the damage to her internal organs. I'm going to try to get in to see her Tuesday when I get to Chicago for our operation."

"That would be good," Jim said as they joined Loop 635 going north. "Maybe you'd get a chance to talk face-to-face with the doctors. I've found that they're not as reluctant to give out specifics when you're standing in front of them. And I'm sure Val would like to know more about what's happening to her."

"Yeah, she's been calling me almost every day," Gene told him. "Speaking of Val, she's been monitoring Robert's condition closely. He did ask if some man had been at their table, and she told him that someone had stopped to see if he was all right. She also told him that she thinks he may have been a doctor."

"That's good," Jim agreed as they approached the exit for Highway 244. "Has he started displaying any of the symptoms yet?"

"She said that he's starting to complain about headaches," Gene answered. "That seems to be pretty much on track for what we know about the progression. Given that, he probably won't start feeling really bad until Wednesday or Thursday. I still wish we could have gotten to him on the first try."

"Me too," Jim agreed. "And if we can't complete our operation Tuesday night, he could be starting to think that something was done to him. If he has any clue or suspects that the man who approached him was other than a helpful passerby, he might say something to one of the guys we're after."

"I know," Gene said. "I've told Val to stick as close as she can to try to dissuade him from thinking it's anything other than a headache. But that will be difficult to do once he starts experiencing the fever and nausea that accompany the headaches."

"Has he mentioned going in for a checkup?" Jim asked as they joined Loop 12 across the top of Dallas.

"Not yet," Gene answered. "And he's still going to work as usual. Let's just hope that he still feels like working until we're done in Chicago. After that, I don't care. Even if he's lucid and coherent when the bodies are found Thursday, he can't impact the investigation enough to change the direction we've planned."

"What about the street cops?" Jim asked. "When will they be targeted?"

"Not our problem," Gene answered. "We'll let CPD take care of them. We will leak certain information, but our tasking was to remove the gangs and Capt. Robert Nelson. One other thing." Gene said as he took the exit for Lemmon Avenue. "We'll be going to New Orleans before we fly to Quantico."

"I guess that means we'll be picking up Marie," Jim replied.

"Good guess," Gene said as they pulled into the Business Jet Center at Love Field. "I needed to get her to Quantico today, and there weren't many options for commercial flights. And since the entire purpose of this meeting is to get you and her working as a team, I figured that an extra hour or so together wouldn't hurt." Parking his Suburban, he continued, "Larry and O will get in this afternoon, and I've asked them to set up the room for the entire briefing that we gave the teams. It'll be ready tomorrow morning, and they'll present it as we have breakfast. I think that's the fastest way to give Marie an overview and enough details to understand the complexity of the operation."

"That's a good idea," Jim said as Gene got his suitcase from the back seat. "Especially since they've probably incorporated all the changes that we've discussed over the last couple of weeks."

"Exactly," Gene agreed as Jim pulled his overnight bag from the car. "And it will give you another chance to spot anything that might need tweaking. More importantly, you can point out where you think Marie should be concerned because of the intersection of several critical actions. It would help if she's looking in the right direction instead of having to wait for you to tell her where to look. Sometimes a split second can be crucial if someone's not paying attention to things."

"Sort of like our waiter?" Jim reminded him as they walked to the terminal.

"Yes," Gene said with a look to chastise Jim's reminder. "Also like someone not having a phone in their hand when a critical call came in. Let's let those dogs lie."

Chapter 60

An hour and a half later, they were taxiing to Signature Aviation, the company that serviced general aviation at the New Orleans airport. As they approached the ramp, Marie was seen standing just outside of the terminal door.

As the ground personnel directed them to stop just yards from her, Jim walked to the door and waited for the pilots to shut down the left engine. Hearing it winding down, he opened the door and let the built-in stairs lower. Stepping down, he walked to meet Marie and took her suitcase. Five minutes later, they were seated with Gene as the left engine was restarted, and they taxied back toward the runways.

"This sure beats the commercial flights," she remarked as they sped down the taxiway. "No fuss. No waiting in line to get to your seat while a hundred people try to put their carryon luggage in the overhead bin. I believe that this is the way I want to travel from now on."

"You and Jim's wife, Jennifer," Gene said, smiling. "If I gave in to everybody who wanted their own personal jet, the company would be broke within a week, and I'd be out of a job. So don't get used to it."

Marie just smiled back and then asked Jim, "And how is your wife? I think I'd be upset if my husband kept leaving on the days he's not already gone for work."

"Trust me," Jim answered. "We had that very discussion this weekend.

"And how did that turn out?" she asked.

"As well as can be expected," he told her. "But I'm afraid that Gene doesn't fully appreciate the immovable force that a man's wife can exert."

"No, I know full well what that lady can do to make your life and sometimes mine miserable," Gene said as he opened his briefcase. "It's just that I can always leave and you can't." Pulling several folders out, he handed them to Marie and said, "We've got almost two hours until we get to Quantico, so I suggest you two start planning on how you plan to manage the operation."

Jim slipped over to the seat that faced her and asked, "How much did Gene tell you about the operation?"

"I guess just the basics," she told him as she looked at the contents in each folder. "Kidnap three members of each of the top five gangs, assassinate two of them, and question the third. Place the blame on a gang from St. Louis."

"That's pretty much it," Jim agreed as she flipped through the pages. "Our part will be more or less to oversee the five teams in Chicago and the one from St. Louis."

"Where will we be while we're monitoring them?" Marie asked. "And what sort of communications gear will we have?"

Gene turned to them and said, "We have rooms at the Holiday Inn Express just off the O'Hare Airport. Jim will have a suite where we'll set up for you guys, and you'll have an adjacent room. All the team members will have rooms there as well."

"Won't that raise some suspicions?" Marie asked. "I mean, that's a lot of rooms for the same nights."

"Information Technology convention," Gene answered. "And it's only thirty rooms, counting you and Jim. And your room is only for two nights, Tuesday and Wednesday. The others will be there starting Monday."

"I thought we'd only be there for Tuesday," Marie said, looking up from the folders.

"I hope so," Gene said. "But if we don't get everything done Tuesday night, we need the rooms for the next night. Jim will be staying at the normal layover hotel and will join us after he gets in Tuesday night. Same for Wednesday if necessary."

"Are you staying there?" Jim asked.

"Yes," he answered. "I'll go up on Monday and meet with Mr. O and Larry. We'll help our communications team set up everything in your suite. Regarding the communications gear, you'll have radios with dedicated frequencies for each of the five team captains, a four-line wireless telephone with speakers, and a computer monitor that will show the location of each of the team captains, including the St. Louis team, from the time it starts for Chicago."

"Okay," Marie said. "I fly into ORD on Tuesday afternoon, and you'll pick me up. Is there anything I need to do while I'm waiting for Jim to get in?"

"No," Gene answered. "Actually, Jim may already be at the hotel when you get there. What time do you think you'll get in, Jim?"

"We should land in Chicago about four o'clock," he said. "Give me an hour or so to get to the hotel and change. I should be ready to come join you by no later than six o'clock."

"Okay," Gene corrected himself. "You may have a couple of hours to look at everything before he gets here. Matter of fact, I'll have Mr. O come join you in Jim's suite, and you guys can go over all the equipment. Jim, your timing should work out fine since Larry won't be leaving St. Louis until around ten o'clock. That way, you can track his progress about the same time the Chicago teams are moving to get in position for their first target.”

“Will Mr. O be with us?” Jim asked.

“No, he’ll be set up in his room with almost the same equipment that you’ll have,” Gene told him. “I don’t want him to distract you since he’s going to be more hands-on with his people than you need to be. But you’ll be able to monitor his progress since you’ve got the radios set to the same frequencies.”

Chapter 61

The next morning, Jim was having breakfast in the briefing room when Marie came in.

"Good morning," she said as she prepared a meal of fruit and a protein bar.

"Good morning," Jim replied. "How was your room?"

Setting her plate on the table and returning to the buffet for a cup of coffee, she answered, "I guess you could call it a room. Only because it has four walls and a door. As for comfort? Not so much. A single wide bed shoved up against one wall and barely enough room to open the door without hitting it. The bathroom is barely big enough for me to brush my teeth and hair. The shower? I don't know how anyone your size can raise their arms high enough to wash. I've seen stalls in horse facilities that were bigger."

"They don't go in for luxury," Jim said, smiling. "Sort of like this room. Tiny."

Marie looked around at the ten-foot-long table with three chairs on each side just a few feet from a lectern. "You're right. I guess I was expecting a few more frills. The company has plenty of funds—at least for private jets, rooms, and cars and high-end hotels and restaurants. You'd think they would spend a little more on accommodations for their people when they need to be here."

"The company doesn't need to cater to your comfort," Gene chastised her, stepping up to the table. "If you've paid attention over the years, you'd have noticed that the company creates the right environment for whatever the situation requires. It could be a five-star restaurant or a low-end fast-food vendor." Getting some coffee and a roll, he sat and continued, "Everything they do is charged to some mission. The few times that we require our people to stay here at the headquarters because of time constraints are indeed Spartan. But bear in mind, although you are technically involved in an operation, this portion isn't generating any income or providing any facade for the mission."

"Good morning, everybody," Mr. O said, walking in with Larry. "I hope everybody had a good evening, and I'll try to get this over with as painlessly as possible." He stepped up to Marie's chair and held out his hand. "I'm assuming that you're Marie since it's obvious that you're the only female in this room and I already know everybody else. I'm O, and this is Larry."

"Nice to meet you," Larry said, shaking her hand. "I'm the guy from St. Louis where the company is trying to shift the blame and ultimately the drug and gang problems."

"Don't listen to him," O said as he got a plate of eggs and bacon. "He likes to play the 'Oh, poor me' card whenever we brief anyone new. He's really as much behind this operation as anybody."

"Why don't you guys get started with the briefing while we eat?" Gene suggested. "Jim needs to get back to Texas as early as possible, and I'm sure Marie has better things to do besides listening to you two rehashing old news."

"My pleasure," O said as he returned to the buffet table for a cup of coffee. "I'm going to assume that you know the company was tasked to eradicate the majority of the drug and gang problems in Chicago."

"More or less," Marie responded as she took a slice of watermelon from her plate. "And I know that you've developed teams to capture three people from five gangs."

"That's a good start," O said. "You're working with Jim to make the final decisions on how those teams are to proceed. He'll also be the final authority to cancel the entire operation tomorrow night. But I'm not sure if you're aware of the time and effort that has gone into this operation."

"I read that the company has been working on it for over a year," Marie answered. "And I did notice that most of the intelligence and enforcement organizations have had an input."

"That's true," Larry said as he set his plate on the table. "You've mentioned the Chicago part. But the St. Louis part is just as critical. Even more so if we're going to succeed in placing the blame on other gangs. The true actors in this little eradication must never be exposed. And that is why St. Louis is of equal importance."

"I understand," Marie agreed, returning to the buffet to get a few more pieces of fruit. "I've been with the company for a little over five years, and the overriding concern has always been deniability. That and safeguarding the people who work here."

"*That* is the most important thing," Gene said as he went to refill his coffee. "Even if it means failing at one of the operations. Every effort is made to protect the identity of our operators. And almost as importantly, the mere existence of either Dark Water or Muddy Water must never become public."

Chapter 62

As Gene retook his seat, O said, "Our plan on the Chicago side has the five teams collecting the top three of each gang, as you know. They'll start with the number-one guy and work their way down. We'll know exactly where each man is, and that information will be relayed to the team captain. He'll be in the van with his four members as they go from location to location, capturing their targets and bringing them to the central facility. I'll be in the hotel monitoring them and their targets' locations every second once the operation commences. You'll be able to monitor our communications, and Jim has the authority to intervene in case we're having difficulty in getting any single target."

"Why don't we control the teams from our location?" Marie asked as she went to refill her coffee.

"The company decided to separate the management of the teams to me," O answered. "It's too cumbersome to try to watch fifteen individual targets as well as the teams. So, the decision was to have me monitoring the targets and Jim monitoring the teams. If a target isn't where he's supposed to be, I'll be responsible for redirecting the team. If it's too time-consuming to go to wherever he is, then Jim can bring the team in without one or more of the targets."

"So, what's the probability of a target not being in the predicted location?" Marie asked, frowning. "I'm assuming that if these individuals were selected and monitored for at least a year, as you've said, then they are integral to the operation. Is that true?"

"Yes," O confirmed, nodding. "But the overall operation can't depend on a single target. If we have thirteen or fourteen of our targets, we can still meet the goal set by the company. As I said, that's Jim's decision."

"What about your part?" Marie asked Larry. "Are you going to continue without some of your targets?"

"No," Larry said. "First off, we've identified several individuals who are members of the St. Louis Vice Lords. It doesn't matter which of them we get. Should one or two not be where we expect, there are several others we can use. Also, we're working with a different time frame. I can absolutely guarantee that we'll get our guys within the hour I've established as the start of our part and when we need to head to Chicago. I'll be with the team the entire time, and I'll decide when to quit looking for an individual if he can't be taken quickly or move on to the next possibility. And finally, even if we're short a single man, we can still perform our task. The Vice Lords of St. Louis will be blamed. Doesn't matter if it's five or fifteen members of the bodies that are found."

"So, you're more or less autonomous," Marie observed.

"Yes," Larry answered. "But Jim will be monitoring our progress just in case we're running late. That could happen if there's an accident on the road between St. Louis and Chicago. Or if we develop car trouble. Neither is expected, but someone has to be able to cancel the entire operation if the unexpected happens. That gives him the option of pushing the time frame to keep it on for tomorrow night or canceling and rescheduling for the following night."

"Okay, let's see if I've got this right," Marie remarked. "You're leaving St. Louis about ten o'clock. The Chicago operation is scheduled for approximately two o'clock. That gives you the four hours you need to get to Chicago. Then if you're running into trouble because of a traffic issue, Jim can delay the Chicago part until you get back on schedule?"

"Let me step in here for a second," Jim said. "Yes, I can delay the start of the Chicago operation. But that may not be necessary just because Larry's team is going to be even an hour late. Once he's on his way, assuming that he's met his time frame, I really don't care if he's an hour or two late. As long as Chicago is running within their time frame, I believe that I'll have sufficient flexibility time wise to keep the operation on track. That's because if we have all or most of the Chicago targets, we can keep them in our facility until we know when Larry will arrive. As a matter of fact, if the targets sit strapped to a chair with hoods over their heads for an extra hour, that might even benefit us. Bottom line is that if Larry can get here up to an hour after we take care of Chicago's operation, we're good."

"Got it," Marie said, nodding. "Now one more thing regarding the Chicago part. I believe that you stated that the five teams will be all together in a van when they go get their targets."

"That's correct," O answered. "We think that the best way to keep the number of our people to the minimum and have sufficient force to get and control our targets is to use vans that have room for the team and their three targets."

"Quick question," Marie responded. "Why not have two of the team members, maybe the team captain and another one, follow in a separate car? They can then be available to go after the individual who wasn't where he was supposed to be. I'm just looking at the increased flexibility. Having an extra vehicle would allow you to go after the missing man while the van and majority of the team go to the facility. The team captain can then find the target and bring him in or eliminate him wherever he's found."

Mr. O looked at her for a second and then looked at Gene. "I think she has a point," he said. "What do you think, General?"

Gene turned to Jim and asked, "It's your operation once it starts, so what would you suggest?"

"I think she's right," Jim told him. "The addition of five cars is a cheap way to have a force multiplier effect. I say do it."

"Good," Gene said, getting up and heading for the door. "We're in agreement. I'll go arrange to have the additional cars at the hotel this afternoon. Is there anything else?"

"Not that I know of," Jim answered for everybody. "But we've still got a few details to go over. Anything for you, Marie?"

"I'm good," she said, smiling at him as Gene left. "Thanks for standing up for me."

"Not a problem," Jim said, smiling back. "You're right, and I'm only interested in doing what's best for the operation. It has nothing to do with who makes the suggestion."

When Gene came back in, everyone was relaxed and engaged in small talk.

"Is that it?" he asked, taking his seat. "Everything taken care of?"

"Pretty much," Jim answered. "Mr. O ran through the basics of what would happen to the targets after we get them to the facility, and Larry covered the effort to blame the St. Louis gang. Marie is satisfied with all that, and so am I. I think there'll always be bugs in the stew but nothing that we can't deal with as they come up."

"Well, then I guess we can wrap this up," Gene said after seeing everyone nodding. "I'll arrange transport for Larry and O to get back home. Jim, you and Marie will be taken home in my plane. It'll take you to Dallas first and then New Orleans since you've got to fly early tomorrow. I guess I'll see everybody in Chicago tomorrow evening." He got up saying, "Except you, Larry. If everything goes as planned, I'll see you for the after-action meeting. And hopefully that will be next weekend. Jim, if you and Marie will come with me, I'll get you to the plane."

Chapter 63

As they were sitting in the leather seats facing each other in the plane for Dallas, Marie said, "I really do appreciate you supporting me about the additional car. That means a lot to me. This is my first time to be in on any of the planning parts."

"Like I said," Jim replied, "you were right. That's what I supported. The idea. That's something that someone should have thought of long ago."

"Still, I appreciate it. I'm somewhat surprised that the General wanted me in on this," she said, crossing her legs. "I've always been a sort of bit player. You know, sort of like I was at the restaurant. This seems like I've suddenly been recognized as something more than a distraction."

"If it makes you feel any better, I was a sort of bit player at the start too," Jim said, glancing down at her legs. "I was just part of the end. I either administered the *judgment* or assisted in it. Maybe not a bit player as you've described but more like the hammer that drives in the nail. This is going to be the first time that I'm sort of like the construction manager. I'm now directing the workers who pound the nail that builds the wall. I'm not the architect, but at least I've had a look at the blueprints.

"You know who I admire?" Marie said, crossing her legs again and watching Jim's face. "Val."

"Why?" Jim asked, thinking back to when he and Jennifer had had the plane to themselves for the flight to Virginia.

"Because she seems happy with her part of the operation. I know I haven't had much time to talk to her, but she seems to genuinely like dealing with the men," she explained. "I don't think I could ever do that. I mean, I'm not a prude or anything, but to have to get involved like that—I just don't think I could."

"I guess she looks at it as just a job. We're all sometimes asked to do things that seem contrary to the way we were raised," Jim told her. "I mean, if you'd asked me before I went to Vietnam if I'd kill someone for money, I'd have said, 'Hell no.' Now look at me."

"Maybe so," Marie replied, sliding down slightly in her seat and crossing her ankles. "I've had several relationships with different men since my divorce, but there has always been a mutual attraction. And I've gotten to know them before anything sexual happened."

"I'm not so sure that Val's involved sexually with all the men she's assigned," Jim suggested. "Maybe they just enjoy being in the company of a beautiful woman. Sort of like you are with the men you've been in relationships with before it became sexual."

"I guess that's possible," Marie said as she began to rhythmically squeeze her knees together. "She is a very sexy lady."

"Yes, she is," Jim said, unable to not watch the obvious display that Marie was performing. "But beauty can't keep a man's interest forever. There has to be something more."

"What do you think the 'something more' is?" Marie asked, relishing the effect she was having on Jim.

"Brains, a sense of humor, and I guess that old-fashioned thing called love," Jim answered. "What do you look for in a man?"

"Of course, I want looks," she answered. "And brains. And a sense of humor. But there's always something that's almost unexplainable that makes certain men attractive. I can't explain it better than that. But I know it when I see it."

"I think I understand," Jim said as a feeling of desire descended to his groin. "I've seen women whom I thought were extremely attractive who weren't actually pretty by normal standards. Something about the way they look at you. I guess it's a lot in the way they act. Sort of inviting yet not. Demurely. No, more like coy. Yeah, coy. Like you said, almost unexplainable."

"How does that make you feel?" Marie asked, tilting her head slightly.

"How does having a woman sort of invite me but not make me feel?" Jim asked. "I guess I'd have to say conflicted."

"Conflicted?" Marie asked. "What does that mean?"

"Conflicted because I'm married," Jim told her. "Having a strong desire that I know I've got to resist. But I guess I could also say it makes me feel good to know that a sexy lady is interested in me. Maybe that's how Val keeps men interested but doesn't necessarily have to get involved sexually."

Marie started to say something when the pilot came on the intercom and announced that they were starting the descent into Dallas for the landing at Love Field.

Jim sat up and said, "I guess we'll just have to wait until the next time we see Val to ask her how she does it."

"I guess," Marie said as a slight look of disappointment crossed her face. "Maybe we can revisit the subject while we're in Chicago tomorrow night."

Chapter 64

Jennifer was waiting in the small lobby of the terminal when Jim stepped down from the plane. Watching him walking across the tarmac with his small overnight bag, she wondered if she was being too critical when he spent time with Gene. Knowing that the two men shared something that she could probably never understand, she vowed to never complain about his infrequent trips, and truth be told, she hoped that she'd get to go with him more often. The weekends she'd spent with him in Virginia had been wonderful.

"Hi, stranger," she said as he entered the terminal. "Miss me? Glad to be home?"

Jim kissed her on the cheek and replied, "Always. Especially when I'm met by a beautiful lady who probably brought a cold beer for the ride home."

"You're going to have to settle for a beautiful lady," she told him as they headed for the car. "But I can promise you all the cold beer you want when we get home. How was the trip?"

"Fine," Jim answered as they got to the car. Tossing his bag in the rear seat, he asked, "Want me to drive?"

"No," Jennifer told him, opening the driver's door. "You just sit back and let me. What do you want to do for dinner tonight?"

"I don't care," Jim said as he got into the passenger seat. "What would you like?"

"I think I'd like to go to Venice Pizza," she said as they pulled out of the parking lot. "I haven't had good lasagna in a long time. Is that all right with you?"

"Fine," he answered as they entered Loop 12 heading east. "How early do you want to eat?"

"Oh, I guess around five or six," she answered. "Is that okay, or do you want to go earlier? I know you've got to get up early in the morning, so I figured we'd eat a little early and have a quiet drink at home. Maybe a movie."

"That sounds good to me," Jim said as they sped around the loop. Looking out of his window, he knew that they were only a couple of miles away from where he'd almost been caught in Leonard's house. *Carelessness*, he thought. *A moment's inattention. That's all it takes.* "Would you like to get the lasagna to go and eat at home?" Jim asked. "We still have a bottle of the wine Gene brought."

"No," Jennifer answered as they took Loop 635 south. "I want to save that wine for another steak night. Plus, eating out means no dishes. I want to have some quiet time with you since you'll be gone for the next three days."

"That's fine with me," Jim said. "I just want to take a nice hot shower and get some clean clothes before we leave the house. You wouldn't believe the room they had for me at Quantico."

"No fancy hotel and restaurant?" she asked, approaching the exit for their neighborhood. "I'm sure Gene doesn't reserve them just for me."

"No," Jim explained. "Sometimes we do get to stay in a nice place. Maybe not as nice as we did in Alexandria. And we certainly don't always eat as well. But these short trips where I stay at the company headquarters are just one step above living in the field."

"I guess you'd better make sure I get to go with you then," Jennifer said, smiling. "Then they won't treat you so poorly."

"As much as I'd like that, I don't think Gene would approve it every time," Jim said as they pulled into their driveway. "Maybe he'd be more receptive if we stayed in rooms like I had last night. We'd have to share a single bed, and I know you wouldn't like the bathroom. No vanity table for your makeup. Barely enough room for a toilet and sink. But if you want, I'll mention it to him."

"That's all right," she told him as she got out of the car. "I'll let you boys rough it. I want at least a three-star hotel, but I'd prefer a five-star. And the same goes for the restaurant."

"Then I think you'd really be disappointed with the meal service we had," Jim remarked as Jennifer unlocked the front door. "Most of the time, the company provides a buffet. It's pretty good, usually. But it might only earn a two-star rating at best."

Tossing her keys on the end table beside the couch, Jennifer replied, "I may not be ready for 'living in the field,' as you put it, but I can remember a few times when we first got married that we stayed in some pretty miserable motels along I-10 driving across New Mexico and Arizona. You go get your shower and change. I'll have you a cold Ziegen Bock in a frosty mug when you get done."

Chapter 65

The Eleventh

On Tuesday afternoon, when Jim and Rob checked into their hotel in Chicago, the desk clerk handed Jim an envelope along with his key and wished them a good evening.

"Anything important?" Rob asked, motioning at the envelope.

"Probably not," Jim answered as they approached the elevator. "My wife was supposed to leave me a message about where she was going to be tonight in case she went to see her mother."

"Well, my offer for you to join my friends and me stands if you change your mind," Rob said as they hit the button for their floor.

"I appreciate it," Jim said as the doors slid open. "But I'll take a rain check. Maybe tomorrow night or on the next trip."

"Sure thing," Rob said, stopping in front of his room. "See you in the morning."

"You bet," Jim said, unlocking his door. "Have a good evening."

After setting his suitcase on the bench at the foot of his bed, Jim sat at the desk and opened the envelope. Reading the phone and room number on the single sheet of paper, he picked up the phone and dialed. As soon as he heard the hotel operator say, "Holiday Inn Express," he told her the room number he was calling and waited.

A couple of rings later, he heard Gene asking, "How was the flight?"

"Fine, sir," Jim said, knowing that Gene wouldn't say much on an unsecure line such as this one. "How's everything going at the convention?"

"Just fine," Gene answered. "I wish you could have been here for the opening ceremony. It was spectacular. Anyway, would you like for me to send someone to come pick you up? Or would you rather wait for the hotel to send a van?"

"I'd prefer to have you send somebody," Jim answered. "I know how long it takes the hotel van. Especially if they have to make several stops to drop off or pick up passengers. I've spent enough time in airports today."

"I understand," Gene replied. "What terminal are you at?"

"G," Jim answered, knowing that Gene would send one of the cars from tonight's operation to come get him at his hotel. "I'll be waiting curbside."

"Good. The car should be there in less than ten minutes," Gene told him before hanging up.

Jim opened his suitcase, pulled a pair of jeans and a T-shirt out, and tossed them on the bed. Hanging his uniform jacket and shirt in the closet, he slipped off the black boots he always wore flying and hung his pants beside the jacket.

Standing at the curb, watching all the cars, taxis, and delivery vans passing, he was taken by surprise when a slightly dirty car pulled up in front of him and stopped.

"Need a lift, mister?" Marie said, smiling as she leaned over and looked up at him.

"Yes, Ma'am," Jim said, opening the door and getting into the passenger seat. "Nice to see you again. And so soon."

"You too," she said as she looked over her shoulder and merged into the almost constant stream of traffic. "Are you ready for tonight?"

"I suppose," Jim answered. "How long have you been here?"

"I got in a couple of hours ago," Marie told him as they left the hotel. "It looks like everything is ready, and we'll just have to wait for a few hours before Larry lets us know that he's on his way."

"That's about what I expected," Jim said, watching Marie maneuver through the traffic. "Since we've got a couple of hours, why don't we stop somewhere before we go to the hotel and get something to eat?"

"Sure," Marie answered. "But there's a pretty nice restaurant at the hotel."

"I'd rather not be seen there too much," Jim explained. "I know we're supposed to be there for a convention, and that's fine to explain why so many people are arriving at the same time, but I prefer not to be seen if at all possible."

"Okay," Marie said. "I think I saw a TGI Friday's on my way here. It should be just ahead. Will that be okay?"

"That'll be fine," Jim told her. "Once we start working on the operation, we won't have much time to eat, unless Gene's made arrangements for room service."

"I'm a little hungry anyway," Marie said as she saw the exit she needed to get to the restaurant. "So, this works out good for me too."

Chapter 66

An hour or so later, as they entered Jim's room at the Holiday Inn Express, they saw Gene talking to Mr. O and heard him say, "We've still got almost three hours before need to preposition our teams, so let's not get too excited about a couple of missing targets."

"Who's missing?" Jim asked as he walked over to where the radios and telephones had been set up.

"The top two of the Vice Lords," O told him. "We had them meeting at a small restaurant on the south side, and then both their cars left. We weren't sure if they were in the cars or if they're still in the restaurant."

"Why is that a problem?" Jim asked. "Aren't you still tracking their cars?"

"Of course," O answered. "And we still have a hold on the satellite that is focusing on the restaurant. The problem is where to send the teams. The cars are both heading more or less to where we expect them, but we aren't sure if the targets are in them."

"Why not?" Jim asked. "The resolution from the satellites is sufficient that you can read the newspaper that a man standing outside of the restaurant is holding. How is it that you don't know if the targets got in the cars after their meeting?"

"The portico of the restaurant extends almost to the street," O explained. "There's only about a foot between the door of the car and the edge of the portico. The position of the satellite is such that the angle from the lens to the ground reduces the visible area to just a few inches. We identified both men getting into the cars before they went to the restaurant. And they were the only men besides the drivers who were inside. And the cars didn't stop until reaching the restaurant. We then saw people exit the cars and cross beneath the portico."

"So, you're positive that the targets entered the restaurant," Jim agreed. "I'm guessing that you never saw anyone reenter the cars before they drove away."

"That's correct," O said, nodding. "Since those two targets are what I'd consider to be our highest value, I certainly don't want to continue the operation without securing them."

"Where did the cars pick them up?" Jim asked, looking at a monitor that showed the positions of the teams.

"Both men were picked up at one of their fronts for their drug operations," O answered.

"And you're positive that they were the only ones who got in the cars?" Jim asked, seeing that all the teams' cars were still in the hotel's parking lot.

"Positive," O told him, nodding vigorously.

"What about if there was another man in the car when it picked up your target?" Jim asked, looking at O. "What if it was that man who entered the restaurant instead of the target? That would leave the target in the car as it drove away."

"That would presume that they were trying to avoid being followed," Gene interjected. "That's something that we haven't seen them do during the entire year we've been watching them. A change in behavior like that would suggest that they're aware of being monitored."

"How sure are you that they don't know about the company's interest and attempts to know their movements?" Jim asked, looking at Gene.

"Almost 100 percent," Gene answered. "We've been performing this type of surveillance for many years, as you well know. I'd say that if they're spooked about something, it has nothing to do with us."

Jim thought for a second and then asked, "What's happening with Robert? He's about the only link that I can think of who would spook our targets if he decided something was hinky because of what we did to him."

"I talked to Val this morning," Gene informed him. "She said that he's starting to get some headaches and a slight fever. He had scheduled an appointment with his doctor for this morning, and she hasn't heard from him since then."

"So, it's possible that he suspects something," Jim said, nodding. "Here's my assessment of the situation. We think our targets entered the restaurant but aren't sure if they're still in there. Then there's the possibility that they're making a radical change to their behavior that suggests knowledge of someone watching them. If they're trying to throw off anyone watching them, then they may have used a substitute to go into the restaurant while they remained in the car and assumed that they wouldn't continue to be followed. So, we have three possibilities."

"I only see two," O said, crossing his arms. "Either they're in the car, which would mean that you're correct about them trying to evade whoever they think is following them, or they're still in the restaurant."

"You're exactly correct," Jim agreed. "But the third possibility is that they've left or plan to leave in another car." Turning to Gene, he asked, "Do I have operational control right now?"

"Yes. As of now, you're in charge of the operation," Gene replied.

Chapter 67

Jim looked at Mr. O and said, "I want the Vice Lords team captain and Marie to go to that restaurant. Have them take a taxi and just go in and have dinner like they're a normal couple." Turning to Gene, he said, "I want the company to provide additional satellite coverage and tracking of any vehicle that stops to pick up anyone leaving that restaurant until we verify whether or not our targets are still there. I also want to know if any cars have come and gone from the time the targets' cars left. If any have, I want them to locate those vehicles and start tracking them."

Jim told O, "You continue monitoring the two targets' cars with the assumption that they're still in them. If you think that you can get two patrol cars to stop them for some valid reason, such as speeding or something that won't make them suspicious, they may be able to verify the occupants of the car before we can get Marie and her escort to the restaurant."

"What if there *is* another man in the car?" O asked. "A standard patrol officer won't know if he's our target or just some passenger."

"Doesn't really matter," Jim said, shaking his head. "If there's anybody in the car besides the driver, something is going on, and I'll bet that our targets are spooked. If there isn't anybody besides the driver in the car, then we'll continue with the assumption that our targets are still in the restaurant. Then our concern is why the cars left without their passengers. That's why I want coverage of any car that comes to the restaurant, especially until we can get Marie into the restaurant. If the targets are there, they still need transportation to go home or wherever they're headed."

"What if they are still in the restaurant?" Marie asked. "What am I supposed to do?"

"Nothing. Just get a table and ignore them. If they're there, O will be monitoring the team captain's radio, and he'll verify their location," Jim answered. "If they are, you just stay and enjoy dinner. That way, we'll have eyes on the targets and will know when someone comes to pick them up. If they aren't there, you can either stay or come back here. That's up to O to decide if he wants all the members of his team here or not."

"I'll leave that up to the team captain," O said, thinking about the impact on his part of the operation if the Vice Lords leaders were about to dramatically change their plans. "If they aren't there, we'll know to just continue following their cars. In any event, like the General said, we still have a couple of hours before we need to commit to where the teams need to be."

"What about Larry?" Gene asked Jim. "What do you plan to do regarding his operation?"

"We still have time to postpone that as well," Jim answered. "As we discussed, his time frame allows him to get here even shortly after we eliminate our targets. I'll contact him as soon as we know the situation with the Vice Lords targets, and we can go from there."

"Okay," O said as he turned to leave. "I'll go back to my room and call the team captain, Tim, and make sure that he's appropriately dressed for dinner instead of for the original tasking of shooting people."

"That's a good idea," Jim said, smiling. "Wearing a full-black assault outfit while accompanying a pretty lady to dinner might raise a few eyebrows. Just make sure he checks his radio before he goes into the restaurant. I'd hate to have Marie and Tim go in and us not be able to know what they find. Matter of fact, have him make a call as soon as you talk to him. I want to know that my radio is linked to his frequency and that I can talk directly to him instead of passing information or directions through you."

"Are you saying that you're going to be directing one of my teams?" O asked, turning back and walking up to Jim. "Isn't that why I'm here? To run the actual teams?"

Jim shook his head and told him, "They're still your teams, O. I'm not about to interfere with your operation. Once the actual collecting of the targets commences, you have complete autonomy as far as directing your teams as you deem necessary. I'm just making sure that I can communicate directly with him regarding this reconnaissance mission. I don't want to take a chance that any miscommunication occurs. I really don't expect to need to talk to him, just know immediately what he finds. I could give Marie a radio and get the same results. But I don't think it's necessary to have two people trying to relay the same information. That could result in even more confusion. You'd be getting two possibly different stories and waste time sorting out any confusion. Trust me, I don't want to pick up any additional duties." Jim looked at O saying, "I have all the confidence in the world in you. You're tasked with the most difficult part in this operation, and I'm more here to support you than anything. I just learned a very hard lesson a couple of days ago about what even a few seconds of no communication or miscommunication can do to an operation. And I don't want to jeopardize what I think is a critical decision point."

"No problem," O said after a second, offering his hand to shake. "I guess I'm a little stressed over the possibility of losing two of our most valuable targets. I've been waiting on this to happen for too many years. Now when we're finally about to take some aggressive action to get these scumbags off the streets, the idea of failure is not an option."

"We're not going to fail," Jim assured him, shaking his hand. "Worst case, we'll pause and regroup tomorrow. But let's just get your man and Marie over there and see what our next move should be."

Chapter 68

"All right, Marie," Jim said as O left. "Do you think that you could identify the targets, or do you need to see their pictures again?"

"I guess I need to look at them again," she acknowledged. "I never really paid any attention to their pictures since I wasn't supposed to be involved at that level. But the other guy, Tim, knows them, so isn't that enough?"

"Probably," Jim answered as he pulled the folder on the Vice Lords from the table with the communications equipment. "But just in case, I'd be happier knowing that you can recognize them as well."

Marie took her time studying the faces of the two men that they were looking for as Jim looked around the table and finally asked Gene, "Can we get an earpiece for Marie so that she can monitor our communication while she's there?"

"Not a problem," Gene answered, pulling out his phone. "Get me a couple of earpieces tuned to the frequency assigned to the Vice Lords team," he said, looking at Jim and Marie. Hanging up his phone, he added, "I'll have them here in a couple of minutes. Why do you think you'll need them?"

"Just a precaution," Jim answered as he watched Marie looking at the pictures. "I want her to know if I'm giving her *date* any instructions. She needs to be aware of any directions I'm giving him so that she's in a position to support whatever he needs to do."

"Sounds good," Gene said as Marie put the photos back on the table. "What do you think, Marie?"

"I think I'm turning into a field operative," Marie said, smiling. "All of a sudden, I'm transformed from an assistant to someone who's just monitoring an operation into an active participant in a possibly dangerous situation. Does that mean that I'm getting hazardous duty pay?"

"We don't have hazardous duty pay," Gene informed her. "But you've expressed a desire for more direct involvement. So here it is."

"Oh, I'm happy to do this," Marie countered. "This is really why I joined the company. Just being arm candy for some guy who's actually doing something has never been what I imagined when you guys asked me to come to work. I never thought of myself as a 007 type, but I've always imagined myself sort of like Mata Hari but working for the good guys."

"Oh, really?" Jim remarked as a knock was heard at the door. "You know that she was shot by a French firing squad for being a double agent for the Germans. You might want to find another heroine. I'd suggest Emily West, better known as Emily Morgan, who spied for Texas during the Revolution."

Gene opened the door and took the package that was being delivered. "Thanks," he said as he shut the door. "Let's give these a try." Pulling one of the earpieces out, he said, "Just slip it into your right ear, and we'll see if you can hear Jim's transmission."

"Do you have one for my left ear?" Marie asked, taking the earpiece. "Since I wear my hair more over the left side, it wouldn't be as noticeable."

"No problem," Gene said, handing her the other one. "Just make sure it fits snugly and won't fall out if you move your head aggressively."

Once she was satisfied with the fit, Jim picked up the radio that the Vice Lords team would be using and spoke quietly, "Can you hear me?"

"Yes, I can," came the reply on the radio. "Who is this?"

"I'm Lashley," Jim said. "We're checking another radio for reception, but I'm glad to know that yours is working as well."

"I heard both of you," Marie said, smiling. "And it appears that my earpiece is just for receiving, not transmitting."

"That's right," Jim said, replacing the radio on the table. "As I told Mr. O, I just want you to be able to immediately hear any directions either he or I give Tim, the team captain. So, if you're happy with things, we'll see if he's about ready for your date."

Just as Jim was about to pick up the phone and call O, he heard the radio announce, "This is Tim. I'm ready to go if the lady is. Since I've already done my radio check, I'll head downstairs and wait."

"Okay," Jim told Marie as he walked over to open the door. "Just act normal and pay close attention to what's going on. After watching how quickly you reacted when the waiter didn't show up last time, I'm not worried. And I really don't expect you guys to need to do anything other than seeing who's at the restaurant."

"Got it covered," Marie said as she headed out of the door. A faint melody resembling "The Yellow Rose of Texas" was heard as she walked down the hall.

"What's that about?" Gene asked as he strained to hear the whistling.

Jim just smiled and told him, "That song, 'The Yellow Rose of Texas,' is rumored to have been inspired by Emily Morgan. It appears that our Ms. Marie has an excellent sense of humor."

"And a knowledge of Texas history as well," Gene said, smiling. "I think that young lady has a bright future with Black Water."

"I agree," Jim said, recalling their conversations and her obvious flirting on the trip back to Texas the day before. "And I'm sure she knows what she wants and isn't afraid to go after it." *And that could be a problem for me*, Jim thought as he sat down to wait for them to get to the restaurant.

Chapter 69

It took only about thirty minutes for the taxi to deliver Tim and Marie to the restaurant. As Tim paid and tipped the driver, Marie reached up and casually checked her earpiece. Turning to Tim, she tapped her left ear to remind him to check his communication with Jim.

Watching Tim speak softly into the tiny microphone that was attached to the cuff of his shirt sleeve, she heard him say, "Check" and heard Jim's distinct voice answer, "Roger."

Tim walked to the door and held it open for Marie. As they entered, both of them swept the room with their eyes as if they were looking for an open table.

Marie was the first one to spot the men sitting near the rear. The only problem was that there was another man sitting with them with his back to the door. She reached over and put her hand on Tim's arm as she gave a slight nod to where the men were seating. Tim glanced toward them and began leading her to a table near the wall and close to the front door.

Tim held out a chair so that Marie was facing the rear of the restaurant and so that he would have a view of both the men and the door. As he took his seat, he put his elbow on the table and whispered into his microphone, "Targets spotted. Third unknown with them. Advise."

"Just sit tight and make an order," O directed. "How do you want to play this, Jim?"

"For right now, they're still your targets," Jim answered. "At this point, I'm just monitoring your team."

"Got it," O said confidently and spoke to Tim. "Just sit tight and be ready to leave if we can't get a handle on how they're going to leave the restaurant."

"Looks like they're about finished eating," Tim whispered as he saw a waiter approaching. "I'll get back to you if we see anything changing."

"What can I get you folks to drink?" the waiter asked as he set menus on the table.

"Just water for me," Tim replied as he turned to Marie. "How about you?"

"A glass of tea would be wonderful," she answered as she picked up a menu. "What's the specialty of the restaurant?"

"Giordano's has the best calamari in Chicago," he informed her. "And we're also known for some of the best deep-dish pizza in town."

"I think I'd like the calamari," Marie said, handing her menu back to the waiter. "And maybe a glass of Chardonnay."

"Excellent," the waiter said with a slight bow. "And for the gentleman?"

"That sounds good to me also," Tim answered, handing back his menu. "Except for the wine. I'll stick with water."

"Very well," the waiter said as he turned to go to the kitchen.

Tim smiled at Marie and asked, "Anything abnormal going on over at the table?"

"Not really," she said, smiling and looking directly at him. "The guys we're after keep looking at me."

"That's not abnormal," Tim remarked. "And I'm sure you're used to men looking at you."

"I'm used to that," she said, smiling and reaching over to touch his arm. "It's just that these two seem a little more interested and keep leaning over and talking to each other after they look at me."

Tim dropped his napkin and turned his head enough to get a good look at the men before he straightened up and said, "Still looks like two oversexed men talking about the obvious tributes of a sexy lady."

Marie looked directly at Tim and said, "I hope you're not making some not-so-subtle pass."

"Not a chance," Tim said, frowning at her. "I'm just trying to put myself in their situation. An attractive lady comes in and sits down at a table directly in front of me and a friend. What I'm telling you is probably exactly what you and your female friends do when an attractive man comes into a room where you are. Let's not go where the road doesn't lead."

"I apologize," Marie said, nodding. "It's just that I get really tired of innuendos when I'm just talking to some guy. I'm sorry. I didn't mean to question your professionalism."

"Not a problem," Tim said, smiling as the waiter arrived with their drinks. "I wish I could say the same. The only innuendo I ever get from pretty ladies is a not-so-subtle rolling of their eyes."

Chapter 70

Scant seconds later, Marie saw the third man at the table turn and glance her way. She almost dropped her wine glass when she recognized him.

"That's the man," she whispered to Tim.

"I know," Tim said, surprised at her response. "I also recognized them. So what's the problem?"

"I'm talking about the man with our two men," she hurriedly explained. "He was the target of an operation we had a few days back."

"Are you sure?" Tim asked, hoping to get a glance at the man's face.

"I'm positive," Marie said emphatically. "He's supposed to be sick and at the hospital."

"Is he tied to this operation?" Tim asked, repeatedly glancing at their table.

"I'm not positive, but I think so," she answered, trying not to look toward the table.

"Does he know you?" Tim asked. "What's his name?"

"I'm not sure of his name," Marie answered. "I only heard him referred to as a Captain with the CPD. And that he had ties to the gangs and drugs here."

"So, he doesn't know you," Tim stated as he tried to figure out if they had a problem or not.

"Definitely not," Marie said assuredly. "But there's an outside chance that he may remember having seen me at the same restaurant where Jim gave him something that was supposed to make him extremely sick before he finally died from it."

"Okay," Tim said, trying to tie all the pieces together. "There's a man whom you think is a Chicago Police Captain with our targets, and there's a chance that he's recognized you. And this Captain is tied to gang and drug activity, which is what this operation is concerned with. Is that about it?"

"All that," Marie said, trying to convey her concern without raising other patrons' suspicions. "And we tried to assassinate him just a week ago."

"Before we overreact, let's just keep an eye on them for a few more minutes," Tim finally decided. "I'm still betting that our targets are making rude suggestive remarks to each other and that the other man is just showing a normal male desire to look at the woman who has drawn his friends' interest."

"Under normal circumstances, I'd agree with you," Marie lectured him. "But the appearance of a man whom I thought we had disposed of? Add in the strange way our targets got here and the fact that they are now tied to a man known to be with the police and tied to their business operations. I'm concerned."

"Okay, I get your point," Tim said, trying to reduce the stress level. "Just how positive are you that the man is the same Police Captain?"

"Almost 100 percent," Marie insisted. "I sat not ten feet from him and got an unobstructed view of his face when he turned to look at me while Jim and I were at an adjacent table. It's him."

"All right," Tim said. "Now does he recognize you? I mean, if he didn't do anything more than look at you once in a restaurant a week ago, I still don't see any reason to get too concerned. I think we need to bring the alert level back down before we go nuclear. Does that sound reasonable to you?"

"Okay," Marie finally agreed. "But I'm still sure that he's the man. I think at least we need to let Jim know that he's here and not in some hospital like we've been led to believe."

"I agree with that," Tim said as he raised his wrist to his lips. "Jim, are you there?"

"Here," Jim answered. "What's up?"

"Not sure," Tim answered. "But Marie is firmly convinced that the third unknown we called in about is a Captain with the CPD. She says he's the man whom you conducted an operation on some time last week. Advise."

"Stand by," Jim told him as he turned to Gene. "When was the last time you talked to Val?"

"This morning," Gene answered. "Like I told you when you got here. She said Robert had a doctor's appointment, and she hasn't heard from him since."

"Call her," Jim said forcefully. "If that man at the restaurant is our Captain and if he knows something is going on, Val could be in danger. And while you're at it, get O to send a trustworthy cop to her apartment to check on her if she doesn't answer the phone." Jim said into his radio, "O, get over here ASAP. Tim, I want you and Marie to sit quietly and act normal for now. And please tell me that you're armed."

"Got it," Tim answered. "And yes, I'm armed."

"Good," Jim said with obvious relief in his voice. "Just tell me that it's one of the guns from St. Louis."

"It is," Tim assured him. "What now?"

"Act normal," Jim told him again. "I'll get back to you as soon as we know if Val's all right. Until then, nothing's really changed except I want Marie's attention on the Captain to see if he does anything to make her think he recognizes her. That will—"

"He's getting up," Tim whispered excitedly into his microphone before Jim could finish his sentence. "What do you want me to do?"

Chapter 71

"Excuse me, Miss," Robert said as he got to Tim and Marie's table. "I don't mean to seem forward, but do I know you?"

Marie leaned back in her chair and looked up at him, saying, "Sorry, I don't think so."

"You just look very familiar," Robert continued. "Do you live around here?"

"No, we're from Nashville," Marie said, trying to keep her nerves under control.

"Really?" Robert kept pushing. "How long have you been in Chicago?"

"Just a couple of days," Tim answered. "We're just up here to visit some friends, and I'm sure we've never seen you since we've been here. Have you ever been to Nashville?"

"No," Robert said, keeping his eyes on Marie. "And you aren't familiar, but she is."

"I don't see how that's possible," Tim insisted. "We've been together every time we've gone out. You wouldn't have seen her without seeing me."

"Amy and I went to a little bar by their house the other night," Marie offered. "Maybe that's where you saw me since you didn't see Sam."

"No," Robert insisted. "You were with another man. I'm pretty sure about it."

"That's impossible," she said, acting incensed. "I don't know any other men up here. And like I said, the only time I've been out without Sam is when Amy and I stopped by the bar when we came back from shopping. Now unless you saw us shopping or happened to be in the same bar, you're mistaken."

Robert stood staring at her for a couple of seconds and finally said, "I don't think I'm mistaken. But it will come to me sooner or later. And I'm damned positive that I've seen you somewhere."

Marie watched him go and finally took a deep breath and let it out slowly. "Crap, my heart's beating a thousand times a minute," she said, relaxing slightly.

"Mine too," Tim said as he turned to watch Robert take his seat. "I'm not sure if I can sit here and eat. That was close."

"I'm not sure it's over yet," Marie said as she tried to regain control. "I'm not sure that I'm ready for field work. This is much more difficult than I ever imagined."

"Don't give up on it yet," Tim told her. "You handled that as well as anyone I've ever known with years of experience. Even coming up with Sam and Amy. That was quick thinking. And who the hell is from Nashville? I couldn't lie my way to a conversation about that town except recognizing places like the Grand Ole Opry. Hell, I don't even know if it's a building or a concert."

"Me neither," Marie admitted as the waiter approached with their meals. "I guess I should have picked a town that I had at least been to."

"Maybe so," Tim acknowledged as the waiter placed a plate of calamari in front of Marie. "But I doubt if it would have made any difference. He seemed intent on knowing that he recognized you from around here."

"I know," Marie said as she picked up her fork. "I'm still so damned nervous that I don't know if I can eat."

"Me too," Tim agreed as his calamari was placed in front of him. "But we've got to stay here until Jim calls and says we can leave. If there's one thing I've heard about the company, it's that you stay and do your job. You do that, and they'll take care of you. You don't, they'll cut you loose in a heartbeat."

"Oh shit," Marie said under her breath as she paused with a forkful of calamari. "He's looking over here again."

"Try to ignore him," Tim advised. "Don't even look his way."

"I'm trying," Marie told him. "But he keeps looking at me and talking to the guys with him. And I'm sure it isn't about how hot I am. It's got something to do with him thinking that he knows me."

"You don't know that for sure," Tim said.

"Maybe not, but I don't like this," Marie said, putting her fork down and picking up her wine glass.

Just as she was trying to take a sip, Robert turned and stared at her. Her hand started shaking, and she spilled almost half of the glass on her shirt. A look of instant déjà vu crossed Robert's face, and he turned to the other men.

"Oh shit!" Marie exclaimed. "He knows. Oh crap, he knows. Tell Jim! Now!"

Tim swung his wrist up to his mouth and almost shouted as he relayed Marie's message, "He knows. What do you want us to do?"

"Get her out of there," Jim demanded. "Now. Just get up and leave."

"Oh fuck," Tim quickly said as he stood up. "They're all three coming this way."

"Get Marie out of there!" Jim shouted. "O, get some of your people in there. Tim, you do whatever you need to do to protect you and Marie."

"They're going for their guns!" Tim yelled into his microphone as he tried to keep Marie behind him and as he walked backward to the door.

"Shoot them," Jim ordered. "Shoot them in the face. Kill the sons of bitches. Do it now. O, get your people moving. Gene, call the sanitation team on their way to the restaurant. This is going to shit in a handbasket."

Chapter 72

After what seemed like an hour to Jim but was, in actuality, only a few seconds, he heard Tim say breathlessly, "We're clear. We're out. I think I shot all three of them."

"Just keep walking," Jim told him. "It doesn't matter which way you go. Just get going. O, where are your people?"

"There's a patrol car on its way," he answered. "The shooting was called in before I could get any of our teams headed there."

"That's fine," Jim said over the radio. "Tim, you and Marie go at least two blocks and let us know where you are. O, get the rest of the Vice Lords team to get the third guy, the CFO."

"I need to get Tim first," O explained. "He's the team captain."

"Promote somebody else. Get the CFO," Jim ordered. "If the first two knew something was up, odds are that he's about to rabbit. And get the other teams headed toward their targets."

"We're almost six hours early," O reminded him. "We can't guarantee where the targets are right now."

Jim turned to Gene and said, "Can you provide O and the other teams with current target locations?"

"It will be updated in less than a minute," Gene said as he reached for his phone.

"Just get everybody to their vans or cars," Jim directed. "Have them make their best guess about where they've been expecting the targets to be and head in that direction."

"Got it," O said. "What do you want to do with the Vice Lords guy when we get him?"

"Take him to the facility and strap his ass to a chair," Jim answered. "We're just accelerating this operation. If the Vice Lords knew something, the rest of them may know. We can't wait until they all scatter. Effective immediately, you have control over everything regarding Chicago except Tim and Marie, Mr. O. Go on back to your room and get everybody moving. I'll send a car to get Tim and Marie. And I'll let Larry know that we're executing our end early."

"Updates are on their way," Gene told Jim. "What can I do to help?"

"If you don't mind, just watch the progress of the teams," Jim asked him. "My biggest concern right now is getting Tim and Marie back safely. Have you heard from the sanitation teams?"

"No," Gene answered. "I told them to head to the restaurant. They could be as much as fifteen minutes from there though."

As Jim began thinking about the cleanup and making sure that neither Tim's nor Marie's presence could be verified as part of the shooting, he asked Gene, "Are your driver and Suburban available?"

"I'll make a call," Gene said as he took a quick look at the monitor showing the teams as they streamed out of the hotel parking lot. "I'll send him to get Tim and Marie."

"Thanks," Jim said, picking up the microphone. "Hey, O."

"Yeah?" O replied.

"Can you monitor the local police channels?" Jim asked. "I'd like to know the condition of the targets at the restaurant and that of the other guy."

"Stand by on that," O said. "I'll retune one of my radios to our dispatcher's frequency. I should have you an answer in a couple of minutes."

"Thanks," Jim told him. "Are you getting the latest updates on the targets?"

"Just got them," O answered. "I've relayed the locations to my teams, and they should be on top of them within the hour."

"Great," Jim said. "I'll let you know when I get Tim and Marie back. Gene sent his driver for them, and he's assisting me up here for now."

"Must be nice to have a General working for you," O joked as he listened to the police dispatcher. "And it looks like we've got three dead at the restaurant. Not confirmed until the medical guys get there, but I believe that you can give Tim his marksmanship badge."

"I'll sign the recommendation myself. Have you heard from the guy you sent to Val's apartment?" Jim asked.

"Not yet," O answered. "I'll let you know when he's there and checks it out. What's your plan for the bodies at the restaurant?"

"We let the police worry about them," Jim answered. "As far as anybody's concerned, they were shot with one of the St. Louis guns, and it won't take too much for someone to tie the captain to the gangs as well."

"That sounds like a scene out of *The Godfather*," O joked. "Are you going to send Tim to Sicily?"

"Maybe Oklahoma," Jim answered. "Nobody ever thinks to look there unless you're looking for a casino. Let me know on Val as soon as you can."

"You got it," O said. "Let me know on Tim and Marie too."

"Do you think you can get the sanitation guys in through the back door at the restaurant?" Jim asked Gene, setting the microphone on the desk.

"Shouldn't be a problem," he answered. "Let me guess. You want them dressed like waiters and to replace everything at Tim and Val's table with clean glasses, plates, and silverware." Pausing for a second, Gene put his hand on Jim's shoulder, smiled, and continued, "I may be getting on in age, but I'm still capable of watching an operation and knowing what needs to be done. That is, if it's all right with you since it appears that I'm working for you."

Jim shook his head and smiled, saying, "I guess you heard that, sir."

"Yup," Gene said. "And I just found out that my driver is on his way back with Tim and Marie. And I directed the company to call Larry and let him know that we're running a little ahead. He's supposed to call here as soon as he can reorganize and get his volunteers from the St. Louis Vice Lords. He thinks he can get here before midnight. You're welcome."

Chapter 73

About ten minutes later, Gene opened the door to see Tim and Marie standing there. "Welcome back." he said moving aside for them to enter.

"Jim's in the restroom," Gene told them as they looked around. "Please, you guys, sit down. I'm sure you're ready to relax a little."

"What's going on with the people at the restaurant?" Marie asked as she took one of the armchairs. "Are they dead?"

"That, they are," Gene answered as Jim came out of the restroom, drying his hands. "We've got a team going in to wipe away any evidence that you were there. Fortunately, the restaurant didn't have any security cameras, and neither did the street in front. The only way anyone could possibly place you there would be through an eyewitness, and that would be discounted since both of you were seen at your homes less than an hour ago."

"Congratulations, Tim," Jim said, walking over to shake his hand. "I understand that you're in for a Marksmanship badge. Three shots, three kills. That's sniper territory. It took the average soldier fifty thousand rounds to kill an enemy during Vietnam, and you simply walk into a restaurant and eliminate a corrupt cop and two gang leaders with three shots. If you can keep that up, you'd kill almost fifty thousand men with the same number of shots it takes the average soldier to kill one man. Hell, a hundred men who could shoot like you could eliminate damn near an entire army with the ammo required for the normal soldier to take out a platoon." Jim stood looking at Marie and finally asked, "Are you all right? Or do you need to go somewhere and have a drink?"

"I'm fine," she answered. "I thought I was going to have a heart attack for a while. But I'm all right now. What do you need me to do?"

"If you're sure you're up to it, come sit over here and listen for the teams to check in with Mr. O," Jim told her. "I want to keep track of where we are regarding each of the targets."

Marie got up and walked over to the chair in front of the radios and asked, "Exactly how do you want me to do that?" Jim slid a sheet of paper over to her as she sat and said, "Just cross off the names as you hear that they've been captured or eliminated. You can start with these two." Jim put his left hand gently on her shoulder and pointed to the men she had seen killed. "Then just let me know when all the names are crossed off."

"Why don't you let me do that?" Gene told her as he looked down at her shaking fingers. "I think you deserve a few more minutes off. Why don't you and Tim go downstairs and have a drink or two? I think Jim and I can handle things up here for a little while. Come back in an hour or so and relieve me. I'll probably need a drink by then."

Jim was watching Tim escort her out of the door when Larry called in, saying that he would be at the facility sometime between eleven o'clock and midnight.

"Great," Jim told him. "We seem to be holding our own according to our revised schedule. Let me know if things change on your end."

As he put the microphone back on the table, he heard one of the team members who had been sent to get the remaining Vice Lords target report to Mr. O that they had him and were heading in.

"Did you hear that?" O asked Jim.

"You bet," Jim answered. "One down and four to go."

"That's my count," O replied. "Is it all right if I assign the team to help any of the others?"

"Your operation, your decision," Jim answered. "And don't forget that the car Tim was going to use is still here at the hotel."

"I guess I could ask him to bring it when he gets back and to give us a hand," O started to suggest. "Unless you need him there for anything."

"That reminds me. He just walked in with Marie a minute or so ago, and I've assigned him to watch over her in the hotel lounge," Jim told him. "I apologize if I stepped on your toes in reassigning one of your men."

"Just let me know if he needs an assistant," O said, laughing as he listened to the other teams checking in with updates on their location and the status of their assignments. "By the way, my guy just called and said that Val was at home watching TV when he knocked on her door. She was surprised to see the cop, and I'm betting that she's going to be calling you pretty soon, wondering about what's going on."

"Probably so," Jim answered. "Now let's just hope that we can get everyone else on our list before Larry gets here. Maybe I'll get an hour or two of sleep before I have to fly back to Dallas in the morning."

Chapter 74

Over the next hour, they had crossed off all except two names from their list.

When O called to see what Jim wanted to do about them, he answered, "What information do you have of the financial operations of the gangs?"

"Vice Lords were relatively easy," O answered. "I guess sitting alone with a bag over your head for an hour makes the mind imagine worse things than we could ever think of. Or at least more than we would probably do."

"Do you think he's given you everything that he knows?" Jim asked as Gene answered his phone.

"I'm pretty sure," O answered. "When do you want the teams to get you the information?"

"How much is there?" Jim asked. "I mean, can it be transmitted over the radio, or would that be too time-consuming?"

"My guys say that there's a shitload," O answered, laughing. "I'm guessing that we better bring in the guys who *interviewed* our guests and get their reports."

"How detailed is it?" Jim asked as Gene hung up his phone and motioned for him to get off the radio.

"Kinda sorta," O answered. "Lots of business names, a few individual names. Don't really know how that worked. Stuff like sports gambling facilities, ball teams—again, not sure how that worked—car washes. The list goes on and on. Most of the businesses were the type we've seen before, but there are a few new ones I've never run across before. They're an inventive bunch of shitheads."

Jim looked down at his list of remaining targets and said, "It looks like the only CFO remaining is from the Gangster Disciples."

"That's correct," O agreed. "We've finally got a good location for him, and the team expects to have him in less than thirty   minutes."
"Okay," Jim said as Gene kept motioning for him to hurry up. "You've still got an hour and a half or so before Larry gets here. I'll call you back as we get closer and see if we can wrap this up before he does."

"You mean shut down our interview process?" O asked. "Won't that throw off the time-of-death issue with Larry?"

"Not really," Jim said. "Don't forget that one of the St. Louis Vice Lords killed those guys at the restaurant. So, they've obviously been actively looking for the rest of the Chicago gangs for at least two hours."

"Got it," O agreed. "I'll get back with you regarding the last two targets as soon as I learn more. Do you want the other teams to bring in their information now or wait until it's over?"

"Go ahead and have one of the team bring it in," Jim directed. "And I assume you have some of the other teams out helping bring in the last two."

"Everybody except the guys left behind to work on the CFOs," O assured him. "And I think we can haul their sorry asses out to the middle of nowhere and dump them. Let them worry about if we're coming back while they try to find their way home."

"Sounds good," Jim told him. "I'll be waiting for the data from the interviews. Thanks."

Putting the microphone down, Jim turned to Gene as he was saying, "That was Val. She wants to come here. Do you want me to send my driver?"

"That sounds good," Jim answered as somebody knocked on the door.

Opening it, Tim and Marie came in, smiling, and Marie said, "You were right. I'm ready to go to work now."

"That's great," Jim said as she came over and gave him a quick hug. "Right now, I'd like for you to go with Gene's driver to pick up Val."

"I'd love to do that," Marie told him as she hugged Gene. "I want to tell her about what happened at the restaurant. She's going to be so jealous. When do I leave?"

"In a couple of minutes," Gene told her. "My driver will be here, and he'll take you down to the car."

"What do you want me to do?" Tim asked, looking at the diminishing list of names.

"Why don't you go help Mr. O?" Jim suggested. "The teams are almost finished out on the streets, and it would be over before you could get there. They're also bringing in their reports from the interviews, and you can bring everything here as it comes in."

"That sounds good," Tim said, nodding. "Interviews. That's a pretty mild term for what I suspect went on. I guess watching the leaders of your gangs have their brains sprayed across your shirt is just a different interview technique. Speaking of that, how did my team handle the *interview* of the Vice Lords guy since his bosses were left at the restaurant?"

"You'll have to ask Mr. O," Jim said as there was another knock on the door. "I haven't gotten that deep into the details yet."

"I'll head on down there and see what he wants me to do," Tim said as Gene's driver came in.

"Hi, I'm Marie," she said as Gene introduced the driver. "You'll have to forgive me if I'm a little verbose right now. I've had quite a day."

The driver simply nodded and said, "No problem, Miss. I understand completely."

"Getting hungry?" Gene asked as Marie and the driver left.

"I could eat something," Jim admitted. "I guess things are slow enough now that we can afford to relax a little. What did you have in mind?"

"Room service," Gene answered, handing him the menu. "I'll go to Marie's room and use her phone so that nobody sees what we've installed here."

"Reuben sandwich with chips," Jim said, handing back the menu. "Dr. Pepper if they have it. If not, a glass of tea with lemon."

"Got it," Gene said, walking to the door. "I'm betting that you can handle everything by yourself until I get back. Shouldn't be more than fifteen minutes."

"Take your time," Jim said, sitting down in front of the table with all the communication equipment. "I'll just sit here and relax. Not much more I can do until Larry gets to town and we get the information the CFOs volunteered to give us."

Chapter 75

They had almost finished their sandwiches when Jim heard O directing his teams to get the last two targets to the facility.

"Yo, Jim," O said over the radio.

"Go ahead," Jim answered.

"I guess you heard that we've got the last two," O told him.

"I did," Jim said, smiling at Gene. "Got a guess at how long before you're ready for the teams to vacate the building and we can send in the cleaners?"

"I'm guessing thirty minutes," O answered. "The Gangster Disciple fellow is shitting his pants right now. The team showed him pictures of his boss and the other guys at the facility. I think the topper was when they showed him the photos from the restaurant showing three bodies on the floor. He even recognized the two Vice Lords guys."

"How did you get those photos?" Jim asked, glancing at Gene.

"I have my sources," O told him, laughing. "Some of our more morbid officers seem to like collecting crime scene photos. The bloodier, the better. Let's just say that a close friend on the force is a connoisseur of the macabre."

"That's all I need to know," Jim said as a knock was heard.

"Hey, guys," Val said as she burst through the door as soon as Gene opened it. "Why didn't you come get me when you saw my good friend Robert at the restaurant? Especially after you guys shot him? I feel abandoned."

"We had a little trouble just verifying that you were all right." Jim said as he heard Larry calling in to say that he was less than an hour out. "Good," he said, acknowledging Larry's call as he watched Val put her arm around Marie. "Everybody's at the party, and all that's left is for you to collect the party favors that your friends provided and then give your passengers a ride home."

"Got it," Larry said. "Anything further?"

"No," Jim answered. "How long do you expect before you're done and your team is back on the road?"

"If all the toys you borrowed are at the party, it'll be a quick turnaround," Larry told him. "I'm guessing an hour and a half. Maybe less."

"Good," Jim said, smiling at Gene. "I'll make sure you aren't delayed on our end. Good job. Hey, O." Jim said as he keyed the microphone for the Vice Lords team frequency.

"Go ahead," O answered.

"Is Tim still with you?" Jim asked.

"Sure is," O said. "What do you need him for?"

"I don't need him," Jim explained. "But I do need for you to take his gun and get it out to the facility for collection."

After a moment's pause, O said, "I'm sending him right now. I guess that particular gun does need to be with the guys from St. Louis. We sort of lost track of it during all the excitement."

"Me too," Jim admitted. "Is he good to drive? I mean, how much did he have to drink when he was babysitting Marie?"

"He says just tea," O answered. "He's good to go, and I'll have him bring back any of the reports that are ready."

"Great," Jim told him. "Please have your teams start wrapping up their assignments. Larry will be there in less than an hour, and I want him heading back as quick as we can get him all the stuff he provided. Speaking of that, have you been tracking which ones have been used?"

"Oh yes," O assured him. "There's only been four, not counting Tim's. They'll all be collected and held for Larry. If it's all right with you, we'll take care of our last casualty and release the other one as soon as they get here. Then I'll leave one guy to wait for Larry and give him all the things he gave us."

"Sounds good," Jim agreed. "Just make sure your guy identifies the used ones so Larry can decide how he wants to handle the others."

"Done," O said. "Tim's on his way right now. I think we'll have our end wrapped up within the hour."

"Excellent," Jim answered. "If you want, why don't you close up shop there and come join us? I've got the same radios here, and you can use them. Hell, we'll even call down and get something for you to eat."

"Sounds good. Just get me a sandwich and a Heineken, if you don't mind," O said. "I'll tell all my teams where I'll be, and they can bring everything to your room."

"Done." Jim said putting the microphone down. "Does anybody else need anything to eat?" Jim asked, looking at Marie and Val. "If so, we'll order it when we get Mr. O's."

"I'm good," Marie answered. "I tried to eat at the restaurant, and I'm still not hungry."

"Me too," Val told him. "I had finished dinner when Marie came to get me. I'd like a glass of wine though. Chardonnay, please."

"Chardonnay sounds good," Marie said, smiling at Jim. "What about you, Jim? Will you join us in a glass?"

"Not yet," Jim answered, seeing the look in her eyes. "I'm still working. Not to mention that I have to be at the airport in a few hours and fly back to Texas. Some other time."

"I'll hold you to that," Marie said as Gene went to call room service. "I think that a drink is the least that you owe me after what I went through today."

A couple of minutes later, Gene came in with O, saying, "The food and drinks will be next door in about fifteen minutes. Marie, if you and Val don't mind, could you be over there and let us know when it gets here?"

"Sure," Marie said, glancing at Jim. "Will you guys be coming to join us, or do you want us to bring it over here?"

"Bring it here, please," Gene told her. "We still need to be listening to the radios."

As soon as they left the room, Gene said, "Jim, I'm relieving you. There's not much to be done except wait for the data to get here and send in the cleaners once Larry is headed home. I think Mr. O and I can handle that. I'm pretty sure that O can handle anything else that comes up, and you need to get back to your hotel. I've already told my driver to have the car out front, so you head on down. I'll give you a call later tomorrow or the next day and let you know if anything unexpected happened. We'll plan on a debrief this weekend."

Jim looked at Gene for a second and said, "Sounds good. I may be a too little wired for sleep, but just lying in a soft bed sounds really good. Thanks."

After shaking Gene's and O's hands, Jim left the room. A few minutes later, Val and Marie came in carrying O's sandwich and their drinks.

"Where's Jim?" Marie asked, looking around.

"He's gone back to his hotel," Gene informed her. "His job here is done."

Chapter 76

The next morning, Jim was in the lobby waiting to catch the hotel van to the airport when Rob stepped off the elevator with his suitcase and kit bag. After tossing his key on the hotel desk, he walked over and sat beside Jim on the vinyl couch.

"How was your evening?" he asked, looking at Jim.

"Pretty boring," Jim answered. "How about you?"

"Much the same," Rob answered as they saw the van pull up in front of the hotel. "Dinner with my buddy. Other than that, just another night in another city."

"I know," Jim said as he got up. "I guess we'll meet our flight attendants at the airport."

"Guess so," Rob said, getting up. "I looked at the weather in Dallas before I came down. Looks good."

"Yeah, I looked too," Jim said as they headed for the van. "You always get the legs with good weather."

"I thought it was your turn to fly," Rob said as they got in the van.

"Oh no," Jim said, smiling. "You flew in yesterday, and you said we'd swap every other leg so neither of us had to fly just the DFW legs."

"Oh yeah," Rob said as the van headed for the airport. "And we'll reverse them next week."

"Yes," Jim said with a bigger grin on his face. "But today it's your leg, and we're at concourse G again. And I'm sure you know what that means."

"You and your damned Cinnabons," Rob said, shaking his head.

"Hey, guys," the driver said as they got about halfway to the airport. "Did you see the news this morning?"

"No," Rob answered. "Why? Did something happen?"

"Oh yes," he said as he glanced back and forth between the road and his rearview mirror. "Looks like there was a major gang war overnight."

"No shit!" Rob exclaimed. "Where?"

"Looks like one of the local gangs decided to take out a couple of their rivals," the driver continued as he passed a copy of the *Chicago Tribune* back. "There were a couple of bodies at a restaurant and a dozen or so in some warehouse. Blood and brains all over the floors. The news probably didn't show the real nasty stuff, but what they did was gory as hell."

"Wow!" Rob exclaimed taking the paper. "Sounds like the news people will have a field day for a few days. How about you, Jim? Did you see or hear anything about this?"

"No," Jim said as he saw the exit for ORD approaching. "I must have slept through it."